Critical praise for *Treasures on Earth*

"Carter Wilson's beautiful short novel is near-perfect in style and form, and fascinating in content. Its power is so great I think we may be witnessing the birth of a classic. Wilson's style is a triumph of simplicity, beauty, and warmth. It bears comparison with Hemingway at his very best, simple and pure and vibrant with far more emotion that the surface seems to indicate. The hero through whose eyes we see the story is one of us, and we feel at home with him. The sound of his thoughts is absolutely honest, and there is nothing showy or self-consciously literary here at all."

—Boston *Globe*

"From the sinuous but disarming manner in which he renders the love affair between two men of such dissimilar cultures to his evocation of the daily life in Peru and the opening of the aperture onto the majestic ruins of Machu Picchu itself, Wilson shapes the shards and records of this exotic expedition into a form that does much more than merely tantalize. He reaches into the rubble of past lives and comes up with a book that moves and entertains us in all the ways a good novel should."

—Los Angeles *Herald*

"Wilson's novel is a coming-out story, but one significantly different from others. It is a tale of one man's struggle to find acceptance; but far more important, it is the story of the discovery of lost realms of the human soul. Carter Wilson has elevated the coming-out experience to grand heights in this book."

—The *Advocate*

"I have read *Treasures on Earth* with great enjoyment and admiration. Most of all, I admire the book for its extraordinarily subtle study of a friendship between two people of widely different cultures — it can stand comparison with Forster's somewhat similar study in *A Passage to India.* My congratulations to Carter Wilson."

—Christopher Isherwood

OTHER NOVELS BY CARTER WILSON

Crazy February

I Have Fought the Good Fight

A Green Tree and a Dry Tree

TREASURES ON EARTH

TREASURES ON EARTH

A NOVEL BY

Carter Wilson

Boston • Alyson Publications, Inc.

Treasures on Earth was originally published in cloth
by Alfred A. Knopf, Inc., 1981.
First quality paperback edition
by Alyson Publications, Inc., 1990.

ISBN 1-55583-172-9

Manufactured in the United States of America.

The events described in this book concerning the
scientific exploits of the Yale University–National Geographic
Society Expedition are based on historical documents.
The characters portrayed here are, however, all products
of the author's imagination; and where the name of a real
person is used (as is the case with Hiram Bingham,
for example) the author has not hesitated to distort
or invent situations and descriptions whenever it seemed
fictionally accurate to do so.

To R. S. M.

PART I

1911

Would anyone believe what I had found? Fortunately, in this land where accuracy in reporting what one has seen is not a prevailing characteristic of travelers, I had a good camera and the sun was shining.

—HIRAM BINGHAM,
'discoverer' of Machu Picchu

If I could tell the story in words, I wouldn't need to lug a camera.

—LEWIS HINE,
photographer

ONE

WHEN he at last reached his destination, the town of Puno on the Peruvian shore of Lake Titicaca, Willie Hickler had no idea what to expect. Perhaps he would find nothing, nobody he knew.

Hickler was the owner of a small photography studio in New Haven, Connecticut. But he was also a habitually itinerant soul and had been already far from home—fifteen hundred miles away in the middle of Nebraska photographing Indians—when he had received a telegram inviting him to come join the 1911 Yale University–National Geographic Society Peruvian Expedition.

The wire was from Hiram Bingham, a professor of geography who was the expedition's director as well as a longtime friend and sometimes employer of Willie's. Bingham had spent several hundred words on persuasion. There were phrases in the telegram meant to evoke memory of pledges Bingham and Willie had made to one another in extreme situations in the past. (Most of the locations of their mutual extremity had been saloons in New York and Bridgeport and *cantinas* in sovereign Mexico.) Reminders of commitments not to grow stodgy or old in spirit no matter how their bodies declined and betrayed them. (Bingham was, in 1911, thirty-six years of age, Willie Hickler thirty-two.) For them, Bingham said, this would be the last great adventure, the one for the sake of all their past adventures together. COME, the telegram concluded, AND SEE FOR SELF STOP REQUIRE OF HICKLER PROFESSIONALLY NOTHING MORE THAN PRESENCE AT UNFOLDING OF THESE EVENTS STOP ONLY RIGHT FINEST PHOTOGRAPHIC EYE IN AMERICAN HEMISPHERE SHOULD WITNESS IF NOT EVEN ONCE MAKE RECORD OF HIGHEST ORDER MARVELS OF THE CON-

TINENTS FINEST CIVILIZATION DAILY REVEALING THEMSELVES TO US HERE STOP EN SERIO AND WITH A MULTITUDE OF STRONG ABRAZOS STOP HIRAM.

The telegram made no mention of salary. But the following day there arrived a notice from a bank in New Haven that Willie was free to draw on Mr. Hiram Bingham's personal account for an amount which looked more than sufficient to cover his passage down there.

Willie traveled by buckboard to Kearney, by rail to San Francisco, then by steamer down to Callao. The means of conveyance from the port in to Lima was a horse-drawn streetcar on steel tracks. In Lima he found a letter only two weeks old which said the others were pushing on toward the ancient city of Cuzco but that Bingham and Christina Long, the young woman who studied archaeology as an adjunct student with Bingham at Yale, and a Peruvian employee of theirs named Ernesto Mena would await Willie at Puno until the last day of March. The photographer took the next available packet farther along the coast to Mollendo, the lower terminus of Ferrocarriles del Sur, the railroad that would lift him into the Andes.

He left Mollendo before noon on March 31. The train ran rapidly through the coastal desert, as if it were trying to escape confrontation with the Goliath of cloud-crested mountains which loomed, a great solid wall, above the left-hand side of the coach. When at last he could see their sturdy green British engine ahead rounding toward the struggle, Willie sighed deeply. He napped some. The mountains they entered were sere and brown. A white powder dust filmed his window and obscured the view.

By six they had come down into the valley of Arequipa, a city entirely under the influence or the imposition of a monstrous and beautifully symmetrical volcano called El Misti. In the station, Willie received news that the train stopped here for the night and would not continue on toward Puno until tomorrow.

Mrs. Hodges's, the boardinghouse recommended to him, turned out to be the place where the entire Yale–National Geographic group had put up several months before. After a meal which included pork chops in an onion-and-bacon cream gravy and a selection of apple and peach pies, Willie was invited into the antimacassar-strewn parlor by two mining engineers who hailed from Pennsylvania. The younger of them was a blond, bearded, tall man with big reddened hands and thick forearms. He said how much they had enjoyed the company of Edmund Foote, a classics professor who had come along to be the Bingham expedition's ornithologist, and the unfailing good spirits of the comparative physiologist Alvin Bumstead.

"Old Doctor Bones-and-Bumps, as he calls himself," the elder engineer said.

The bourbon imported from home which the gentlemen poured loosened Willie up quicker than usual. Arequipa is seventy-six hundred feet above the sea and he was tired as well, having journeyed, he figured, nearly seven thousand miles in the last five weeks.

His hosts wondered could Willie shed any light on the Yale people's *real* purpose in coming to Peru. This Bingham fellow, they said, kept his cards so close to his chest probably even *he* couldn't read them. The Peruvians of course to a man stood convinced the '*yankis*' had in their possession maps which would lead them directly to the well-known hoards of gold and silver the Incas had buried in the 1500's instead of giving them up to Francisco Pizarro to pay the ransom of their captive emperor, Atahualpa.

"In search of treasure? Hiram?" Willie laughed. He doubted sincerely that was the expedition's purpose. Though, from what he understood, there might be a kind of *permuted* truth involved. A trip to South America two years before had intrigued Bingham, like many before him, with the notion that there remained to be discovered in modern times one Inca city the Spanish had never known and hence could not have ransacked. Vitcos was its name and it was supposed to lie somewhere in a place called Vilcabamba down the valley of the Urubamba River beyond Cuzco. (The elder engineer nodded his bald head at the place names. To Willie they meant little, of course, brought to mind no pictures. He remembered the long ones from talks with Hiram only because they were so insistently rhythmed. VIL-ca-BAM-ba, like the melodies of tarantellas the Italians at home were so fond of.) Bingham relied for his information principally on someone Willie recalled being named Calancha, who had described the unlocated Vitcos in a history of the doings of the Augustinian Order in the early days of the Spanish occupation of Peru.

The senior engineer's name was Harris. He got up to bring the bottle around, strangleholding it at the neck. Refilling Willie's glass, he said, "Antonio de la Calancha? *The Moral Chronicle?* That book was written a hundred years after the fact." Contempt and amusement surfaced together on his mobile face, as though Willie had mentioned a very old and dear but also very dissolute friend. "The Yale people would try and tell us in their circles Dr. Bingham was of the highest possible rep, considered heir apparent to Prescott and Clements Markham as the expert on the Inca."

Willie said he thought that was true. Hiram had written a book on South America.

"They all do—least the ones who don't stay long enough to get fuddled by it. I wonder does Bingham know Sir Clements dismisses Calancha out of hand? And even Prescott, in his trusting sweet blindness, could smell a rat when it came to the *Crónica Moralizada.*"

"I'll mention that to Hiram when I see him," Willie said. Thinking then '*If* I see him.'

Harris was persistent. "Our own dear Mrs. Hodges, who tries to keep up on the doings of notables back home, she claims Bingham's a man of huge personal wealth. Pal to millionaires and senators. The son of missionaries who went out early to the Sandwiches and used calico and trinkets to convert the heathen and, more important, get them to sign over their choicest property—as a sign of faith, of course."

Willie said he thought it was a mite more complicated than that, but yes, there seemed to be considerable Bingham family holdings in Hawaii. And Hiram certainly was not the type of professor forced to make do only on his income from the university.

"And the young lady in question?" said the rangy, taller engineer, "those long blond tresses floating along in Bingham's wake? There wasn't anyone here, including Mrs. H, who believed that girl could really be Mr. Bingham's wife. What is it makes you smile?"

"I'm surprised Hiram goes ahead trying," Willie said. "He's never convinced *anyone* I know about of Christina's being his wife. Your suspicions were correct, gentlemen. There *is* an authentic Mrs. Bingham at home in New Haven who presides over five authentic Bingham children at the authentic Bingham dining table each evening."

"Does their papa attend?"

"Always until the children have gone up for the night."

They had worked their way by now down to the last couple of inches in the bottle. Mr. Harris began to ask about how the profession of photography went. Was it, for instance, lucrative enough to keep body and soul from going asunder?

But this Hickler was turning out to be an even more private type than his pal Bingham. The inquiries about himself made Willie wince, and he kept steering the conversation out toward other territory. Both engineers could detect a fine seam of cantankerousness developing in their photographer acquaintance, so they let whatever other questions they might have had go by.

Willie excused himself and stepped out into the night to take some draughts of the citrus-smelling rarefied air. He gazed for a moment at the Southern Cross. It lay on its side just above the white volcanic-stone city, glinting like the crucifix of a rosary discovered, neglected, in a drawer.

Willie had been attracted to the engineers, first to the younger (Tom was his name) and then, when he showed he knew his history, more to the older one, Harris. Generally, Willie could bring himself to trust anyone who like himself had a skill, could make something work. Technical people. But the engineers had by chance pushed almost at once against a soft spot. Willie had left to him, by this stage in his life, very little real family. A sister-in-law, his brother's widow, and two small nephews who lived near him in New Haven. A mother in an asylum near Boston. Uncles, aunts and cousins on his mother's side, all of whom he avoided when he could. So Willie had, for the last years, allowed Hiram Bingham to provide him with access to what you might call a 'ready-made' family. At first it had been with Hiram's wife, Abby, and the ever growing pack of smart Bingham boys. More recently, since the breach, Willie had come to think often of Hiram and Christina together as being dearer to him than any family of the flesh had ever been.

So, when the two engineers had probed their way into the business of who exactly Hiram was married to, unknowingly they had awakened deep and confusing unhappinesses of Willie's. He had for a long time now thought it shoddy on his friend's part to insist on maintaining the double existence. Sweet, dogged Christina and sweet, disappointed Abby, both kept on tenter-hooks, neither free to develop for herself if she could any life which was not somehow a dance in attendance on Hiram.

THE NEXT day's journey began at nine a.m. "*Exactly,*" as the conductor was pleased to point out. "My train runs on English time."

"What's the other possibility?" Willie asked.

"Peruvian time."

"Which is?"

"Always behind, *señor.*"

Willie's seatmate, a sad-looking old Peruvian gentleman in a badly shaped brown suit, cackled loudly and unpatriotically.

Almost as soon as they left behind the dusty biblical whiteness of Arequipa, they began to climb. Cattle ranches and, in spite of the unpromising dry look of the soil, fields for agriculture, curving courses for irrigation water between the rows, great swaths of the earth thus appearing to have been raked by the comb of a giant. Despite his excitement, Willie had a hangover and, as the climb grew steeper, he slept. He dreamed a big bass drum was pounding nearby. Unseen hands continually tightened the head. The drum was bound to break. He woke to find his own blood pulsing hard right against his skin. Out the window there had grown up great rounded mountains which reminded him of the Rockies in Idaho. But either the railroad and the people had gotten very small or the mountains were getting out of control. They were growing too big. Questions of scale. Willie slept and woke up again. It was the altitude, for sure. His breath was short. He had a headache and he felt exhilarated. *Thrilled,* he thought, *from my head down to my toes.* A little after two p.m. the conductor announced, "Crucero Alto." The highest point on the line, Willie remembered, the height of the top of the Matterhorn. The sign on the little stationhouse said 4500 meters. Fourteen thousand seven hundred and some feet that would be. About as high, he had read, as human beings eke out existence anywhere on the face of the world. But, from the train at least, you couldn't tell very much about how they managed. Except near the tiny depots, almost no houses. No trees. Great yellow swells of hills and depressions, cold blue lakes. If you lived on the moon you probably wouldn't have found it much lonelier than this.

But then in an hour they crossed into a slightly lower, browner terrain and Willie caught sight of herds of beasts, small whitish furry ones, shy and swift, moving like clouds of snow against the sides of mountains. *Vicuñas* those were, his seatmate told him. Then herds of staid larger animals with long wool coats and muzzles and big questioning eyes.

"One-el lima's a bean, two-el *llama*'s a beast," Willie said aloud, "and a three-el 'larmer's a *fire.*"

"What's that?" the sad little man asked.

Ah, Willie said, just an English rhyme he had been taught in school. About *llamas*, more or less.

"The Spanish at first called them 'furry camels.' "

More people now too, ladies in bowlers and wide, flounced

red skirts, men in caps with hound-dog earflaps, all spinning as they walked along, drawing out thread from hand to hand and running it down onto spindles swinging and circling at their heels like acolytes' censers.

One of the towns where they stopped a minute was called Maravillas. Willie had often thought simply because of its name he would like to reside in What Cheer, Iowa. But 'Wonders,' Peru—an even better return address.

By late afternoon they had reached the *puna*, a desolate, magnificent plain Willie's seatmate said just went "away, away—thousands and thousands of kilometers—even into Bolivia." Then the old gentleman repeated "away, away" dreamily, waving the back of his hand toward the train window as though he was trying to shoo death or love or something equally momentous off his doorstep.

The train sidled toward the low near mountains on the right and then rather suddenly seemed to decide on an end run to the left. They rounded a long curve and came to where the track was only a few feet above the edge of a vast piece of luminous pewter-gray water. Lake Titicaca, an 'inland sea' as proclaimed, for Willie could make out only horizon, no farther shore. Above the Lake rose great spumes of cloud. They looked like they came from a fire or were the smoke of volcanoes. The sun had gone behind the mountains on the side where the town of Puno was. They ticked along past the beginnings of adobe and tile-roofed buildings, now, it seemed, in a race against darkness. The afterglow of the sunset mounted and mounted and became a thickness of swarming golden light—it produced halos around the felt-hatted heads of Indian women standing beside the tracks—and then, like a curtain descending or a miracle drawing to its close, it was over and the night begun.

Lamps had not yet been lit at the depot. For all its strangeness and the hubble-bubble of the crowd pressing around him to greet the arrivals, Willie saw at least one familiar sight: the granite terminal itself with its broad eaves and high windows must have been built by a gringo, because detail for detail it was the same as the station in Milford in darkest Connecticut.

Otherwise, things seemed as he had feared. Willie arriving on the scene a little too late. April Fool's Day. The only other obvious foreigners on the platform were a couple sporting identical light-colored bulky overcoats and broad-brimmed hats slouched against the breeze blowing in off the Lake. They had as guardian one of those new shepherd dogs from Germany, a wolfish-looking animal of the type the very well-off at home had recently taken a fancy to.

Willie pushed his way through in the general direction of the baggage cars. He wanted to make sure his luggage and equipment got off safe. All of the throat-tightening excitement of the past weeks—anticipation augmented to a near-intolerable limit in the last twenty-four hours by the bodily changes the altitude had rung on him—was in flight, seeping from him. 'Away, away,' as the old gentleman on the train had chanted so morosely.

At the end of the platform he stopped, thumb hooked in the watchpocket of his vest, considering whether to get down in the rich red mud in order to get over to the baggage cars. Better to wait and see how many of his well-labeled possessions the Indian porters came up with. They had begun bringing things along to the steps in quite a regular little antlike procession.

Some disturbance. A hand seizing Willie's, lifting it, holding hard. Nothing subtle this time around. The touch of the pickpockets in ports of call like Buenaventura had been ever so much lighter. So now, almost automatically, the heel of Willie's left hand came over to strike the man's wrist away.

But Willie was off balance. Being yanked back into the dense choke of people whose shoulders came only to his waist nearly toppled him. His fist struck air. His assailant's grip had gotten tighter. The man grinned back at Willie. A brown-and-white wool tasseled Indian cap. Long nose with flaring nostrils, handlebar mustache, big gap between the front teeth, one of them half broken off, identifiers in case there was a police force in this place and Willie could get to them.

"This way!" the man shouted, "this way! They are over there!"

Then Willie understood. The couple with the dog he had assumed to be Germans had turned and were waving at him and were not, of course, Germans, but his friends. Hiram a good deal thinner than when Willie had seen him last. His face darkened, tan. Christina Long was blotting her cheeks with a handkerchief. The sight of her made Willie realize that he too was primed and any moment now would begin to cry.

Someone had led a heavily burdened little horse right out onto the platform. The animal stood directly in their path. People around them were berating its owner both in Spanish and in a rapid Indian language. The man he had thought was a thief dropped back and put one arm around Willie's waist and the other hand on his elbow as though Willie were some precious cargo and steered him behind the horse's trembling flank and forward into the crowd.

"Ernesto Mena. At your service."

"I know you," Willie said. "Hiram wrote to me about you."

"We've come down to meet all the trains for the last two weeks. We had lost hope. But now here you are."

Willie and Hiram closed and embraced, a bear hug with both arms in the Mexican fashion. Hiram was warm and smelled some of alcohol.

If Willie had had any doubts about undertaking the present voyage, the longest and farthest from home of his life so far—and there had been many nights aboard ship when alone on deck he went beyond hearing the voice of himself tell him he was a fool and into a full-fledged, many-voiced panic which prophesied that this whimsical cutting-loose from all his usual moorings was the precipitant act of a man intent on driving himself mad—those doubts had all washed away in an instant. Some of our greatest certainties we come upon only by indirection. It wasn't Christina's red eyes or even the faint heaving in Hiram's chest which told Willie he had for once done the right thing. Rather, it was looking over Hiram's shoulder and seeing their satisfaction mirrored in the face of their new helper. Willie in himself, after all, was a stranger, meant nothing to this Mena. Yet the little man in the Indian hat was beaming and his eyes too were filled with copious tears.

TWO

THE WORD *'hueco'* as Willie knew it from Mexico meant a hollow or small cave. In Peru a *hueco* was a bar. Or, better translated, any hole-in-the-wall where the owner provided a colorless cheap raw brandy called Pisco together with a narrow bench or a chair to sit on while you drank it and maybe a table and a candle stub for illumination and not a lot more.

Late in the evening, after an extended celebrational dinner in the dining room at the hotel and after Christina had gone to bed, Hiram and Ernesto Mena led Willie to a *hueco* called La Captiva near the Lake's edge.

Where, some time still later, Willie sat thinking his only remaining problem was how, in this old business of boozing with Hiram, to reckon what his compensation for the altitude should be. Very much like the experience of driving someone else's lighter rig and better horses. Initially you are excited by the new speed at which the familiar sights flash by. But then so quickly you adjust, forget, until you reach the midpoint of a usual turn of the corner and wake up to the truth that you are taking it too fast, cutting it too sharp, are too far leaned over on the rims of your inside wheels.

Hiram had begun explaining to Ernesto something of Willie's career. Though in a disconcerting way. He talked about Edward Curtis and about Curtis's mammoth endeavor, but without mentioning exactly what the endeavor was. Nothing about the planned twenty volumes of photographs, only names of supporters like E. H. Harriman and J. Pierpont Morgan, which had little effect on Ernesto. The roll call made Willie uncomfortable, as though a biography of him was being constructed out of facts, but the wrong ones.

At last, perhaps realizing that Ernesto was not mightily impressed, Hiram pulled his trump. "*And* our Willie here was summoned to the White House in Washington to make a portrait of no less a figure than President Theodore Roosevelt."

"Together with all the children and the damned dogs and the children's pony and the pony cart," Willie said. "You should mention too that the only reason *I* went was because Mr. Curtis was down with swollen tonsils on the day of the appointment."

"Which is another thing," Hiram continued in Spanish. "Circumstances force our Willie here to slave for another fellow. This *pinche Señor* Curtis gets all the credit, while it's really our friend here who's actually doing the work."

"What work is that?" Ernesto asked.

"Making photographs which convey all the scientific information we need about the ordinary, the day-to-day in the existence of the Indians in North America."

Indians in the United States? The Peruvian didn't quite understand. Hiram and Willie tried to explain. After a few minutes, Ernesto's eyebrows went up. "*Ah, los retskinis!*" He knew about them from dime romances about the West that had begun to appear in Peru. But he had imagined, as he said, by now the cowboys and the cavalry would have murdered them all.

"Only almost," Willie said.

Hiram went on about how it was one thing to be able to record life raw on pictorial film, but Willie, however, was another, rarer beast. His Indian photographs were *works of art*, no matter whether you cared about the subject matter, as indelibly impressive and eternally memorable as any painting by any so-called Old Master.

"I see." Ernesto made a hard appraisal of Willie's face. "An artist, then."

"Not on purpose," Willie said.

Hiram got to his feet and started across the little room to get their Pisco bottle replenished.

"Taking pictures is my trade is all," Willie said in a low voice. "Artists have a finer sense of themselves than that."

"More delicate." Ernesto nodded.

"I have a mother, you see, who—"

"It's the human case, isn't it?"

"I suppose."

Willie was in a way glad Ernesto had stopped him. He wouldn't have had the Spanish to explain what he meant to say anyway. How his mother had become one of those poor unfortunates who must dwell in the retreats of the insane (was there a word *asilo?* or would you say—certainly more evocative—a *convento?*), and that she had also been one of those who had needed to attach herself by hook or by crook to what she called 'the world of beauty'—or, more simply, Art. Hence how, in his chosen trade, Willie walked a thin line, always conscious of the fact that his own motive was only separable from his mother's by his denying at every turn it was anything so abstract as 'beauty' he was in search of.

Willie said, "I hold with the belief that it's only the ordinary worker, just trying to get his daily bread and with no *idea* of his own importance, who may prove in the judgment of time to be an 'artist.' "

"I think that," Ernesto said.

The *hueco*'s only other client was a young man standing at the counter in a drab-green tunic with brass buttons. A policeman or soldier of some sort, fairly drunk. Hiram was insisting he come join them at their table.

"Is there any possibility of seeing your photographs? Did you bring them?"

"I'm sorry, I didn't." Then, suddenly, Willie added, "Not the ones Hiram's talking about. But I do have a few with me, three or four pictures I could show to you if I ever get located somewhere and get to unpack my things. No '*retskinis*,' I'm afraid."

"What, then?"

"Orphans."

"For my own reasons I especially like photographs of little children," Ernesto said.

"Well, *not* little children in fact. In fact just pictures I've made I think I like best because no one else seems to care for them at all."

"Oh, I see—*your* orphans."

The soldier at the counter was saying that no good could come of this invasion of the motherland by the English and the '*yankis,*' the Germans and, worst of all, the pernicious Jew moneylenders. Hiram said well at least the railroads were a sign of progress. No, the soldier said, only the chosen instrument for the rape of Peru.

"Proudest people in the world, us Peruvians," Ernesto said. "*Señor* Bingham showed me what a Frenchman who came here a hundred years ago wrote: 'Among all the capital cities of South America, it is only in Lima that one notes how even the *dogs* parade proudly through the streets.' "

Across the room, Hiram was wondering whether the soldier knew of places in Puno where men might meet girls.

At fiestas, and on Sunday afternoon in the park there was a *paseo* where young ladies walked out with their mothers or their *dueñas,* the soldier said.

No, Hiram meant places where a dumb foreigner without pretty words could find love with a woman in just one evening.

The soldier stood straight up and raked a shock of black hair up off his forehead. "Such places as you mention are not permitted in Peru, *señor.*"

"See?" Ernesto touched Willie's elbow.

Willie might otherwise not have noticed. What Ernesto had pointed out was a pink line of scar above his brow the soldier revealed in pushing back his hair.

"The truth is," the soldier announced, "that the 'dumb foreigner' you speak of, *señor,* only remains in our mountains long enough to extract the ore and the riches and to take them away. There is in Peru no opportunity for finding love. Not for him."

Ernesto's hand was still on Willie's sleeve. "It's been difficult for your friends here."

"Difficult how?"

"Oh," Ernesto turned his head, "nothing. Except we had an out-of-the-ordinary rainy season. The professor off exploring the islands in the Lake, and then we were down at the ruins by Copacabana for quite a while. So Miss Long was left alone a great deal of the winter."

"What about that?"

Ernesto considered his reply. "Nothing. The walls of the rooms in the hotel got moldier and moldier until you could see the damp shining through. A bad period. Things will be better now you've come."

Willie was puzzled. Whatever Ernesto had mounted up to tell him, he had then shied off.

Hiram was back, having convinced his soldier acquaintance to join them. Up close Willie could see the buttons on the fellow's tunic were each stamped with a simple human face, stolid, blank almost. Perhaps meant to be the uncaring visage of the Sun Himself.

Dinner, something at dinner tonight. Oh.

Willie had thought they were all going in together to eat in the big empty dining room at the Hotel del Lago, Hiram and Christina, Willie and Ernesto Mena. But in the hall they had perchance met up with an army officer, trim mustache and pointed goatee elongating further an already long face, who was introduced as *Teniente* Leopoldo Agustín Ávila de Mara y something something—the last few names Willie hadn't quite caught—and then all of a sudden it had developed Ernesto had some 'things to do' and so instead it had been Leo Ávila who had joined them at table. From some palaver they had had back home about Hiram's 1909 trip across South America, Willie recognized Ávila must be the Cuzco gentleman who had taken leave from his army post to guide Hiram to the Inca ruins of the southern highlands that first time. And what caused Willie to think of him now was that Ávila too had had a row of shiny brass faces down the front of his uniform. But the image on the lieutenant's buttons was much more elaborately etched, full raised round eyebrows, a mustache waxed into upward-curling ends, a rayed nimbus surrounding the face, a mocking Spanish-conqueror Sun which looked as though it could have been modeled on the features of Leo Ávila himself.

When Hiram presented the soldier to them now, Ernesto was not even polite. He gave the newcomer nothing more than a curt incline of his head.

Because the man was drunk, Willie imagined. In Mexico they would talk about 'The Point.' A lady, for example, might drink a bit, but by definition a lady never goes past '*El Punto.*' The soldier had obviously reached the point and was gone, gone beyond. He held his empty glass up between thumb and forefinger, waiting. Hiram refilled it.

"And you, my—my—*compatriot* I suppose it is? What uniform is this you wear?" The soldier reached out to touch the pompons on Ernesto's cap. But Ernesto pulled his head away. "Ah, I see. You must be one of these 'friends' to the poor little Indian, his picturesque costume and his charming, backward ways. But not such as to ever allow a *real* Indian—which I happen to be, *señor*—to lay his filthy hands on you."

"Not because you're an Indian," Ernesto said in an even, almost kind voice, "but because I have *never* let myself be touched by anyone, especially people too drunk to know what they're doing."

The soldier stared at Hiram, then at Willie, as though one or the other of them would come to his assistance. When neither of them moved, the young man put his arms on the table and lowered his head onto them.

Ernesto removed the cap and regarded it. "It's interesting the number of simple ways there are to offend people," he said.

"You should go on and wear it, though," Willie said. "It's very handsome on you."

"You must know we are still Spanish enough here to have the custom: if a visitor admires what you have, it becomes his." Ernesto offered Willie the cap.

"I had forgotten," Willie said. "And I forget still—is there some way left for me to refuse and still equal you in your politeness? if I thank you? tell you what a kind, elegant, gentlemanly act?"

Ernesto laughed. "Yes, that would more than satisfy the conditions."

"Friends, then."

"Yes, with pleasure."

Willie and Ernesto shook hands. There should, Willie knew, be a toast now. But the bottle was empty again.

He was about to get up when Hiram said, "The immediate task before us, Willie, is convincing our friend Ernesto here to come to the States with us at the end of the year, once our season is finished. I've tried him, but without much success. Maybe you can be more persuasive."

Ernesto said to Hiram, "Without any English I wouldn't survive long certainly."

"But obviously—in America you will be our guest," Hiram said. "And Willie here keeps comfortable bachelor quarters where there is plenty of extra room. So if you got tired of living with Christina and me, you could always move over and stay with Willie. Isn't that so, Willie?"

His *hueco* was Ernesto's *hueco*, Willie answered.

Though actually he didn't have much heart for it. It had been Hiram's practice wherever he went in the world's backwaters to draw to him excellent men, guides, go-betweens, informants, interpreters, and then to insist on taking them home with him. What happened to these people once Hiram had transported them to New Haven, often at a dreary expense of time and money to get them either legitimate or bogus travel documents, was nothing. Or somehow worse than that. After the big welcome and the *abrazo*, Hiram promptly forgot them. If he trusted they were developing no intentions toward his lady, they lived in the servant's room in the back of the flat Hiram kept for Christina and himself. Otherwise, in little cells he rented them in boardinghouses. Exotic birds shivering in cold shopwindows.

Ernesto stood and picked up the Pisco bottle. "I'm sorry," he said. "It must seem very ungrateful of me to resist your kind offer of a journey to the north. Also," he nodded to Willie, "your hospitality."

Hiram said, "There is no kindness involved, Ernesto. You give to me from your exceptional ability. I happen to have the resource of education at hand. If I offer that to you, it is a matter of simple return."

Ernesto shook his head. "I draw my salary. So we are even there."

The soldier was through with his nap, trying to see out of the barest slits his eyes could open. He waved his finger at Hiram and tried to say something. Ernesto lifted him out of his seat and whispered to him, "Come. There is something *very* important I want your opinion on." He steered the fellow across the room, unbolted the front door, shoved the soldier out into the night and closed the door after him. Then he went behind the counter to refill the bottle again. The *hueco* owner was dozing on a stool with his back to the wall.

"Ernesto," Hiram said, "is the only other person I've come to know in all the years since I met you who doesn't want something *out* of me."

"Not true in my case either," Willie said.

"Oh? I didn't know. What are you in it for?"

"The talk, Hiram. I like the quality of the talk you and I achieve sometimes."

"But beyond that—I will insist on it. You, and now this Mena."

"And Christina?"

"Where there's passion, love between a man and a woman, you can't say that we are free of designs, each on the other, can you now?"

"I suppose not," Willie said.

They shared up what was in the bottle Ernesto had brought, but Willie found it hard to take part in the conversation. He was very drunk now himself and what Hiram had said about designs began to seem more and more true to him about all our relations, whether man-and-woman, carnal or not. When he had first got Hiram's telegram and made up his mind, Willie had decided to take Hiram at his word—REQUIRE OF HICKLER PROFESSIONALLY NOTHING MORE THAN PRESENCE. Then at the last minute, the cases with his cameras and darkroom stuff already marked for shipment back East, he had remembered. It was true of Hiram that he cared more about drawing people to him than he did about being with them. The greater the distance, the higher the obstacle, the more fired-up he became. It was as though he could measure the extent of your love for him in miles. And once he had you, once you had proved what he needed to know, some form of neglect was inevitable. So Willie had rewritten the labels and had his photographic equipment loaded instead on the train to San Francisco.

They went out into the cold night, Hiram and Willie first, Ernesto staying a moment to settle up with the *hueco*'s proprietor. He came along half a block or more behind them. Willie had no idea of the time, but the streets were dead, left to an occasional scavenging dog (none of them, he thought, at this hour particularly proud).

Then, rounding a corner, the great colonial mass of the Hotel del Lago before them, Willie and Hiram came on a man slouched drowsily against a wall.

Willie didn't recognize him until too late. It was the soldier. Willie stopped, but Hiram stumbled on a bit and the soldier had time to get the stick out from behind his back and to turn before Willie could grab for him. The soldier's elbow came up under Willie's chin. Willie's teeth slammed shut on the skin inside his mouth and in the pain he tasted a warm flooding. The soldier, free, clubbed Hiram over the head. There was a suspended moment, silence all around, and then Hiram groaned heavily as though the wind had been knocked out of him and his legs buckled. Willie grabbed again, but the soldier was all motion, the stick coming down again on Hiram's head. Willie heard footsteps behind, Ernesto running, and at the same time long shutters right above him sprang open and there was a very old woman—only her moon-white face, the rest sheathed in black—screaming, "Murder! assassins! help! they are killing my son!" Hiram was on the cobblestones. The soldier kicked at his ribs. A look of such amazement on Hiram's face. Willie waded into the soldier and threw his arms around him. Ernesto was there then. For some reason he had in hand the bottle they had been drinking from at the *hueco.* It hit the crown of the soldier's head and splintered a million ways and the soldier drooped in Willie's arms.

The old woman's alarm had carried. Shutters were popping open all around, heads appearing, men in undershirts holding up their pants stepping sleepily into the street.

"The foreigners! they've killed my son! look, everybody look!"

Willie still embraced the limp body. He could find in himself no hard feelings about what the kid had done. Hiram's subtle goading seemed fair enough reason for the attack. Willie spat out warm blood and gently let the soldier down onto the pavement.

Ernesto was squatted over Hiram, brushing sparkling shards of glass off his face.

"We should send for the police," Willie said.

"Oh no. Come, if we can get him up together, we can at least carry him to the hotel."

They tried lifting Hiram, but, like any drunk's, Hiram's body resisted the force of other wills. His eyes came open and he said very reasonably, "I only came to know his country, and for that he wants to kill me. Can you figure that one, Willie?"

"Not at the moment," Willie said. He had just discovered blood all over his hand where he had been holding the back of Hiram's head. "But I'll discuss it with you if you can help us get you up now."

"Of course."

They tried again to lift Hiram and this time, with his assistance, they got him on his feet and his arms pulled around over their shoulders. The soldier's mother had gone from cries to bitter complaint. Her neighbors were trying to rouse her son for her. As the foreigners and Ernesto limped by, people turned their faces away. Behind them Willie heard shutters banging closed.

THREE

NOW THAT they had Willie firmly in hand, Hiram had announced last night, it was imperative for them to get out of Puno as quick as humanly possible. The other members of the expedition, fifteen or so scientists and assistants, were already ensconced in the Hotel Central in Cuzco, another long day's train journey away. From the secretive and separate telegrams they sent, it was obvious they were at loose ends about how to occupy their time in their leader's absence. Taking the opportunity, as Hiram put it, of the cat's being still at Titicaca to bicker mightily amongst themselves.

The only impediment to sudden departure was a mountain of gear. Willie did not fully comprehend the magnitude of the problem until he came up in the morning to find out how Hiram's head was faring. In the narrow room on the hotel's ground floor he was sharing with Ernesto Mena, all the walls were neatly stacked with painted wooden containers Hiram called 'unit-food-boxes' because they had each been packed to his specifications by Fortnum and Mason with tinned goods and staples enough to feed two men for eight days. Once the food was gone, the boxes became good cases for botanical specimens, geological collections and whatnot. Hiram and Christina were occupying a sort of suite, two high-ceilinged chambers connected by an open doorway, much lighter, airier and larger than the rooms downstairs. But, though bare of furniture except for an armoire, some chairs and a huge mahogany bed in the inner chamber, these rooms were nearly impassable. Willie was reminded of the quarters of privileged, well-outfitted boys once they have grown up and gone away. Only here the fishing rods, telescope, nets and traps, the picks for climbing in ice, were the latest professional models, not toys. The center of the outer room was strewn with baskets specially woven from the reeds that grew all along the Lake. Christina's proper field of study was the material culture of native peoples. Together she and Ernesto Mena were packing the collections she had made through the winter from the households of Aymara Indians. Both of them were nearly up to their knees in a kind of hemp Ernesto had located which, when shredded, had the quality of good Malayan raffia.

They were, Christina explained, in a real push because Leo Ávila, the lieutenant Willie had met last night, was due to arrive momentarily to take everything off to the train station. Ávila was going down to the coast for a short stay and the plan was for him to find appropriate storage for all the stuff accumulated so far, either in Mollendo or, better, in Callao or Lima.

"But take a moment to look at this, Willie." Christina pointed to the seat of a chair drawn up next to her. On it were three little herds of *llamas,* one group left earthen color, one glazed white and the third black, none of the animals more than three or four inches high. "These people delight in miniatures," Christina said, "you find them everywhere." She reached over and slipped a cigar box from under the wadding in a basket already packed. Inside, nicely nestled in cotton, were tiny sets of crude dishes and bowls, a doll-sized poncho and a knit cap with flaps like Ernesto's which was so small it fit snug over Willie's big finger.

Christina was looking up at him. Willie always thought her a pretty woman, but she had times—this was one of them—when she grew incandescent. When it happened, whatever sophistication eight years' living in the East had given her dropped away and you saw underneath the girl off the Missouri farm, her unselfconscious access to amazement and pleasure.

Hiram was in the inner room. He had allowed Benito, his police dog, to get up and curl at his feet on the mahogany bed. Together they looked like souls marooned, cast away. The whole archaeological collection surrounded them. Willie had to pick his way between pots and carved stones and steel-banded boxes.

"Let's see."

Hiram leaned forward from the bed pillows and delicately probed in his hair with his fingertips. There was, at the crown, a shaven patch almost as big as a monk's tonsure, covered with white adhesive bandage. The work had been done by the Scottish wife of the hotel owner, a woman who had served as a nurse in South Africa during the Boer conflict.

"Nice job," Willie said. "How many stitches?"

"Three, " Hiram said.

"Hurt?"

"More I think from the banging my head took than from the cut. I'm all right. Have a chair if you can find one, and pour yourself some beer." There were four big bottles, two of them already empty, on a little table by the bed.

From experience, Willie could predict which sort of day it would be. Hiram had really only two kinds. There were mornings he rose not much after the sun, all steamed up with purpose. On a dig, the helpers would have to yank themselves out to the site to keep their boss from destroying their careful work with the blade of his impatient shovel. In the office, page after page of scientific reports, journal articles and pleas to friends and potential patrons Hiram hoped to enlist in his schemes poured off whatever surface he was using as a desk and had to be rescued from the floor. By noon of such days, Hiram would have accomplished what a lesser man might be pleased to finish in a week. But other mornings, no matter what plan or timetable he had set, Hiram proved incapable of rousing even himself, much less of providing motive force for anyone else. Almost inevitably such occasions followed nights when H.B. had gotten drunk. He would stay abed thumbing through novels, and no one could gain an audience with him except Christina, who was usually too put-out to want one. Or Willie, who would sit at the foot of the bed or in a chair beside it while Hiram, unclean, still smelling of alcohol, naked except for his uncollared shirt, thrashed about, pulling the mess of sheets and blankets up over him in different ways, trying to find some comfortable position first on one elbow and then the other, drinking beer, coughing, swearing one minute cigarettes were the whole of his problem and the next reaching over to pluck one out of Willie's pocket (despite Willie's having told him long ago he found this habit discomfiting, even a bit humiliating).

Ernesto came in from the other room carrying a frame and backing he had constructed for an intricate little snatch of Inca weaving which had been discovered in a good state of preservation in a cave. He wanted to know if it was protected well enough. Hiram thought so. Then, "Glass of beer, Ernesto? I need to thank you for saving my life."

Ernesto turned down the beer. "And it wasn't *your* life that was the question," he said, on his way out. "Our friend the soldier needs to learn to be more careful of himself."

Willie struck a match. The smell of sulfur reached his nostrils and made them itch. He lit his own cigarette and held the light over to Hiram.

"That business of bringing Ernesto to Yale? I'm set on it, Willie."

"I could tell." Willie's chest felt heavy. "How'd you locate him?"

"Luck. Sheer luck bagged us Ernesto. Well, more than luck, I suppose. Back in Arequipa while we were preparing our assault on Coropuna—did I tell you we had done that one?"

"Done what?"

"We were the first to scale Mount Coropuna. From some sightings I took the last time I was down here I had calculated it was a candidate for being the highest mountain in Peru. Which, when we got up there, turned out not to be the case. Short by some fifteen or twenty meters of Mount Huascarán in the north."

Willie smiled.

"Well," Hiram said, "none of us would stake good American dollars on my eventual reputation being that of great geographer, would we? No Humboldt he!"

"No," Willie agreed. "But possibly a great—well, something else."

Hiram shrugged. "*Posible.* Anyway, the long and short of it was that to *get* to the base of the mountain we had to cross desert, which I knew would require mules for transportation. So I took Leo Ávila along to the market with me, knowing as a gringo I was bound to be cheated, but hoping Leo could make sure it wouldn't be by overmuch. The mule-drivers, the *arrieros* of Arequipa, they're an infamous lot—cowboys, gypsies and hoodlums all rolled together. Known especially for the outlandish care they take gussying up their animals. And themselves as well. The others swarmed all over us, but my attention went to this one man who hung back. A certain conspicuous *neatness* about him. Not of a physical sort, really, though I noted he was clean too, which I didn't give a hang about. More his separateness. Discretion. His mules drawn up in a nice attentive squadron beside him. Turned out he and Leo knew each other. Ernesto's mother has been the lifelong maid and companion to an aunt of Leo's in Cuzco. Raised together, brothers, until the inevitable moment when Leo had to start acting the master and Ernesto the servant."

Willie was nodding. "That the reason Ernesto stayed shy of you and Ávila in the market?"

"*One* of them. There are plenty more. As you are bound to discover, Ernesto's whole life is a series of mysteries, one Chinese-boxed inside the next. Plus the proverbial sea of troubles as well."

"What troubles?"

"A wife and four little kids in Cuzco. The woman moved out, went home to her family, supposedly because Ernesto couldn't support her. Then there were threats and demands for money from the father-in-law, a lien placed on Ernesto's salary, so he decamped for Arequipa."

"And does he know Cuzco is the next stop? that you're planning on taking him back there?"

"Oh yes. He's quit on nearly a daily basis for a week now. Giving his notice is Ernesto's favorite weapon. Soon as I got through the whole rigamarole of purchasing his mules and engaging his services, which here, as in Mexico, involves a good deal of drinking and affirming that you have read the other fellow's character and have found it to be of sterling quality et cetera et cetera, just, in fact, when I thought we were all settled and ready to move on Coropuna, Ernesto comes back to me with the news he is up for a job as head wrangler for some rancher in Arequipa who breeds fine horses. His proposition was that *if* he got the other job, *then* and only then would he come work for me."

"I don't understand that," Willie said.

"Neither did I. Simple, though, once you become familiar with the man's logic. *If* he proved indispensable in the rancher's eyes, *then* we would all have the necessary evidence that he was worth what I was offering him."

A soft cool breeze brought in with it noises of the street below. There would be loud talking and the rumble of carts and then spaces, complete calm through which Willie could hear, as now, the far-off tooting of a whistle or a cat voicing a mild, questioning meow. He reached for new cigarettes and shook two out of the package. "Stress," he said.

"How's that?"

"The means there is to apply tension to the situation, to pull on the extremes and see where the stress lines appear. To my mind, not the happiest way to conduct human affairs."

"Nor to mine."

Willie couldn't help a small sniff and then a grieved little smile. Hiram laughed. There was between them a strong shared memory for certain things they had said to one another over the years. Willie, at least, was recalling Hiram's telling him once how emotions *must* be facts of some sort and that an experimentalist like himself only recognizes as fact what can be proved today and again tomorrow, even if tomorrow is a Sunday.

"It's a forceful tactic, though," Hiram said.

"Oh yes, the one of princes. And scientists."

"You learn quick and cheap what people *really* care about instead of what they *say* they care about."

"Or is it that when you put a fellow on the spot the only thing you're likely to find out is how mean he can be?"

31

Willie's question went unanswered. There was suddenly much commotion in the street below, clopping hoofs mixed with the sweet pure sounds of the brass bells which *llamas* wear around their necks and on their bridles. And then someone shouting Hiram's name.

Christina was at the doorway. "Leo's come," she announced happily.

Hiram said, "What? no trumpets to precede him?"

"Nearly." She went to the window and pushed the shutters full out. "You all should come look. He's some sight, for sure."

Willie got up and went over to the window. Below, though not very far because he was mounted on a giant black horse, was Leo Ávila, dressed precisely, crisply, in a green *kepi* with a lacquered black visor and a newly pressed green military tunic. Drawn up behind him was a pack of about twenty *llamas*, their leads in the hands of five Indian porters. The entire entourage was decked out in elaborate finery, the beasts in their tassels and bells, the men in bright striped woolen caps and *ponchos*.

Hiram was behind Willie, hidden from the sight of those on the street. "Could have loaded it all on our own damned mules," he said in a low voice.

"Hiram?" Leo Ávila called. "Ho! is there no one up there?"

"Is the other room packed?" Hiram asked.

"Almost," said Christina.

"Good."

Hiram all at once swung into action. Finding his pants on the floor, he was into them in little more than a single motion. He pulled the black galluses up over his broad shoulders and let them snap in place, then said, "Willie and I will step out for a bit then."

"But Hiram, it's you that Leo will want to talk to, make plans with."

"I'm sure," Hiram said. "Take care of it, my dear. You know I trust your judgment in all things, in this as in the others. Everything will go just fine. I gave him all the money he'll need yesterday. So not another *sol.*" Hiram put his feet into his boots and, without stopping to strap them up, charged into the outer room.

Willie was about to follow. But he hesitated and then, very calmly, as though his own slowing could bring the pace of the morning back to a walk, he touched Christina's arm and said, "That's quite some procession *Señor* Ávila got up."

Christina only nodded.

"I mean if the locals are already suspicious the gringos mean to cart off their ancient treasures, *Señor* Ávila's certainly doing all he can to fan their fires."

"He doesn't care what *they* think," Christina said fiercely. Then, in her more usual voice, "Leo imagines it's his duty to show us the glories of Peru. Whenever in his eyes it doesn't measure up, doesn't all seem as wonderful as it really is, he gets afraid we'll be unamused, so he takes it on himself to provide the additional spectacle—gilt for the lily."

They heard the hall door opening, and then Hiram telling Ernesto to meet him and Willie at some place called Rayas del Sol as soon as he was through here.

Christina went into the outer room. "Hiram, what about the archaeological pieces? I thought they were so special you wanted to pack each of them yourself."

"I've changed my mind, my dear. You do it. I'm sure Leo or our friend Ernesto will be glad to— We've agreed to that, haven't we?"

"To what?"

"That we are free to change our minds. Coming, Willie?"

Hiram went out. Willie nodded to no one in particular and went to the door. There he turned and said apologetically to Christina, "I should go along and see can I keep him out of trouble."

Christina didn't respond. She stood in the middle of the room gazing down on her hands as though they were strangers to her. On her face there was an expression Willie had seen a hundred times before. Not anger at Hiram, at least none showing. Rather, a daze. The intelligent child who has been slapped trying to find the reason for it. Benito had come down from the bed in the other room, all alert, ears up, and now insisted his big head against his mistress's side. She let her hand stroke his muzzle.

They looked posed for a photograph, the sort laundry-soap manufacturers put on their calendars. 'DEVOTION,' it would probably be called. And the only saving grace, Willie thought, would be if you could somehow hit the contrast—the purity of the dog's devotion against the sad confusion brought on by the woman's turning aside into that solitary path.

ERNESTO missed Willie and Hiram at Rayas del Sol, but managed to track them down at the third place they stopped. By then they had already switched from the dark, full German-style beer to more serious Pisco and the afternoon and even the rays of the actual sun were gone and there was only half-light remaining out over the Lake.

One of the men at the next table had left for a few minutes and now returned with a plateful of rich-smelling pieces of meat broiled on sticks. The sight set Willie's insides to rumbling. He hadn't eaten since breakfast.

"Are you interested?" Ernesto asked.

"Only to know what it is," Willie said.

"*Anticuchos,*" the Peruvian said.

"Beef heart marinated and cooked over charcoal," Hiram said in English. "Delicious." He fished in his pocket and brought forth a whole wad of *soles,* which he put on the table before Ernesto.

Getting to his feet, Ernesto sorted through the bills and chose one, then handed the rest back to Hiram and started for the door.

"Wait, Ernesto," Willie called after him, "I didn't mean—" But the man had already ducked out into the street.

"I didn't want him to imagine he had to attend to my every wish."

"That he will not do anyway," Hiram said. "Though at times, when it pleases him, you'll find he may *insist* on waiting on you. Here, give me your hand."

Willie held his out and Hiram covered it with both of his larger, fleshier, warmer paws. He was red in the face, head lowering, at least a full step beyond where Willie thought himself to be on the drunk's descent (or ascension, whichever it was), at a place that, whenever *he* reached it, Willie knew he was either about to pass out or lose whatever was on his stomach. Hiram, though, could linger at this stage for hours when he wanted to.

"Welcome." Hiram's hand squeezed Willie's.

"Welcome yourself."

"No, I mean this, Willie." Hiram's head swung up a little. The bottom rims of his eyes were damming tears. "I've wanted you to know one thing: your pal H.B. is dying."

Hiram's oldest song. How many times had Willie heard it? Public performances, private ones, poetically in telegrams, such as the occasion Hiram had run amok in El Paso and wired Willie repeatedly about 'going over,' meaning into dementia, into death, as well of course as taking the blasted train into Mexico. Despite this history of false alarms, Willie now addressed Hiram seriously. "Dying?" he repeated, "what of?"

"I told her—I told them *both*—'Do as you like. Stay or go, as you wish. But not in my company, please, for I will not be *reduced* bit by bit, destroyed, by anyone else.' " Hiram wiped tears off his cheeks with the back of his hand. "The whole time here, Willie, it's been so awful."

Willie remembered Ernesto last night starting to give a warning, then backing off. And Christina today, surrounded by all the neatly bound-up boxes and baskets, Benito pushing against her skirts.

Then he knew. "The lieutenant," he said, "what's-his-name, Ávila. Is that it?"

"Given who he is and who we are, how could he *not* be drawn to her? The gold of her hair, the knowledge we aren't really married, which to his way of thinking makes Christie a woman of easy virtue, the possibility of having his revenge on the *yanki* who took him up and treated him like a— Oh," Hiram shuddered, "an impossibly rich mixture of motives."

"But why would Christina be taken in by any of that?"

"It's flattery. No, better, it is *attention*, Willie, of a sort I don't think you and I even know how to lavish on anybody. Not in our northern way of doing things. In our terms, 'shameless.' But for Christina, like nothing she's ever known."

"Certainly from what she's said, nobody in that blessed family of hers ever took a moment. Nobody before you, Hiram."

"And with me, well, it's been time now and things famously erode in time, you know, so now when *I* tell her— Besides, he's handsome. And young. And *of* the place, *of* the Peru kept secret from us by dint of our being outlanders."

"Was there actually an affair?"

Hiram's breath caught and came out in a deep groan. He wiped his eyes on the back of his sleeve and looked up again. "You were brought up Catholic. Even better than I you must know a sin is a sin whether of the body or dwelling only in the mind."

Willie gave a little laugh. "That was the exact point where I began to fall away, Hiram. When the weight of responsibility for my meandering fancy descended on me. What is and what I wish are so very far apart I can't hold myself accountable for both."

"God, I'm happy you're here. In the worst of it I prayed to you, Willie, actually did pray that you would see clear to coming. You're the only one in the world I can unburden myself to."

"Let me ask this: when you found out what was going on, why didn't you give this *Teniente* Ávila the sack?"

"For a time I thought I'd have to kill him."

"I meant something less dramatic—simply telling him his services were no longer required."

"Leo's from the impecunious branch of the great Ávila clan. But that doesn't keep him from being well connected. All the permissions to dig where we want and remove archaeological objects we signed in Lima bear the seal of Leo's uncle, who happens to be the cabinet minister for interior affairs. What I've done instead was use every means available to prove my contempt for him."

"How's that?"

"Leo thought things should continue between him and me in the way they were when I was here last time. So I set about and built Ernesto up, made *him* my right-hand man. The notion that I could rely on anyone else, particularly a fellow who taught himself to read and write and whose mother is a kitchen helper, that has become a widening, contaminated wound to Leo's endless pride."

Willie laughed. "Where's the evil in that?"

"Creating enmity between two men which will linger long after we're gone. Poor Ernesto will have no defense against Leo once we leave."

"But what could he do?"

"See to it Ernesto's mother loses the only employment she's ever had. Also, there's universal conscription here and Ernesto's never served."

"But he must be my age, Hiram. That's a little past usefulness to the military."

"Not legally. Not if Leo wanted to inform on him. Which is why I *have* to take Ernesto back to the States with me and see to it he gets some training in something. Armor against his life here. Because at the moment he is in the vulnerable position and I am the one who put him there. Which is where *you* come in, Willie."

"How so?"

"I mean to give Ernesto the greatest gift I have to give anyone."

The man in question was coming in from the now black street bearing a tin plate laden with steaming *anticuchos.*

"You're in luck, Hiram. Here's Ernesto himself. Tell *him* what his bonanza is to be."

Hiram would not be so easily jostled out of his conspiratorial seriousness. "But the gift is you, Willie! I am going to give Ernesto *you* to be his friend."

"Jesus!"

"What's there?"

It had been anger, a pang of it, sharper in Willie's gut than the pangs of hunger. But now passing. In a calm voice, as though speaking to a novice, Willie said, "Hiram, you can't *give* people to each other. Not any more than you can 'give' them those other favorites of yours, their 'freedom' or their 'pride.' You picture yourself the great democrat, fair disregarder of a man's class and antecedents. But what you have in fact is a royal sense of yourself. You the possessor and dispenser of all the king's touches. If Christina leaves you in the end, it won't be for greater swagger and youth, but because of the way your thinking diminishes the rest of us. Here, eat."

Willie passed the plate. Hiram looked at the *anticuchos* blankly. Ernesto shook his head and reached instead for the Pisco to fill their glasses.

Beef heart was not in general Willie's favorite food. But under its carbon crust this meat was juicy, vinegary and sweet at the same time. It had been soaked a long while in something spicy and had none of the ammoniacal taste he had half expected.

Ernesto was sitting straight up on the bench and gazing evenly at Willie. "I have made my decision," he said. "It will be impossible for me to go to the United States. Not because the offer isn't grander than I am worthy of—surely it must be—but because of considerations in my personal life."

"What are those?" Willie asked.

Tears ran down the Peruvian's cheeks, so plenteous that before he could speak again they had run out to the broad ends of his mustache and made them wet. Willie thought of cats, of a fullness they get about the jowls and whiskers when they have been out hunting.

"Our friend here," Ernesto nodded toward Hiram, "has explained to me how in your profession you must become an expert at reading another man's character in an instant. Otherwise you could not make the portraits which have brought you fame."

"I'm not exactly—" Willie began.

But Ernesto held up his hand. "Please, allow me my moment. So by now you must have figured out that in this world I am a man who counts for nothing. Which is true."

Again Willie opened his mouth. "Please," Ernesto said, "just the moment. What you may not know is that, though I take no pride in myself, I am in fact the father of four little children. And in them I have a certain pride. Where are these offspring then? you ask. Not here. Not dwelling in the security of their father's love. Then what pride can I rightly take in them? None at all. My little ones orphans, or worse than orphans. I know how it is growing up without a father, for that was my own situation as well. But why, then, if I feel so strongly? Because my wife has locked them away from me." Ernesto stopped to drink. "She even got an order lodged with the police in Cuzco which prohibits me from loitering in the street outside my father-in-law's house where I might catch a glimpse of them! So I went away to Arequipa, thinking in time it would be less painful for the children to believe their father had abandoned them. But it hasn't worked out. My mother visits them. So I hear what lies they tell even my little namesake. And I know too what my wife would say if I went off as far as North America. The final desertion, the ultimate proof there was in me no love for any of them. I am sorry."

"And there's nothing to be done about all this?"

"When we reach Cuzco we can see," Hiram said. "There are bound to be legal ways to pry the children loose from their clutches, even if only for an hour at a time."

"But there's no use," Ernesto said. "By now my wife will have them poisoned against me completely."

"That's not certain, Ernesto," Willie said. "Remember the capacity children themselves have for believing. That fact is on your side. In my own case, my father—"

But this wasn't the time.

What had come to mind, clearer and brighter than reality, was a picture of Willie's own father fairly dancing down the middle of Maple Street in Cambridge in a hat ludicrously small for his big head and an open overcoat too heavy for the October afternoon. He was leading on a rope an imposing horse of the sort brewers have pull their gilded wagons in fairs. This would be 1887 or so, Willie eight years old. Probably neither he nor his younger brother had seen the old man for a year or more. To other children they accounted for his absence by claiming he was a sailor on a ship, though between themselves they usually understood this was a lie. He had come to find out who would like to go for a ride, their father said. Both boys already up on the animal's broad slippery back, legs sticking straight out, when their mother appeared at the door to ask their father where he had stolen the horse from. 'Borrowed, my dear,' his father had sung out. 'Well, and when are you planning on returning my children to me, Jack?' 'In a trice, my dear, in the twinkling of an eye' was the reply, the last thing Willie could recall about his father alive. When he died they had been taken to the wake and had been led up to the coffin, little Danny and little Willie, but the paraffin-still face inside was not anybody Willie would ever admit to knowing.

"Hope!" he announced to Ernesto. "We think we can give our children all sorts of things, money et cetera, a start in life. But there is really only one thing useful for the journey parents can outfit their offspring with, which is—"

Speaking, Willie heard the quivering timbre of his own voice and knew he had reached his moment. *El Punto.* In Willie right now, heart fluttering, chest, whole body lifting, rising, *this car going UP!* the attendant says, Willie trying to fix on Ernesto's large eyes while he mumbles "—my own father too busy to stop for anything except to teach me—" Willie in tears now, too. Tasting them. Catching the bug. Third of three tonight. A thought he had had yesterday at the depot. Willie Hickler at large in the land where men cry. Amazement at Willie: after such a long long time of the other, so very very *happy.*

"Spit it out, old man." Hiram speaking English.

"Hope," Willie said again, in Spanish. "The ability to look forward to our lives with real, unwavering hope. That is all we can pass on to anybody else anyway."

FOUR

A RASPING sound, a spark, a little jump of light, a round flame first freely floating in the darkness, then, cradled yellow in Ernesto's cupped hands, brought over and put to the lamp wick and trapped in the bottom of the glass chimney.

Home to the room they shared in the hotel.

Willie moved forward till his chin hung directly over the lamp, hairs of his beard lifting in the upflowing warmth, the smell of kerosene.

Willie so very drunk. So keyed up.

Ernesto lay stretched out on the board floor in the narrow passage between the two beds, eyes closed, back of the hand which clutched the box of matches to his forehead. For statues and actors, the sign of the distraught, the sorrowful, those in mourning.

Willie plunked down next to him. "A question."

"And from there—an answer."

"Beyond whatever money you make from Hiram, what is it *you* want out of all of this?"

Ernesto's eyes came open. "Only to help *Señor* Bingham, to make sure he has the best chance to complete the work he came to do."

"But for yourself, Ernesto, what?"

"Nothing. Except to live a little harder, stronger, to the very limit of my strength and endurance. They have been extremely good to me, Hiram and Christina both. They have shared their secrets with me. Both. And I have told them mine."

Ernesto's eyes closed again.

Tiny man. Little feet in beat-up muddy boots. Larger through the shoulders, base to a big head. The face, so active, mobile in the daytime, now at rest was all worry, fret. A sea of troubles, what Hiram had said. Protestant hymns: 'Deck thyself, my soul, with gladness . . .' the tune as well as the words running through Willie's fuddlement, 'Leave the gloomy haunts of . . .'

Was it that? the *sadness* Willie found so powerful, so attractive, so *like* his own? Ernesto the little father, the brother, calling out to the self inside Willie which did not duck, which faced up to the terrible brevity of it all, to the promise of Doomsday being any day, not so grand, no trumpets, no graves yawning, only an ending tailor-made for each and every one?

"Ernesto? let me say a little, one traitorous sentence, and then never again. I promise. I want to warn you: try not to be drawn in by Hiram's great belief in his own importance. I'm speaking from experience. It's not a life for a life. The danger is giving up your own cause because of the great demands of his."

"I have no cause of my own. I am a whore."

Soy puto.

The words shocked Willie. "That's not true," he said quickly.

"A servant, then."

"That's not so either."

"A servant of God. Aren't you?"

"I don't know anymore."

Silence. What Willie had said hanging before him. No way to know whether it had been heard. Ernesto's breath shushing out, drawing in. He had passed out.

Willie gathered him up and lifted him onto the bed nearer the window. He loosened Ernesto's shoes and brought them off his feet. Some kind of raggedy dirt-crusted socks with holes. He unbuttoned the top of Ernesto's shirt.

Ernesto stirred, protesting, tried to rise, sank back. Tried again and made it. "Towel," he said. He found one on the foot of the bed, then lurched to the door and went out.

Willie hesitated. Came into the hall a moment later. Pitch dark, dank-smelling. His leg brushed something, cloth, bulk. It stirred. Indians huddled against the wall to sleep. Given a night's *posada,* rest. Give me peace. Somewhere nearby the sound of water. Willie moved ahead toward it, his hand streaking the cold wall to guide him, foot tentative, probing each step so he wouldn't trip over people again. Hand on the knob of the door of what must be the washroom when there came a shout, an agonizing cry. Willie stopped. Cold. In the silence he could hear his own heart going. A dream. A drunk off somewhere hallooing into the night. To plug the black emptiness with at least something. Or mayhem. Or a soul hailing Charon.

He turned the handle. Inside, light, a faint gray square high on the far side, a small, divided, tiled room filled with warm vapor. A shoulder-high barrier, Ernesto's pants and shirt flung on a little bench to Willie's side of it, the man himself dim, hidden by steam and water gushing from an arched pipe halfway up the wall.

"Ernesto? may I come in with you?"

"Yes, come on."

Willie got out of his own clothes. The floor tile cold. Willie's cock was nearly hardened. He put his hand in front of it to shield himself, then let it go. Willie ashamed, then not ashamed. Ernesto moved away from the pipe and Willie, shivering, got under and drenched his head, then hungrily turned himself back and forth to get the heat to run everywhere. The drain was clogged and the water came up to their ankles. Willie stepped half aside to share the stream, his penis brushing against Ernesto's side. Ernesto's body all muscular, tight, his shoulders directly below Willie angled planes, like armor, glowing softly. The smaller man reached out and up to the window ledge where there was a stone bowl and brought back a handful of something. A small circumcised penis he had, a little drawn-up scrotum. He offered his hand to Willie full of soft tallowy soap. Willie took some and Ernesto spread what was left in a big circle on his own stomach. Willie asked could he put the soap on. Ernesto said go ahead. Willie brushed the coarse hair up off Ernesto's neck and started at the prominent knob of bone at the base of the head, running his hands out along the shoulders and down the arms, then returning and going down the back to the slight outcurve of the buttocks. He left off there and, turning Ernesto toward him, swept soap up from his belly with one hand to his nipples, then down into his pubic hair with the other, touching and briefly holding first the little cock and then the light sack so he could feel the round moving of the testicles. Ernesto stood still through this, head bent forward into the stream of the water. He stepped out again to scoop more soap from the bowl. "Now I'll do yours?" Willie said yes, do it. Himself stood still, felt Ernesto's hard smooth palms moving rapidly over him, efficient, down his back, around to his stomach, circling there. Ernesto's head inclined a bit, as if he had to look at it first, was curious, then his hand cupped, moving out Willie's penis and back, drawing off the foreskin, once only, the slick feel of soap. "There," Ernesto said, "done. You wash off now."

Willie sluiced more water over himself, brushing it hastily down his body. Ernesto was beyond the half-wall wiping off with the towel. Nearly imbedded in the cement Willie found a large valve key. Burning to the touch when he turned it. The water squeezed off to a trickle.

Ernesto had gone, leaving the door half open. Willie mopped himself quickly with the towel, which was sopping now, put on his clothes without fastening anything except the top button of his pants, and barged out into the hall.

In the room, Ernesto stood fully dressed in the warm lamplight, looking around him for something.

"What is it?" Willie asked.

"I have to go out," Ernesto said softly.

"I'll go with you, then. Where to?"

"Nowhere. I just have to go."

"Ernesto, I—" Willie's throat hard with the beginning of a full apology. He didn't know what the words of it would be.

"Excuse me," Ernesto said. *Disculpame.* "I have a secret life I can't let Hiram and *Señora* Christina know about." Ernesto got on his knees between the beds, looked under one, then the other. "You go to sleep now. It's very late."

"I'd like to come with you," Willie said. "That is, if it's no trouble to you." Trouble, *molestia.* In Mexico, at least, this would be the way to trap Ernesto. In politeness, he would have to deny that anything Willie could ask would be a *molestia.*

"Trouble?" Ernesto said, "of course not. What trouble?"

Willie suddenly let go to sadness and disappointment. If he had to use tricks to make Ernesto take him along, it wasn't worth going. He picked up the boots off the chair in the corner where he himself had put them and held them out. "Are these what you're looking for?"

Ernesto nodded and took the boots. While he was getting into them, Willie removed his own clothes again, leaving the pants on the floor where he stepped free of them, the shirt dropped beside it. He pulled back the blankets and got into bed, burrowing down in its lumpy hillocks, his body seeking the contours of the resting place it had made for itself the night before. The last he remembered was Ernesto close by him again saying Willie? in a whisper, and his asking what? and Ernesto asking should he kill the lamp? and Willie saying no, he'd prefer it left to burn itself out. Though this, like everything which came after it, could also have been dream.

POUNDING on the door jolted Willie awake. "No," he managed to groan, some part of his mind alerted, racing to find the Spanish for 'not now.' But before the words could come to his lips, the knob turned and the door swung open and Hiram pushed into the room all smiles, his mustache freshly brushed, a big capped bottle of beer tucked in the crook of his arm and another, foaming, thrust out toward Willie.

Christina was behind Hiram in a white shirtwaist and pearly-gray skirt. Could she come in as well? Willie pulled the covers up over his chest and said now it was all right.

"Ernesto not sleep in?"

Willie raised his head. The bed across from his was still fully made up. "Seems not."

"Damn!"

"What's wrong?"

"Only that when I woke up this morning it came to me that we're free, old friend. Free. Now that Leo's taken the *equipaje*, there is, as they say, nothing that need detain the experienced traveler a moment longer. Serendipitously, the train departs Puno for Cuzco at two o'clock this afternoon and we—" Hiram brought from his pocket four pieces of elaborately gravured green pasteboard and flourished them for Willie and Christina to see "—we happy few are aboard. It's the last departure for the week and I even went ahead and arranged the space for Ernesto's damn mules." Hiram plunked down on the bed opposite Willie and drank from the bottle of beer in his hand. "Well, what'd the man *say* when he left? Maybe we can track him down."

"I don't know. Some urgent piece of business came up about two this morning."

"Two? Well, we know what sort of business *that's* likely to have been, don't we?"

Christina blushed and pressed her hands to the front of her skirts.

"Sorry, my dear."

But she was half smiling, not really offended. She sat down beside Hiram on the other bed and put her hand over his. She was fresh too, recently bathed. Fresh from making love, Willie supposed. And likely that as a result of making up their quarrel. Neither seemed to notice Willie's clothes from yesterday underfoot.

"You'll find life with Ernesto full of this sort of thing," Christina said. "Sudden disappearances. I don't know whether he's told you, he misses his children so much—"

"He was off on the subject again last night," Hiram said.

"So *we've* become family to him," Christina said, "which helps him forget his troubles, I think. But then when the memory of the little ones comes back, the distance he has to fall is all that much greater and he has to run away from us for a while. Don't you think that's so, Hiram?"

Considering, Hiram brought the beer to his lips and, finding he had emptied the bottle, set it on the floor by the nightstand. "I think what's so is that that's your theory, my dear," he said. "For myself, I try not to immerse myself in the atrocious morass of human motive. Action and reaction are enough for me. In the case in point, *my* action for a time will be to wait. Then at some point if *Señor* Mena has still not shown his little whiskers, I shall take a look for him in the various stewy purlieus of this place. If he hasn't come to light by a quarter to two, I shall pin a note for him to the ear of one of his fabulous mules. One thing Ernesto can be counted on for: at some point today he will remember to go and water his animals. They are more than his meal ticket, they are his pride and his joy." Hiram got up. "Come join us for breakfast quick as you can, won't you, Willie?"

When Hiram and Christina had gone out into the hall, Willie noticed that the lamp wick was languishing in barely a hair's breadth of kerosene. But the flame continued, entirely subdued, blue, rounded, tiny.

Willie swung his legs out of the bed and his feet hit the cold floor. Shirt and pants crumpled there. The feeling through the whole trunk of him was of things grinding. Of hunger, also of hollowness. It was surprising and ugly, a mean fact, that people still passed in the street outside the room, that he should be privy to the noises of their lives moving straight on ahead when it had been proven to him that his—

The first bits of what he had dreamed in the night had begun to reappear before him. He and his brother, Danny, in reality dead now, packing leather valises for a long trip. It was revealed they were going to fight the Spanish, though whether in Cuba or at Manila Bay was not yet clear. There was a big girl Willie knew as a glass-washer in the back of a bar in New Haven, but in the dream she was in Boston in a little room along a row of door-ajar little rooms, lolling back with her hands behind her head, wearing a felt vest open to show her large slack breasts and the rolls of flesh below them. In the other cubicles, cribs, men and women were grappling with one another, in twos, in threes and fours, in great parties. In the dream Willie's thought had been part in Spanish: 'The whole world fucking. *Menos yo.*' Less me. And on the stone wall at the end of the corridor the tattered half of a poster from a circus, a red wagon with a whole band of identical-looking men clutching their brass instruments for dear life, their white marble eyes staring out at the camera, all with little bristly mustaches, none wide and drooping like Ernesto's, and, above them, a cancellation notice which read 'IT HAS NOT WORKED OUT.'

Willie got out the last of his clean clothes, underwear and a shirt mangled and starched rigid aboard the steamer he had come down on. He paused a moment, wishing he didn't have to wear them, these last pieces of evidence that once he had managed to live somehow in order. Then he went ahead and dressed. His brown worsted suit was beginning to smell. Not so unpleasant, though, he decided. More dusty than dirty. His own odor becoming thinner and vaguely exotic in the thinner, exotic atmosphere. An elusive talcum-powder smell.

Why, although he made no appearance there, did Hiram's presence penetrate every image in the dream? And, deeper, more vaguely, a more distant watcher, the face of Willie's mother?

He was with Hiram and Christina in the hotel dining room eating slices of papaya when the answer began to emerge. There were large windows on three sides of the room which provided a panoramic view of the Lake. The sunlight this morning, thin, astringent, brought every detail nicely clear and exact. The reeds down by the shore stood up in precise parallels like the half-hatching for shadow in a lithograph. The low-lying reed boats slipped over the flat surface, poled by the natives so effortlessly that they created no discernible wake, only perfect slow-expanding circles where their poles came out of the water.

The key was this: the life they said had not worked out was his mother's. In childhood, when he got up the courage to ask why it was she couldn't stay with them at home, his aunts and his grandfather would answer him, 'Poor woman,' or maybe 'A bad match, your father,' or, once, 'You too will learn some day, Willie, that it *does* happen in this world, there are simply some unfortunate souls whose lives don't work out.'

As a child, obstinate, hopeful, he would not believe. Twenty-some years afterwards on visits to the state place at Waltham when his mother was neither down and out nor on her high horse about the indignities she suffered at the hands of the attendants, Willie always found it strange that she herself was of the same opinion: 'You know,' she would say, 'I have nothing against any of them anymore. If they could forgive me—and I include the dead ones too—I would, for my part, gladly let it all go by. I'm only a sad person, you know, Willie. Somehow I couldn't make it come out right for me. Not anything to mourn after, dear.'

Mourn for her life? No, that he thought he'd never really done. Instead he had taken it for a fable and used its morals to construct as his own a story which was as unlike hers as he had the power to make it. Helen Danaher had offered herself up on the twin altars of Art and Love. About Art, Willie was as wary as a barefoot boy in a field of fresh cowflap. About Love: His mother had loved to distraction an Englishman of great charm named John Hickler, who, through no fault of his own it seemed, was not capable of the protracted balancing act which is called marriage. Whereas for Willie, around the time he came of age, he also came to understand that he probably would not marry. His body (and even his soul, if he possessed one) longed for the touch of other men. As an idea this did not surprise him. He knew the poet Walt Whitman had believed that men could achieve together not only a satisfying and holy union of their separate selves, but also a universal fellowship of comrades which would hasten the coming of a true democracy to all the world. About the international camaraderie, the band of brothers, Willie was distantly and mildly skeptical. About the possibility of the physical and spiritual union of two men, he thought perhaps. But for himself, no. He had tried. In several different cities he had gone to the bars along the waterfront where men danced together. At first the sight of them—they openly caressed each other's bodies as they moved, bit at one another's ears—would excite Willie till he trembled. But he could not imagine Willie into the picture even though it was right there before his eyes. The ladylike ones, though endearing in the way they came over to say their grandiloquent hellos and to tug his beard, only unsettled him. He would not have minded, he thought, had he come into the world a woman, but he dreaded the idea of himself as a flimsy parody of something he was not. The others, sailors or husky mechanics with their sleeves rolled, he experienced a heavy physical longing for. But even then he could not believe *they* might have designs similar to his. He assumed they must come to such places only out of hardship, strange ports, horns honed by months at sea and no wages to spend on girls. So Willie had reconciled himself to the notion that he was not ever going to be able to have the kind of love he wanted. And because of the moral he drew from the story of his mother, the sadness of this capitulation, of giving up, had brought with it a measure of relief. She had always said she prayed for her firstborn to see clear to becoming a priest. Willie had gone as far as taking the vow of celibacy. The burden of responsibility for the mysteries he had so far managed to evade.

But now what? Clearly the life constructed out of contraries, by avoiding the traps in his mother's life, hadn't worked out either. Within thirty-six hours of his arrival at the verge of Lake Titicaca, Willie Hickler had found a man he had thought it possible for him to love. And had so disgusted the fellow with his advances that the man had run away. Willie was so ashamed of himself and fearful of their finding out that he could hardly bear to look up from his plate at either Hiram or Christina. The only solution he could think of for the moment was to ask if he could be taken out and done away with.

"What?"

Hiram had asked him some question.

"Sorry," Willie said, "I got distracted."

"I was noting that you seem to have disregarded instruction and went ahead and brought your camera stuff along with you."

Willie attempted a smile. "A photographer hardly feels himself without a couple hundred pounds of equipment strapped about his body."

"We were wondering, Christina and I, if you would consent to a little portraiture this morning? That is, unless you had something else on the agenda."

"No," Willie said, "nothing at all planned except trying to lop off this bulbous, burdensome head I got myself somewhere."

Christina said, "You know I wouldn't ordinarily trouble you, Willie, not for the world. Only I finally had courage—I think the distance away from them was a help—to go on ahead and let my parents know most of what I think they've long suspected about Hiram and me. They wrote and asked for our photograph. Which seemed to me brave and forgiving, at least for *my* folks."

Willie went back to the room to unpack his 8 x 10 camera. No sign of Ernesto. Returning, he set Hiram and Christina at a table by the east window. Except for a small patch spilling over Christina's shoulder, there was no direct sun on the couple. But the light was hitting the white tablecloth before them and provided a strong inferent glow which illuminated their faces from below like a row of theatrical footlights, knocking out Hiram's extra chins and the pouches under his eyes.

Willie tried one, but, as usual when the situation was pleasing to him, his subjects responded badly. Told that they should expect to sit still for several seconds, both went rigid, Hiram as fish-eyed and unforgivingly formidable as any paterfamilias, Christina arrow-straight in her chair and absolutely stricken. As soon as it was over, however, Willie said, "*Excelente*" and pretended to make a minor adjustment of the lens and to say he would like to try it again at a different aperture just for sureness' sake.

His own tone of voice surprised him. It was that pleasant, reasonable song he had sung to hundreds, maybe thousands of folks day after day in the skylighted little studio in New Haven. Making his bread and butter. That was it, of course, the solution. He would go home, take up the existence familiar to him. Tell Hiram for some unknowable reason Peru just didn't excite him.

Did not suit. And hope Ernesto would keep mum. No cause for doing himself in. The real canon against self-slaughter is that ceaseless rambling prayer called ordinary life.

Hiram ordered a glass of brandy and drummed his fingers on the tablecloth while he waited for it to come. Willie put in a new negative and got the bulb in hand again without even a second glance in the back of the camera. He could do that. Once he had it framed, a picture stayed in mind for him. He had a certain contempt for any photographer who had to keep peeping and peeping again at his composition.

The waiter had just appeared and set the brandy before Hiram and Willie had drawn in breath when Christina broke out delightedly, "There he is!"

"Who?" Hiram turned in his seat.

"Ernesto. Coming out at that door. Down there in the side street. Oh. He's disappeared now."

"Well, so we know he lives," Hiram said.

"Folks, please," Willie said softly, closing his fingers on the rubber bulb.

What he got then was both Hiram and Christina turned to the side toward something bright, Christina only half settled back in her chair, the spot of direct light blotted by her head and providing not quite a nimbus but an airiness all around which made her hair shimmer. And Hiram very dashing, a cavalier. It was not clear if his pleasure was with the same sight as whatever pleased the woman, or whether he was satisfied simply by the vision of her. The qualities of the photograph were movement, surprise and, most of all, expectancy.

Willie was gratified enough by the print he made for Christina to send her family that, once he had it fixed in the hydrochloric and had set it to dry on a blotter, he locked the negative and a new sheet of paper together in the wood frame again and took it out into the courtyard to expose a copy for himself. No need to bother timing it on his watch. The first one had taken a little less than the period of half a cigarette. He leaned back against the wall, smoked, then closed his eyes and turned his face up toward the light. Almost immediately faint water-colory circles began swirling and exploding against the insides of his eyelids.

"The Indians call this 'the time of day when it is so quiet you can hear the lizards gulping down the sun.' "

Willie's eyes started open. Ernesto stood before him.

"Where'd you come from?"

"You are about to burn yourself, William."

"What? Oh." The cigarette had tilted down in his hand and was furiously consuming itself. Willie dropped it and brought his fingers up to his nose. Bad yellowish smell. Then he remembered. "Jesus!" He stooped and turned the print frame face down.

"What sort of thing is that?"

"I was cooking a picture," Willie said. "Finished now. Are you all right?"

Ernesto said, "I am fine, thank you."

The skin all around Ernesto's eyes was darkened, papery. He looked exhausted. His thick black hair was smoothed down wet to his scalp. A morning bath for him too, like Hiram and Christina. Ablutions, restitutions. Willie brought his watch out of his pocket and flipped open the lid. Startling, disconcerting that it was only eleven twenty. Already such a long day.

"So we are leaving this place finally."

"You saw Hiram?" Willie said.

"In the hall. You will be happy in Cuzco, William." In Spanish it sounded as 'Weel-*yum.*' "Excellent ruins for you to make photographs of, the fortress of Sacsayhuaman—"

"Ernesto, I'm not—" Willie stopped himself.

"Not what?"

He had been going to explain that he was not a photographer of ancient edifices. At least he would never be by choice. But he heard even in his beginning truculence some anger and, of course, hurt. And those were things in himself he preferred not to portray at this tenuous moment.

"In Cuzco I can show you everything," Ernesto went on.

"After all, it is my place. I know Cuzco like the palm of my hand."

Willie regarded his own long fingers, the nicotined crevice between the first and second.

"Why do you smile at that?"

"Only because in English we usually say we *know* things like the *back* of our hand and I looked at mine and all at once it seemed very foreign to me."

"Oh. But it is yours, isn't it? You put on the right one when you got out of bed this morning, didn't you?"

"I think so. Think it's mine." Willie turned his hand back and forth in the sun. Ernesto looked at it with him.

What the hell? Willie thought. Being sold, being played by the very man who had in the night, he was sure, turned from him. And Willie liking it, flirting back, holding out. How, unless he could read minds at a distance, did Ernesto even know there was any question about whether Willie would be going on with them to Cuzco? How know to wait it out through this silly, lingering little bit of conversation? What at stake, of interest, for him? Willie remembering his own thought in the shower, Ernesto standing, soft runny soap in his hand, head inclined a bit in the stream of hot water, inclined a bit to look at Willie's hardened penis before he touched it. Curious.

"Oh, I forgot." Ernesto dug in his pocket. "I found something for you."

What he brought out was a knit Indian cap, nicely folded with rich strings of black, brown and white tassels showing.

"Here, smell," Ernesto said. "It's new. They mostly use wool from *llamas* to make these, but this one I noted because it was *alpaca.* Much softer, finer. 'And big too,' I thought the minute I saw it, 'the woman must have been dreaming of a big man when she made it.' Here, try it on."

Ernesto handed over the cap and Willie put it on. It fit. The earflaps hanging down bothered Willie, so Ernesto folded them up and tied the strings of the tassels together on top. Willie squatted and slipped the wood backing into the print frame so no more light could get on it, then turned it over. The glass side gave a clear reflection of Willie against the faint sky. Princely, he thought.

"Well, if we're going today we don't have a lot of time left, do we?"

"Not if I mean to get my animals watered before I put them on the railroad. Here, shall I carry that for you?"

"No, it's all right," Willie said, getting up. "I can manage."

AT THE time he died, Willie's brother had had a wife, Sara, and two boys barely out of infancy. The three of them lived now in New Haven near Willie. Sara ran the photography studio and took over the portraiture part of it whenever Willie went off wandering. At Juliaca, the crossroads of the southern line, the travelers were told they would have to wait, perhaps all night, because the train from Arequipa which was to meet theirs was detained, so Willie had the opportunity to write something to his sister-in-law.

He told her directly about Ernesto. Almost as soon as the fact had become clear to him, he wrote, his next thought had been, 'Then I will need help,' and he had thought of her. "And then I laughed at myself, realizing that I have *always* called on you from the field when laid low by some strange malady. Do you remember the delphic wire you sent me in Papago territory? CARE WILLIE MORE STOP DAILY EPSOM SALTS FOOTBATH STOP SARA. I was well in a week. Swollen feet and love—there is not another person in the world whose advice I would care about on those two subjects."

He described to Sara a dream he had had rocking in his coach seat an hour before:

"I watched Bolivia across the Lake. It would appear and then would appear to disappear, as though I were a latter-day and lesser Moses subject to fluctuations in my faith in the existence of the Promised Land. Bolivia was mountains and clouds uniting and becoming great striding figures, giants. They were, I realized then, returning. Drawing near, attending, then withdrawing. But now they had come back for good, not withdrawing really for any length of time, merely stepping behind a scrim of pearly clouds some moments, behind bars of light at others.

"Clearly gods. But I couldn't tell which ones. They seemed classical mostly, yet also New World somehow in their diffidence, their distant sweetness. All I could tell for sure was that *they* were waiting for *us*. For us to make the right move, the right gesture. A sacrifice? A change in our ways?

"I got myself a little double-ended reed boat of the kind the natives of the Lake build and loaded on all my camera equipment and set out for Bolivia alone. But the wind was against me. It battered me. The little boat lapped against the reeds growing at the water's edge.

"Then Ernesto Mena had come into the little boat with me. He began tugging in the sail and letting it out so it made a sound like a wheezing, sighing lung, and we were going again. Ernesto was my guide, but we did not yet know much of each other's language, so most of our 'talk' was by signs and motions of the eye. He indicated to me the only way we would ever get across the water was on these short tacks. But I was afraid the gods would mistake our necessary zigzagging for meandering, for irresolution, for wavering faith, and, though I was afraid of going to them, I felt we *had* to, that it was incumbent on us at this moment to fly to them in joy, to welcome them with open arms!

"There was in all of this dread, and also the highest excitement. A hovering, the atmosphere dense with electricity, ready to burst into flame, like the moments in the near West, Oklahoma, Nebraska, when you sense before seeing it the storm about to break, the dome of heaven about to crack and break open over your head, a phenomenon which always brought me back to believing, with my Indian friends, that their Old Ones haven't gone away really. They remain, immanent. Though now in sadness, still continuing, dwelling in all things.

"I just now told Ernesto in my dream the old gods came back. His only question was 'Which ones?'

"I told him among others Eros. Not meaning the tricky little cherub with the darts, but the encompassing, compassionate, vital spirit of renewal and regeneration, the healer-up.

"Write to me please as soon as you can. This is not because I have much fear about what you will think of me. I recall you and the boys going with me to the depot this last time, none of us of course knowing how extended the present separation was to be, and something in your face, some flicker, caused me to tell you not to fret yourself, I would be all right. Your response was 'I only worry about what if something happened to *us*, Willie. I do wish you had someone of your own.' Well, now that has come about."

FIVE

CUZCO," Hiram said. "In his great *Commentary*, Garcilaso de la Vega claims that, to the Inca, the word meant 'navel.' Cuzco, the navel of the universe. A belief found all through history: that there are some few centers of human commotion and concern, focal points in the not-yet-mapped geography of the soul, to which we are drawn over and over by who knows what impulse. Jerusalem. Alexandria. Mecca. Rome. Mexico City. Cuzco. The cradles, or matrices, the moldering flowers which become the seedbeds for each new blossoming, each revolution in mortal thinking."

They were running late, and a misty rain had brought the evening down early. Looking out the coach window, all Willie could tell was that they had come into the bowl of something immense and dark, a valley.

He smiled. "You remind me of all those little towns in Oaxaca and Chiapas. The people there called their village proper 'the navel of the earth' too and, especially at the peak of fiestas with the bands playing and the bells ringing and the rockets going off overhead, all that concentration of human purposefulness would make me feel it too, that we *were* all together in the belly of this whatever *and* all afire. Then the next day I'd be sober and penitent and it would come back to me that these belly buttons of the gods were to be found about every fifteen or twenty miles down the road."

Ernesto was half sitting on the arm of Willie's coach seat facing Hiram and Christina. Hiram asked him what the Quechua for 'navel' was.

Ernesto looked away, then touched his finger to a place right above his belt and, clearly pleased with himself for having retrieved this one, announced, "*Puputi.*"

"Well," Hiram said, "lexical items for body parts shouldn't change much over time. So we cast doubt on Garcilaso and his omphalos."

Then they were slowing into the station.

As they got down to the platform, there was a stir in the crowd, as though royalty or divinity were moving among them. A way came open and down it sailed a tiny woman with a walnut-wrinkled face. She seemed wrapped, rather than dressed, in bolts and bolts of black silk, like a doll or—it pleased Willie to think this—like the mummies of the Inca rulers Hiram had been reading to them about on the journey, swaddled and preserved in temples of their own and carried out in procession for their livelier descendants to view on holy days. Two servingwomen came along right behind this ancient personage. The elder kept the lady's train up off the ground and for some reason was on the border of tears. The younger shaded her mistress with a black umbrella, needlessly, since the platform was protected from the rain by a roof.

"*La Orejona,*" Ernesto said softly.

"Ah—"

Willie knew about her. Leo Ávila's great-aunt. Growing up in the back corridors of her house, Ernesto had said, he and his older brothers and sisters had always called the mistress 'Big Ear,' the name the Spanish had given members of the Inca nobility for the custom of distending the lobes of their ears by inserting gold circlets in them. In this *Doña* Laura's case also because she was an inveterate eavesdropper. She had more or less singlehandedly set in motion an artistic 'renaissance' in Cuzco forty or fifty years ago, collecting traditional Quechua songs and composing elaborate oratorio settings for them, with titles such as "Symphony of the Descent of the Golden *Llama*" and "Incaic Reminiscences," which she then performed in all the principal cities of Peru. These concerts must have been odd affairs, as Hiram had pointed out, since, being a lady, *Doña* Laura could never perform in public. So the occasions had taken place in the salons of private homes with orchestras of a hundred, audiences of perhaps fifty notables and the *diva* singing to them from behind a painted screen in an Indian language the listeners would not admit to understanding even if they mostly did in fact.

When it came time for Willie to be introduced, he was offered a knobby little hand crusted with jewels. To kiss it, he had to lower himself somehow, and the way he did that was to go down almost on one knee. The crowd tittered and Willie wondered why all his democratic common sense had forsaken him so suddenly. But then from their sporadic clapping and murmuring nods he could tell the onlookers approved his gesture greatly.

On their slow progress out toward the street, Hiram gave full vent to his considerable ability at framing florid praises in Spanish. More than a pleasure, what a singular *honor* it was to them, *Doña* Laura's willingness to come out to greet them despite such inclemency in the heavens.

The lady said matter-of-factly that in her nephew Leo's absence from the city she considered it only proper that she represent the Ávilas in this moment.

An enclosed coach waited beyond the portico. *Doña* Laura's women began gathering up the back of her skirts to get her across a muddy patch to it.

"You! Martín!" the lady demanded, "come hold this umbrella up for me."

Ernesto ran to lend a hand.

Willie should have figured it out before. Yet it was only then, when the lady was settled in her coach and the older of the servant women turned to give Ernesto a furtive, clumsy hug before climbing in, that he realized what had transpired. Besides their welcoming, the occasion was also Ernesto's homecoming after several years' absence—but the social situation dictated that he and his mother and sister could not even exchange a greeting except behind *Doña* Laura's back.

When the coach had rumbled off, Willie said, "Martín?"

"My saint's name, what they called me when I was little.

When I was twelve and left home the first time, I started using Ernesto. *La Orejona*, however, would never recognize the right of someone as low as me to change things around like that. So she calls me Martín." Ernesto shrugged. "She's old, after all, ninety they think, and it's not as though I have any great power behind me to insist on the other. So it doesn't matter."

But Willie could tell of course it did and, because he was himself the child of servants, he thought he knew exactly of what cankerous, never healing sort the hurt would be.

It was a Thursday evening when they arrived. Saturday at midmorning, Ernesto found Willie at the Hotel Central and led him off through the narrow streets to the market. They zigzagged between the *puestos* of the Indians with their lodes of tomatoes and cabbages and potatoes of more sizes and colors than Willie had ever seen before laid out on the cobbles, and around behind the Spanish women in black with their baskets hung from their arms, their hands clasped white over the mounds of their stomachs. It was not the main market Ernesto was interested in, but the flea market, which took place on a little street below the last stalls of the butchers and the tinsmiths.

"When I worked in Cuzco, I'd always make up an errand for myself Saturday morning so I could come down here for half an hour or so. There's treasure here sometimes, if you have the eye to find it."

Willie applied himself to the hunt, imitating Ernesto, scanning what the vendors sitting along both curbs had before them, suddenly squatting to finger an item or to lift aside one thing to see what lay under it. One man had laid out on his cloth only large old keys, bolts and rectangular door locks. The fellow next to him specialized in brass, spurs as thin and graceful as wishbones with their rowels missing or blunted or bent into claws, a dark lantern door, simple sun-faced buttons like the ones on the uniform of the soldier Hiram had come to blows with in Puno (though none of the mustachioed pop-eyed officer-suns such as Leo Ávila had, Willie noted). But in many of the arrays the sense of what went with what was totally baffling, at least to a foreigner. One woman offered mostly hats, tattered little caps for babies, the color nearly all washed out of them, varnished white straw hats of the kind Indian women wore in some of the towns, crowns collapsed or brims mangled now, one or two bonnets, an interesting collection Ernesto pointed out of clay faces, quite old and probably taken from broken pots, small porcelain or perhaps wax dolls' heads, some with thin strands of human hair still clinging to them, some missing their noses or with the features all smudged out with age or too much childish attention. As Willie continued staring without moving toward any of the objects displayed, he could feel the woman's eyes stealing up on him. Just as he began to turn away, she laughed and flicked her shawl aside, revealing, next to her other stuff, a box containing three or four glass eyes and a skull, small enough so that if it wasn't a monkey's, it would have to be that of a baby.

Willie shivered.

Farther down the block, in the collection of a toothless old woman, Willie recognized something. It was the torn upper half of a sheet of foolscap with the embossed roman letterhead of the National Savings and Trust Company in Washington, D.C., "chartered," as it said, "by an Act of Congress 1867." The burden of the letter itself was to congratulate Avery Hillman, a Yale undergraduate along on the expedition, on the attainment of his majority and to offer the bank's services in continuing to manage funds left in trust to him by his grandfather Jardin Avery Sanger. All this Willie knew because when they reached the Central Thursday night, they had found some of the gringo party in the midst of a celebration in honor of 'Avery's finally getting his hands on some of his *pizoos*,' as their burly cartographer, Clement Bailey, had proclaimed in a toast. Avery had then read the letter aloud, including the amount due him, well over a million, which some in the group had considered a callow if not uncouth thing to do. Willie was thinking of buying back the top half of the sheet and returning it to Avery as a sort of joke. Then, bending toward it, he saw the blond ringlets of Avery's hair lying on the ground. And for just a bit, maybe because the woman who specialized in things of the head had spooked him so, it occurred to him this lady must have stolen Avery's soul and these were his physical leavings. Near. In fact what was on display was the entire contents of the wastebasket from Avery Hillman's hotel room, including the sweepings from a haircut Avery had had and a matted dirty pile of fluffy dust from under the new millionaire's bed.

As he was beckoning Ernesto to come see, Willie glanced again at the woman. She was huddled back against a closed door, her gums working constantly, her eyes giant. Very hungry, probably, chewing what life there was out of a gooey green wad of *coca* leaves and—Willie felt he could always tell this fact about a person—certainly dead crazy.

When Willie pointed out what he'd discovered, Ernesto shook his head and said, "*I* wouldn't be comfortable knowing she had anything that was mine in her possession."

Ernesto offered her money for Avery's trash. But oh no. She mocked them. She wasn't interested in selling. Not today.

They went on down the street. "There were others like her before," Willie said, "but I thought it was my fault being a gringo that I couldn't find anything of any value in their collections."

"I've always liked the mad ones' being there," said Ernesto, "no idea left in *their* heads of any difference between what's useful and what's garbage. Laughing themselves sick over all the rest of our fine, sane decisions to choose *this* piece of junk instead of *that.*"

Soon it began to seem to Willie only logical that the first thing a person born and mostly bred in Cuzco as Ernesto was would want you to see would be its flea market.

For Cuzco, this navel of the mother earth, was, as a city, a junk heap. A place where you had to move with care and not be singleminded, because here history had come unglued. Bits of different pasts flitted like lint across the plaza. Pieces of the scenery from various tragedies and religious and historical dramas were stashed face to face in no particular order. At the tedious business of excavating centers of human enterprise which lie under one another, the archaeologist depends a good deal on death or destruction, because these usually act like layers of lead to separate and distinguish the eras. Cuzco had no such markers. For eight hundred years its life had been continuous. So, in its corporate form, the city was like the individual of perfect memory—that is, unhinged, child and man and ancient in the same breath.

It therefore behooved the visitor who wished to understand what was going on round about him, Willie thought, to become a bit unhinged himself, to detach the head and shake contents vigorously.

Or at a minimum, it behooved and amused a slightly-underemployed-photographer-with-some-time-on-his-hands-while-he-waited-for-Ernesto-Mena to sit in the park facing the cathedral and there to peruse Hiram's copy of Carlos Zárate's *Account of the Conquest of the Empire Called Pirú*, published in Spain in 1534, and from time to time to look up and squint and try to imagine things not as they were, but as they had appeared to a friar in the sixteenth century.

This Zárate and two of the soldiers were the only Europeans to visit the Inca holy city before it fell to the Spanish. Atahualpa, the Inca, had been tricked and captured by Francisco Pizarro with his troop of about a hundred and eighty at a place since called Cajamarca six hundred miles through the mountains to the northwest. For his ransom, Atahualpa promised the invaders a storehouse full of gold. And though the stuff began to flow in daily from all parts of the realm and mounted toward the mark they painted along the walls of the chosen room, the Spaniards grew impatient. They continued to hear from traitorous informants the fabulous accounts, including the hardly believable tale that Cuzco's mighty temples were faced with plates of gold. But Atahualpa's general in the capital, one Quisquis, had yet to forfeit a single precious object.

Zárate was ordered to go along with the other two because he could write. Their job was to reconnoiter and estimate the potential size of the riches still to come.

They were carried the two hundred leagues of their journey in litters, hammocks borne on poles by relays of straining men. And so, almost incidentally, became the first whites to travel a large portion of the Inca Highway, an engineering wonder of the world which tied together the mountain heights and the chasms with a ribbon of stone causeways wide enough for two men to pass on the run and endless, carefully hewn stairways and thick-roped footbridges.

Though the Spaniards had arrived from the north and Willie had approached from the south, Zárate's mounting excitement with the *increasing order* of the landscape was very much like Willie's own feeling had been on the train:

> On the twenty-second day since setting off from Cajamarca, we at last attained a vantage point beyond which even the most scrupulous eye would not be able to detect a single mote more of wilderness, only terraces built one upon another up the sides of every mountain, a geometrician's paradise, the walls and pavings all regular, the road at times passing through tunnels carved in the living rock, watchtowers set atop pinnacles already remote, commanding and grand.

The main square of Cuzco, large and airy in the present day, would have been almost twice as grand when Carlos Zárate first saw it from up the hill. Where it was bound on the southwest now by a row of whitewashed shops under an arcade, a stream called the Huaytanay had flowed—'mirthfully' was how Zárate had heard it—over rocks in an open channel, it and others like it throughout the city carrying off the effluence of the inhabitants, yet maintained so well the Inca and his attendant ladies often came down to splash and bathe in the crystal water. (Once the Spanish took control, cleanliness, like the orderliness which so amazed Zárate, had been among the first things to go. Fifteen years after the Conquest, writers were complaining, as though there were a native conspiracy, that the Huaytanay stank to high heaven and had strangely become clogged with filth.) Beyond the stream had been a second graveled plaza used for public entertainments and festivals. The near side had been flanked by high-walled enclosures or *canchas*, the palaces the Incas built themselves which had been kept as their mausoleums and memorials when they died.

Willie stood a moment to stretch his legs and to get from his pants pocket a two-inch square of white stone he had bought in the market. Then he sat again.

As he had thought, he was once more under careful scrutiny. Across the paving from him was an Indian woman crushed against the curlicued arm of an empty park bench, an infant sleeping on her lap with a cloth shielding its face from the sun. Whether doped or drunk or simply tired, to appearances the woman had seemed beyond curiosity about anything. But the moment Willie moved, twin sharpshooters had begun to follow him from the black void under the brim of her bowler.

He rubbed some at the red dust still caked on the stone. He had paid for it half a *sol*, two bits, which Ernesto thought too much even for one so nice. To bring the price down, Ernesto had begun running figures past the seller faster than he could follow. Willie had become embarrassed finally and cut off the bargaining. The stones were called *ayus* and the Indians buried them with their dead as symbols of wealth and contentment to carry on to the next life. Lovingly etched on what might be a low grade of marble was a look-down-in view of a walled settlement, the thatch of the house proper, the roofs of the granaries and the backs of the sheep and kine in their prosperous rows. An '*ayu*' Ernesto translated as a 'homesite; you know, the people who live together as one—' here the Spanish must not have seemed adequate because what he had come up with was 'unit,' the first English word Willie had heard him borrow.

Maybe, Willie thought, the *ayus* were really souvenirs, tokens, miniature remembrances of how *rich* the great enclosures of the Incas had been. Not unlike the little White House and the Capitol in glass snowstorms he had brought his nephews once from Washington.

The woman across the walk was staring at him unguardedly now.

On the stone platform to the right of the cathedral, in front of the chapel called El Trionfo, which had been the Spaniards' first church here, two members of Willie's own profession were plying their trade. Each gentleman had a backdrop strung up, a patio in one case, a chocolate-wrapper view of Mont Blanc in the other, and there, like spiders, they awaited the opportunity to capture grim-eyed newlyweds and hasty baptismal parties as they came from inside.

Bad place for a photographer, Cuzco, in Willie's humble opinion. Hell, if Hell is in fact where the punishment fits the crime. The whole bag of tricks Willie had collected through time about how to recede *toward* if not exactly *into* the scenery proved useless in a situation where the whole of the citizenry were themselves ceaseless, omnivorous watchers.

The Indians especially. Just an hour ago Willie had come into serious collision with a passerby. He had assumed the man wandering along with his mouth hanging open was, like the other Indians fresh down from the mountains, merely entranced with him as yet another of Cuzco's marvels, and had realized, too late to get out of his way, that the fellow was completely blind. At the hotel this morning a softly unobtrusive young lady with her hair braided in shiny plum-colored ribbons had come to deliver him coffee and hot milk. And somehow, between door and writing table and back, she had managed to trip twice over the end of Willie's bed, so intent was she on collecting every possible detail of him she could in her brief passage through his room.

The reason they were so watchful, Willie thought, was that they had never actually surrendered possession of the stage. Foreigners were only actors in an interlude which so little amused the Quechua descendants of the Incas that in almost four hundred years they had not even bothered to learn the language of the little drama bound, as they thought, so soon to pass into oblivion.

Other places in the world Willie had been his question was always could he be seeing what he saw? Here the *things* asserted their reality so grandly, so far beyond question, that he began to doubt instead the reality of the viewer. For ten days now he had been feeling slight, insubstantial, a pale and vulnerable underground being forced out into the strong light. No matter how odd or badly formed or actually unbelievable the woman across the walk might find him, he was no more strange to her than, in the mirror, he had become to himself.

The bell for two o'clock sounded. Willie was no longer even pretending to read the Zárate account. Above the old letters jumping about on the page white-hot in the sun like water in a skillet, Ernesto darted into view, coming out of a narrow street walled in original stone called, Willie thought, 'The Narrows.' He was holding up tight to him the heads of three of his mules. At the curb the animals' eyes went wide and they pulled back, nearly lifting Ernesto off the ground. What frightened them was an Oldsmobile, one of the first cars to reach the city, brought up from the coast already assembled on a flatbed railroad car. It throbbed along toward them, relentless and implacable as the future.

Willie let the touring car go past and then waded across the street to Ernesto, who made apologies, *disculpas*, for being so late.

Willie laughed. "How do you do it? Wait around the corner until the bell rings the time you say you'll be here and then come out from hiding?"

"No," Ernesto said, "it's only that being late is so easy and being *on the moment* is harder, so I prefer it of course."

Willie wondered about the third mule. He had no idea where they were going. Last evening Ernesto had asked only if he wouldn't like to 'partake of a little adventure to see something out of the ordinary.' *Fuera de la normal,* it was a phrase Ernesto employed constantly.

Ernesto brought up to Willie's room at the hotel woven striped satchels the size of saddlebags to pack what Willie laid out on the bed. He wanted to know the name in English for each piece of gear, plus its use. Without having been warned, he seemed to understand about photosensitivity. Anything which had a latch he would not open until he had asked if it was all right.

He peered into a black leather box which contained lenses, each fitted into a circular indentation of smooth-shorn green felt. "You have equipment of very good quality, then."

"The best." Willie nodded.

"But as Hiram explains it, you aren't paid by the university and you're not a rich man."

"By the standards of the gentlemen here, no," Willie said. "But from the beginning I have always outfitted myself as best I could, even if it meant going without in other ways. I worked through a summer at a portrait gallery in New York without ever taking off my jacket because under it I had no belt, only a piece of rope to hold up my pants. All for the sake of that piece of glass to the left there. Excuse me if I seem proud."

"No, I can understand that perfectly."

Glancing around for what else he might need, Willie spotted the edge of a portfolio stashed upright alongside the clothes in one of his cases. "Want to take a moment to look at something?"

"Are these your 'orphans'?"

"Yes."

Willie laid three photographs out on the bed. His own first impression was of pleasure. In each of these he had wanted at least one small area of pure white, and his memory had been that he hadn't quite got it. But now in the thinner, higher light they shone for him—the ruff at the terrier's throat, the top step of a marble stoop—the soft, nonmetallic-seeming whiteness of platinum, since Willie preferred a paper made in England which was sensitized with palladium, a malleable, lighter form of platinum, to the silver-coated papers Eastman and the Germans put out.

Why did he call these his 'orphans,' he wondered, when he'd hardly shown them to anyone? had not worked really on finding them homes in other people's imaginations?

'Orphans' because, much as he loved them, he had never before had any real hope that anyone else would see in them anything to get excited about. People, he thought, care about photographs of themselves, of their loved ones (including pets and relatives, usually in that order), pictures they took themselves, no matter how bad, photographs composed exactly like famous paintings, which relieve the viewer of the need to make any response other than 'Oh, that's just like the Whatchama'callit by What'shisname,' and photographs which have only one possible moral, such as 'The wench may be having a high old time now, but in the end she'll have to pay' or, favorite of the middle classes, 'Isn't that sweet?'

None of the pictures on the bed met any of the requirements on Willie's list. Each was taken in New Haven on a quiet morning, early, Willie having had a bath and on his way to do something else, tripod balanced on his shoulder. The dark arch of trees over Bradley Street, the ordinary brick row houses, two neighbor women out washing their low front steps. He had liked the reflections along their freckly arms, the glow in the space between a bucket and a black skirt. The pictures were composed in a bland, balanced, inartistic way which somehow made for a generally *generous* view of the world. Like penny postcards with no monument, nothing to 'wish you were here' for except the moment itself. Each time squeezing the bulb, Willie had felt airy, accepting, thankful for being present—as though he were an open door and light in a bar was passing through him in a solid silent torrent, or one of those window-like stone Inca frames alone on a hill, whistling to itself, all things free to blow through him at random. This even-tempered openness was the only 'emotion' Willie felt he had ever succeeded at rendering unequivocally first on film and then on paper. All three of these were proofs. No pushing, no polishing or retouching, minutes in the darkroom instead of hours.

Ernesto still had not given any opinion.

"*Hijos naturales,*" Willie said. Bastards. Opening the portfolio again, he took out the photograph of Christina and Hiram from Puno and added it to the three on the bed.

"Well, I like that best," Ernesto said.

"Think because you know the subjects?"

"That, yes. But also because these others— Is this where you live?"

"Yes, my very street."

"I thought so. Well, these others, there's something a little sad about them, you know. You'd think they were taken by someone from the southern America, not by any *yanki.* But in this," Ernesto pointed to Hiram and Christina, "there is understanding. Not everyone can tell how much those two are in love. You have provided the proof. More—it is also clear how much the man who took it loves the couple."

"Or loves something. Do you know what they're looking out for?"

"Whatever is happening down on the Lake, I suppose."

"No. Ernesto Mena has just gone in a door in the street below them."

FIFTEEN minutes later, after they had crossed through the Plaza de Armas and were trotting along a road going west out of Cuzco creating a cloud of white dust behind them, Willie found himself coming to the end of a sadness (the one he had expected, that Ernesto wouldn't take to his favorites either) and the beginning of a new idea.

What if?

What if you let the feeling for Ernesto order the making of pictures here? The record was unsullied so far, since the one item taken contained him in reflection. Ernesto, what he sees, Peru through Ernesto's eyes.

It seemed very good. For an idea. As ideas go. In a place of such confusion, at last an organizing principle. Ernesto as Willie's organ of sense, his only interpreter. So in the end for Willie the reality of Peru should turn out to be solely the reality of having known Ernesto.

Heresy, of course. Saddling yourself to only one way of seeing things when you know there are more.

And saddening too, a bit, since the new plan would mean giving up on the method which had produced his orphans—waiting, going easy, staying loose in mind and body, having no purpose, *not* wanting.

Ernesto was going ahead. Willie, more used to horses, shook the reins and clucked to his mule. To no effect.

"Kick!" Ernesto called back. "They're deaf."

Willie drove his heels against his mount's underbelly and it broke into a trot. He felt a pull back on the lead rope to the third mule and then it too came along. Drawing abreast, he said, "*Deaf?*"

"Forty-five hundred meters up on Mount Coropuna, they got sick from the altitude and I had to puncture their ears to give them a little relief, poor things."

Ahead was a wooden bridge and a wide but shallow river, and beyond that a little town dominated by a domed church Ernesto said was called San Sebastián. As they clopped onto the trestles, Willie saw at a little distance a whole elbow of the stream was bright orange. Oxcarts were drawn up on the bank and men and children were bending over, working in the water.

"That can't be gold."

Ernesto looked back. "No, carrots. They're washing the dirt off."

Willie drew up. Though he tried to keep what he had learned from looking at paintings out of his work, there were of course times he wished he had become a painter. Whenever it was color which organized things, as the orange did here. Still, if he played it right, the intensity of the carrots against the softness of the browns in the clothes and the lowering sun would give him—

"We should go on now," Ernesto said. He pulled his Indian cap down in front and kicked into his mule so hard the animal fairly leaped ahead.

They jounced at a quick trot down into San Sebastián, through the square and along toward the outskirts. Willie thought he must have made some error. Ernesto had been troubled by something. As soon as he saw no carts or travelers coming toward them, Willie pulled up alongside again to apologize. There were lines where tears had run down through the dust on Ernesto's cheeks.

"Did I do something?"

"Oh no." Ernesto wiped at his face with the heel of his hand.

"What, then?"

"My two oldest boys were down there working. I had forgotten their grandfather owns fields out here. I didn't want them to see me."

"But wouldn't this have been your opportunity?"

"How? so they could report to the little ones, and the little ones could wonder why, if he was back in Cuzco, their own father wouldn't even come to see them?"

The road went generally west and a little north, climbing above the path of the river. The valley began to narrow. Once or twice Willie caught sight of the tracks they had traveled coming the opposite direction on the train up from Puno. The sun reached the peaks of the near mountains above them, flared a brief moment and went down. Then quite quickly two things happened. The crumpled-paper mountains on the far side of the valley grew pink, blushed violently and began to grow dark. And the temperature dropped. Ten or more degrees in three or four minutes, Willie figured. He reined up and got out his jacket. A little ghost of a whirlwind was coming down the road on them. The mules began to turn to the side to give way to the busier traveler, but as it neared them the spiral of air and dust moved off to the left and went crackling into the dry corn, where it expired.

Ernesto undid the lead rope from Willie's saddle and, holding the third mule up to the nose of his own, set off again at a much faster pace. Venus appeared in the still-white wake of the sun. She hung there solitary above them motionless as they moved along, until her courtiers came and began to group themselves about her for the evening.

IT WAS well past nightfall when Ernesto led the way off the main road and they came into the single crooked street of a village. The houses looked strangely like people, some leaning across the narrow way to catch a word of gossip, others drawing back in shock or disdain. Their liveliness came from the fact that none of them was in plumb, no line straight, all the adobe walls either bowed or sagged.

The place they stopped the night had been for three hundred years the principal inn for wayfarers between Cuzco and the town of Urcos. With the advent of the railroad, its value as a hostel had declined, and the huge old structure had fallen into the diminutive hands of an unusual couple, he a squat man named Cente, for Vincente, and she a little waddling lady called Domi, a nickname for Dominga. Though they were brother and sister, Cente and Domi had a big brood, eight or nine children, each Domi's *recuerdo* or memento of a different traveler who had stayed at the inn.

When Domi ran into the courtyard, Ernesto reached out to take her hands. She smelled at them, then shook her head and said no, she'd been cooking *chicharrón* all day and they were covered with grease. Ernesto insisted. Domi sniffed again and then, lifting her filthy gingham apron, began assiduously wiping her fingers on her dark red skirt. Ernesto grabbed her hands and kissed them both. She laughed and laughed. "Oh *compa'*, now you're just like me, all onions and grease, and nobody will want to kiss *you* anymore either!"

Willie's thought was, 'Not so, not so.'

They were led into a large, high-ceilinged dark room and seated at a long table. The smaller children at once gathered around Ernesto. A little boy in a baggy sort of gray long-john suit, got who knows where, pushed in between his legs. Another knelt on the bench and draped his arms over Ernesto's shoulders. The older ones hung back a bit so they could feast their eyes on the stranger.

Cente brought bowls filled with a brown liquid and set them on the table. *Chicha.* Ernesto rose and made a speech in Quechua, which included several bows and light handshakes with Cente and the right few drops poured out on the floor for the old god Pachacamac before he drank. When his turn came, Willie took up his portion and offered some thanks out loud in Spanish, and then in English a silent prayer to ward off any little organisms lurking in the murky depths. The *chicha* tasted sweet and cool, with a nice fermented biting.

The lady Domi, pushing steaming iron kettles about on the great hearth at the far end of the hall, called out to ask if Ernesto's friend's knowing *chicha* meant he also was acquainted with *coca.*

No? then, they agreed, it was time for Willie to learn. Domi brought to the table a cloth containing a good-sized heap of oval, bay-shaped leaves and a dry cake of some burnt ash. Ernesto showed Willie how to choose three leaves and arrange them one behind the other, small, medium, large, between thumb and forefinger. These you held before your mouth and "breathed across them" a little combination of prayer and gratitude, to the others present, to the leaves themselves and to the spirits in everything around you, mountains and roads and rocks included. "Like a telephone," Ernesto pointed out, "but with no wire or limits to who you can call up."

Once blessed and having blessed you, the three leaves were folded and placed between your teeth and the inside of your cheek. More leaves were added, fifteen or so, until you had a nice manageable wad. You bit off a small piece from the cake of ash, which tasted tart and stung a little, and the whole mass you then held and moved about and generally worried, sucking and chewing it some now and then.

Fluffy-furred guinea pigs, called *cuy,* were allowed free roam of the dirt floor. They were everywhere, in corners, scrambling across your boots under the table. When Domi and her girls dropped potato parings, they didn't even bother picking them up, since the *cuy* would be on the scraps in a moment. They were treated as pets as well, held and stroked, and given names.

It happened that, bringing in new bowls of *chicha,* Cente precipitated a little tragedy. He stepped on a black-and-white *cuy.* The *cuy* let out a tiny piping squeal so shrill it set the dogs in the house to barking. The toddler in the long johns burst into tears and dove down under the table to retrieve the wounded thing and ran with it to his mother's red skirt. Domi held the *cuy* up by the scruff of its neck to examine it and then, very seriously, asked the boy to tell her what this one was called. Monkey-face, he said. Well, said Domi, now he'd have to call this one Cojo.

"Cojo?" Willie didn't know the word.

Someone with a bad leg, Ernesto explained. Limper.

"Ah."

"Domi asks how the *coca* suits you."

"Tell her fine," Willie said. "Actually, though, I don't think I feel anything. My mouth's a little tired, but that's probably from speaking so much Spanish. And, oh—"

"And what?"

Willie got out his cigarettes, passed them to Cente and Ernesto and took one himself. "And nothing. Only at some moment, at the right time, I want you to tell these people I feel tonight as though I've fallen out of the orbit of the hard world for a moment and—you need not repeat this part—down where it's only us, the mice and other defenseless animals of the field making up our own pleasures to celebrate the ruination of empires. Just us, outside of normal time."

Ernesto struck a match, held it over to Cente, then used the light to scan Willie's face before putting it to his cigarette. "*Fuera del tiempo normal, eh? Certain* you don't feel anything?"

"Well, maybe a *little,*" Willie admitted as he leaned toward Ernesto's match. He smelled something bad and familiar. Hair singeing. He pulled back and tamped at his mustache and then at his beard with the palm of his hand, laughing. "Certainly that wasn't precisely what I meant to tell you at this moment."

"What was, then?"

"That I hope you understand what a rare thing this friendship of ours is. For me, at least. I'm not a man who comes easily or very frequently into the kind of faith I feel in you, Ernesto."

"In Quechua they say *coca* pulls the knot between friends tight."

"This is more than *coca,* I assure you," Willie said.

"I think I know," Ernesto said. "Coming back to Cuzco this time, I've been struck over and over by one thing. Here I am, on my own since I was twelve, off learning things, how to fix shoes, how to make people pay up on their bills, how to get drunk in a bar without having a penny, by doing a little magic. My secrets, my tricks, some legal, some less so. But all knowledge which is mine now, which they can't take from me. Then in the street I meet the friends of my childhood, all set up now with their little families, their secure jobs, and I compare what they have and what I've got and it looks like mine is nothing next to theirs, nothing at all. Except when I'm around you, or with Hiram and Christina. Then I believe again what I've done with my small time here has been worth the effort. You know that Professor Foote, Hiram's friend?"

"Yes."

"He's a very learned man. We were talking one night and he told me our word 'planet' is from the Greek for a wanderer, a vagabond. When I met up with Hiram I thought 'visitors from another planet' and I wondered why we should get along so well. Now I understand it's just because we are all the wanderers."

Willie asked, "Why was it you began traveling—wandering, if you like—so early? Twelve, you said."

Ernesto looked Willie in the eye. "Because I was a bad kid, always in trouble. When you're the youngest, you're always the culprit, whether you committed the crime or not. I made my poor mother suffer, so much finally I knew I had to go away. There was a mule-driver taking goods down to Arequipa, and I tagged along after him and learned to make myself useful on the way. When we got there, the man said, 'Now what are you going to do?' and I told him my father lived there in town. Which was true. But he had left my mother before I was born and had never come looking for *me,* so why should I express an interest in *him* now? Instead, I went to Lima, just because I had promised myself I'd see it once. When I landed there, I had to my name one extra pair of pants and two apples. When I had eaten the apples, I sold the pants to buy bread, and when I'd eaten the bread and had gone down to Callao and had satisfied myself with a look at the ocean and still couldn't find work, I went back to Arequipa."

Domi now pushed herself between Ernesto and Willie in order to lay plates heaped with food before them.

"And your father took you in?"

"In a manner. He works at leather goods. I went to the factory where he was and he came out. No embrace, no kiss, only 'So now you're here,' as though I were bad news he had been waiting for a long time. He got me a room and said, 'You'll sleep here' and took me to the lady who ran a kitchen and said, 'You'll eat here.' Never to *his* house, of course. He had another woman by then, who didn't know anything about a previous family. He got me a job too, selling glass bowls in the market. We were supposed to claim they were crystal. For a year I lived like that, and then I told him he had proved his case, I *was* better off *not* having a father, and we left it at that. Go on, William, eat."

There was braised pork and half a cob each of *moto,* the large-kerneled Peruvian corn, potatoes and hot green chili sauce called *ahí* laid on a little bed of sliced onions. Willie ate, though with a connoisseur's diffidence, since between the *chicha* and the *coca* he felt no real hunger, only a calm, slightly distant *interest* in his supper as yet another of the myriad *interesting* things of this world.

Well-being, *bienestar.*

Willie looked down and was mildly surprised to find he had eaten every bit of food on his plate.

And what about the contrary movement, like the tide of a murky river crossing the bluer, clearer water of an estuary—the devil in Willie not content with this being enough, saying *no* to the *bienestar,* to the period of grace, demanding he push on to declarations, to cards on the table, to talking love and bodies instead of friendship and glances, even if that meant the dissolution of everything?

Willie had no answer, no idea how long he could keep one water from clouding the other, or whether that was even a question of his own will.

The children had slowly dropped away. The older girls were eating, and even Domi had banked her fires and come to perch on the bench. Cente draped his arm over her shoulder and tried to persuade her to have something.

No, she was too worn out to eat.

"Just some eggs, then."

Domi turned her eye frankly on Willie and said to Ernesto, "I'm so *tired* of these same old brown eggs day after day. But I wouldn't mind at all sampling those red eggs your stranger has there in his pants."

Cente and Ernesto howled, Willie blushed and the girls giggled.

How old could Domi's joke be? Willie wondered. When born? In a world as sad as this one, any cause for laughter must have a certain durability, greater probably than the durability of the andesite or porphyry of the Incas' building blocks. Usually what you read of the Conquest was about the passion for riches, the pillage, the suffering of the Indians, the disease and the enslavement. Hardly ever anything about the joys there must have been for some few in the shocking discovery of other beings so *like* themselves and so amusingly *different* all at once.

In his *chicha* hospitality Cente was insistent that nothing would do but that the honored guests should sleep in the '*cama de la Infanta.*' It was called this, he told Willie as he led the way down the dark corridor, because the bed had really been fashioned as a wedding gift for one of the princesses of Spain. But before it got very far out of Cuzco, the gentleman whose present it was had fallen into disgrace and had ended up spending the rest of his days at their inn, selling off his possessions one by one to pay his keep. Cente had no idea when these events might have taken place. The bed itself was boxy, busily carved in black with tatters of velvet still making a partial canopy over it. Willie assumed it must have been made some time in the early seventeenth century.

When princesses came in much smaller sizes. He had to curl a bit on his side to fit and Ernesto, lying on his back, was so close

Willie could hear the high singing of his breath as it passed where Ernesto was missing part of his front tooth.

"Would you like to talk a bit?"

"Of course."

"Strange thing about me," Ernesto said, "there are periods I don't much like being around people. When I was a trader and went from village to village on a mule or, earlier, on foot, the journeys by myself were always much better than being in the towns. On Sundays my wife would want to go stroll in the park with all the babies in our arms and I would have been quite happy sitting in my room sewing buttons on my shirts, oiling harness, thinking about things. But certain times, often late at night when it's hard to find, I *need* conversation."

"My brother was that way," Willie said. "I think it's the reason he became a journalist."

"That night in Puno when I had to go out late? it was because there was someone I had to see. A prostitute, actually, but the sexual act wasn't the question. We just chatted, hours and hours, about everything, until it was time for me to go back to work. And with you, Willie. When we knew for sure that you were coming, Hiram said, 'He is the easiest person in the world to talk to.' And that turned out to be true."

"If so, a large part of it is your doing."

"How?"

"It's something about you I've felt from the beginning—that no matter what I tell you, you will understand, accept it as part of life, not think badly of me."

"What are these things you want me to know?"

Willie's silence then seemed very long to him, though he knew in some part it was likely only a few seconds. "Are you aware of the kind of friendship between men which has a physical aspect?"

Ernesto laughed. "Oh yes. I have had the experience."

"With men?"

"Once, when I was eighteen. In Arequipa. Do you want to hear it?"

"Yes. Who was he?"

"A singer. They call them gypsies there, though I don't think they really are. Only people from down on the coast who sing in the *huecos* for tips or a meal. There was a troupe of them, including a girl I thought was wonderful, fantastic. Finally this fellow my own age and I were drinking and he told me how to find the room where she was staying. At that point I didn't have anything—no place to live, no job, no money. But I went. And when I got there it was very late at night and only this same fellow in the room. Maybe he was her pimp, I never found out. First he said the girl would come back soon and then he changed it and said she'd gone off with some rich man and it was going to be him and me if that was all right. I said it was, unless he meant only for convenience, in which case I would have to leave."

"Did you care about him?"

"Oh yes, for a while."

"How long did it go on?"

"A week, maybe more. I don't remember."

"And what happened?"

"We didn't fit each other, that's all. Will you sleep now?"

"Yes. Only may I ask a favor, my friend?"

"Friends don't have to ask."

"May I feel your heart?"

"Of course, doctor."

As Willie was moving his hand, Ernesto grasped it and directed it up beneath his woolen undershirt to the place. Ernesto's chest flat and hard. Like armor, Willie remembered thinking, standing there in the steaming water at Puno. One softer spot beneath his finger which must be the nipple. Under Willie's palm Ernesto's heartbeat came heavy and slow. And his own was in fact peaceful too, calm now.

"*Contento?*"

"*Contento,*" Willie whispered.

SIX

IT WAS not yet full light when the travelers came into the main hall, but Domi had already stuffed her cheek with a wad of *coca* and was busy building her fires.

Without her children around to talk to, the lady relied instead on her *cuy*, laughing back at their squeaks, picking them up and scolding them. Oh yes, she said, she loved them just like human children. "I give them all the names of the real babies I wanted but couldn't have because life is so *short* and so sad—Luisa here, Aquiles, Salvador, Maní. I'll name one after your stranger there if you'll tell me his name."

"WE-LEE" it came out in Quechua.

Then, as they were finishing their coffee, Domi took the lid off a large pot of freshly boiled water and, without a tear or a moment's hesitation, dropped in two of the *cuy* she had been talking to a little before and slammed down the lid. Then she began to sing rather loudly and tunelessly.

Up beyond the end of the village there was no road, only a well-traveled rocky path made of tight switchbacks. They climbed fast. The mules adopted a kind of hop up on the front legs followed by stretching through their midsections and a second wrenching hop up on the back legs. Convinced the double disjointing movement would throw either him or his gear, Willie prayed, as always more earnestly for the camera than for himself, since he would take a fall better than it would.

Well before he could see it, Willie heard the high merry tinkling of a pack train coming down from above, the Indians calling to each other, "*Pisi pisi yamanta,*" go little by little. Anticipating them, the humans in the procession had pulled off to the side of the path in the tall grass, but when Ernesto and Willie rounded the bend the long necks of the *llamas* rose and their big eyes opened wide. A young boy in a big floppy felt hat was riding atop the full bags on one *llama*'s back. When he saw Willie, a little catching, surprised groan escaped his throat, what in an adult would only have been the sound of an unexpected sudden release of pent-up physical desire.

Willie called out as Ernesto had taught him, "*Sumahk p'unchay!*" Good day!

Silence, the supreme silence of the morning, then through it the constant breathing of the wind, punctuated only by the straining of the mules' leather trappings and then by the far-off cackle of some starling-sounding bird.

"*Sumahk p'unchay, virakocha,*" called the oldest of the Indian men finally, touching his forehead with his fingertips.

Then Ernesto ahead turned and the little party with the *llamas* was out of sight.

"*Virakocha?*"

"Man, gentleman. The Inca name for God. And what they called the Spanish from the beginning," Ernesto said. " '*Vira*' is also fat, like pig fat, so we must assume the old people found their new lords all fat, greasy types."

The sun was up and the mists nearly gone when they reached a partly crumbled stone wall set against the hillside. There was a flat place wide enough to leave the mules. Somewhere out of sight Willie could hear water falling.

They were very high up now, overlooking the Oropesa Basin. Vouchsafed the upper-ranging birds' vision of the narrow crack of the valley below and the steep slopes of the mountains on the other side. A good distance above even the highest of the *temporales*, Ernesto pointed out. *Temporales* were those fields the Indians planted higher than the places there were springs, hence dependent on the chance of rainstorms, on faith rather than their skills as farmers.

Over the top of the far ridge Willie could make out a row of tiny, sharpened white teeth glistening in the distant shimmering atmosphere. Could they be the snow-covered peaks of the Cordillera Real, the range in Bolivia which, after Puno, Willie had dreamed were the returning gods? It didn't matter really to him whether they were or not. Remembering they must still be there was, in this so rapidly evolving, chancy time, enough to make him happy. He had told Ernesto about the morose old gentleman on the train, so now he waved languidly toward the horizon and said, "Away, away," which caused Ernesto to smile.

Ernesto carried the camera and much of the equipment, Willie not much more than his walnut tripod and the cloth bound up at the corners which contained the food Domi had forced on them. There was a flight of steps in the wall. At the top, Willie found they were at the foot of a slightly down-sloping plane of immense dimension wedged in the long U of the surrounding steep hills. At least seventy-five yards wide and several times as long, the plane was planted in little squares and rectangles of different crops, principally corn, withered now, and waist-high rows of *quinua* with their wavering top cones, to Willie reminiscent of the plumy flowers of a butterfly bush, and all in brilliant color still, red and thick maroon and orange. As they traipsed along the margins of the careful small fields in silence, Willie began to recognize that the enterprise had been much greater than he had first thought. Except at its mouth, the plane was set below walls surmounted by series of terraces, all overgrown with brush and weeds, many of them tumbled now, a complete geometric reshaping of the little valley into a stadium of some sort. Or maybe, from the higher wall like a battlement at the top end and the waterfall there, some kind of shrine.

Ernesto had gone off toward steps along the side terraces, and now was lost from sight. Willie hurried to catch up. The risers were steep, some over a foot high. And treacherous, since the cube-shaped stones dislodged easily. Each time he achieved a higher platform Willie paused to wipe his forehead with his kerchief and look about. No Ernesto. Then, near the top, he found scratched in the dirt a big 'E' with an exclamation point after it and, a little farther on, in answer to his question about which way to go, an arrow of twigs in the dust pointing to the back wall. Willie proceeded along through the brush and came out where a channel emerged from the hillside, cut under the wall's edge and, from out a square spout, sent a heavy stream of clear water booming down into a large rectangular pool about thirty feet below. Ernesto was sitting waiting.

"So you received my messages."

"Two. Were there more?"

"Maybe." Ernesto shrugged.

They bent over on hands and knees and drank from the channel. The water was so cold Willie had to maneuver it with his tongue to keep it from getting to his teeth and setting them to ache.

"And no one knows about all this?"

"The Indians who plant the fields," Ernesto said. "Me. You now."

"But why hasn't it been discovered?"

"Would it be because it was never lost?"

"Fair enough," Willie laughed. "And you, how did you come to know it was here?"

"From childhood. *Doña* Laura would go off on her tours for months at a time, once she was gone more than a year, and she would never leave my mother enough to get by on. So Mother would send us out here, first with my sister, then later just by myself or with other kids from the city, and Domi and Cente would watch out for us a little and we'd scavenge potatoes left over in the fields. *Doña* Laura may be inhuman in her assumption that poor people will root like pigs to keep from starving, but she isn't exactly wrong. I was down in the valley below here when the earthquake hit in '86."

"What was that like? I've only been in little tremors, in Mexico."

"I was digging away and I felt a kind of seasickness and my friends and I looked at each other and then we saw a kind of dust and smoke rising up together. The Indians call an earthquake 'the anger of God.' That's exactly what you think is going on—the whole world coming apart. We ran down to the river because we thought somehow it would be safer there. Then when the worst was over, we started back toward Cuzco, and after a while the road was filled up with people running away from the city and when we asked them they said the city was totally destroyed and they were the only survivors. And I sat down just where I was and cried and cried. My mother. Everyone I loved in the world. But then we went on. There was nothing else for us to do, and I found her, of course, finally. *Doña* Laura's house was in ruins and unsafe to stay in because the tremors continued a long time, and my mother salvaged some straw ticks from someplace and for almost a week we slept out uncovered in the hills above town."

"What day was the earthquake?"

"July 9," Ernesto said promptly, with no effort of memory.

From the beginning Willie had known he and Ernesto were near in age. Night before last, in a bar, he had found out Ernesto was born a month and a half before him. Since then he had taken to asking for dates from Ernesto's accounts and figuring out where he had been—what Willie was like—at the same time. The summer he was seven his aunts and uncles had taken him and his brother to the shore at Nahant, but instead of making Willie forget or overlook his mother's absence, the vacation had been dominated by a series of dreams in which he was searching for someone lost in a tenement fire, among the overturned, elephant-like coaches in a railroad collision, along an empty road.

He sat smoking, the wind alternately ruffling and smoothing down his hair. "You haven't told Hiram about this place yet?"

"I tried. But Leo Ávila was there with us at the time and when I mentioned the possibility of digging at Tipon, which is what the Indians call this place, Leo said, 'Oh yes, of course, Tipon. A *tambo* or something way up above the road toward Urcos somewhere. But, my dear Ernestito, ruins bigger and better than that are to be discovered in any cornfield you could choose at random anywhere about us.' "

"Still," Willie said, "I suppose Hiram should be informed."

"Leo's the guide. My job is providing transportation, packing crates. But I *did* think maybe if you made a photograph or two here, maybe we could interest them in coming out to excavate."

"Better yet, I could show you and you could take some."

"From below or up here?"

Willie surveyed the scene. "I don't really see which yet. Let's go down and regard it all from another point of view."

They climbed back down and walked over to the pool where the water fell. All along its stone edge grew a rich green tufty plant. Ernesto snapped off a sprig and passed it to Willie, saying it was good to eat. The leaves weren't rounded, but Willie recognized the taste and the fresh crunchiness of some variety of watercress.

"Here?"

"I don't know," Willie said. "Usually it's very easy to photograph buildings of any sort, because human beings can't easily avoid providing a single point to draw the eye. A church forces attention on the place where the priest will perform the mystery. The stages in the theaters of the Greeks were often courtyards before walls like this one. Up there where we were was heaven, where the gods walked. But the wall would have doors in it, palace gates or whatever, for the actors to come from, a focus. But here, what are we supposed to concentrate on?"

Willie disliked the sounds of pontification, the tired knowledge he heard in his little lecture. Perhaps it was because actually he had small enthusiasm for the proposed photograph, none at all for Hiram coming out to dig in the Indians' discreet little gardens. Any reconstruction would be too costly and time-consuming for an effort like the Yale–National Geographic Expedition, and would never strengthen or quicken anyone's regard for this particular spot.

Ernesto was considering. "They must have meant all this to celebrate the blessing of water itself. For it to be so abundant and constant way off up here beyond where there are any other water sources at all, *that* the old people must have thought was more than a stroke of luck."

"Anything beyond luck is sacred."

"I think."

They set about finding a place to position the camera. Ernesto wanted it far enough to the right to show most of the major structure, the gush of water and the pool, and as well at least to indicate the extensiveness of the tiers of terrace. This took a good deal of jockeying and moving the camera about. Ernesto was initially very fussy, but as they got closer to what he wanted, he changed, becoming more silent, his actions more assured. He came out from under the shroud, took the plate Willie handed him and smartly rammed it home.

"You want to do it?"

"No," Willie said, "this is yours. You go ahead."

"How long?"

"Midday sun? Count slowly to two and a half."

In Ernesto's nonchalance Willie recognized a certain degree of imitation. Of himself, yes. But his own performance with a camera was not really so snappy. Some of the motions were borrowed from the photographers who worked the Plaza de Armas in Cuzco.

"How do you think it will look?"

Willie squinted at what Ernesto had chosen. "Fine, I think, though the water won't appear as lively as it does to you and me now. If you wait a half-hour and take one more, the sun there will have crossed the wall and started to shade it, but the water will still be in light and you might get something better."

Willie returned the exposed negative to his film box and then came to sit by Ernesto.

"Do you think anyone would care if I took a little swim?"

"No."

He pulled off his boots and socks, then stood to let down his galluses. He yanked out the tails of his shirt before unbuttoning it. Ernesto was crouched, eyes pinched against the sun so the long lines at the ends curled out both down *and* up, tragedy *and* comedy, smoking and watching Willie. Willie breathed and rubbed the hair on his chest, the heel of his hand touching both nipples in passing, and brushed loose some of the salty dust that had accumulated on him. Then he took the shirt off and let it float out on the grass. He stepped quickly out of his pants, shook them hard once and folded them along what crease there was left in them. He felt his backside, under his hand warm from the sun, internally nearly insensate after yesterday and this morning's time on board the mule. His penis was slack, pressed against his scrotum. Willie loosened and pulled at it once.

At its green, overgrown and strangely calm corners, the pool offered a strong black glass reflection. You could not tell at all what the bottom might be like, whether creatures inhabited the depths or not.

Like most solitary people, Willie was well acquainted with the idiosyncrasies of mirrors. By now he knew, for example, that after you reach a certain age, staring straight down at your own reflection, as he was doing, produces a hangdog vision of yourself old and dissolute. He knew as well that he had reached the point where, having contemplated the text so long, having committed it all to memory, he had little left to question about it. If not happy with himself, he was at least, as he and Ernesto had avowed last night, *contento.* Thankful even that, given so unnecessarily large a frame, the parts went together as well as they did. Arms a little scrawny, hips a little wider than he would want and cradling always a belly, less when he was in the field, more when he was in New Haven. He wished his genitals were more impressive. He admired the way some men swaggered down the street as though what they had in their pants gave them certain rights or at least a self-confidence about all things. But from his limited experience he understood that men of his size and physical type were not likely to have imposing organs. Proportionally, his own penis grew more when it came erect than some he had chanced to see.

But the chief question his own reflection could not answer for him was whether or not his body would ever be in any way attractive to any other man.

He turned. Ernesto still where he had been, crouched, still watching him, at ease, desires indecipherable.

Willie stood a moment grasping the stone border of the pool

with his toes and then jumped in. He bobbed up mouth already open and gulped air, his entire system shocked, heartbeat thudding loud and, it seemed, incredibly slow. He made for the edge, lifted himself half out and yelled. Ernesto was laughing. It was the coldest water Willie had ever been in. He sank back and swam in a single stroke over to the water's downpour and ducked under it. Even a foot or so below the surface it pounded hard on the top of his head.

Out, he shook drops from himself like a dog and ran up and down until he could feel the blood surging again through his arms and legs.

"Are you cleaned?"

"Washed in the blood of the lamb," Willie huffed.

"Then it must be my turn."

Ernesto shucked off his clothes very quickly, businesslike, then sat on the edge of the pool and let his legs into the water. A shiver went through his shoulders, down his smooth back, its brown pale, creamy in the strong light. His backside was squared off, neat against the stones. He eased himself into the water, dunked his head once and came up brushing off his streaming mustaches. Then he climbed out and lay on the pool's edge, breathing fully and slow, one knee raised, the other foot dangling just above the water surface, elbow up and across his eyes to shield them from the sun.

Willie stretched out on the grass. It seemed as soon as his eyes closed that the dreaming began. He was at the edge of the ocean somewhere. It was twilight. A teacher of his from early on, a Jesuit named Joe Larkin, had asked Willie to draw a picture of 'the worst that could happen.' With no hesitation, Willie outlined North and South America in the sand, elastic, fluid, the two subcontinents pulling away from each other, toward breakage, an amoeba in the final stage of dividing itself. Willie broke a twig and stuck half upright in the sand by Connecticut, the other almost midway down the spine of the lower form, where Cuzco would be.

So much land and sea separating the two figures so much

alike. Each alone in his portion, not knowing the story of the other was also his own story. It was magical, heart-lifting, to contemplate the two meeting, banding together to carry the search forward, beyond the Hirams and Centes, the Edward Curtises and the Father Joes, beyond even Manuel Mena, living, and John Hickler, deceased, deeper and deeper into the caverns where the mummies of the fathers are hidden. And conversely pathetic, 'the worst that could happen,' should the twins go apart, return to life as depicted, nonheroic, unpeopled, random.

Willie was awake, thinking of what Ernesto had asked him the first night in Cuzco: 'Do you ever have the sense that you are no one?' For himself, Ernesto had said, it would overcome him briefly, a few moments of feeling completely alone, especially when he was fighting with everyone, especially with his mother and his sister. The sensation made him realize first how much courage it would take to commit suicide, and then how suicide *could* occur—if the moments like the ones he had became longer, or occurred over and over.

How do you convince someone else that he *is?*

Willie smiled. Obviously *he* had responded to that question some time ago with the perfectly adequate answer 'Photography.' Which, he thought now, was a form of the more general process called 'Remembering.' And which in turn (he recalled his only bit of Plato) was a form of the even more general phenomenon called 'Love.'

Willie got up. He moved in silence. But not skulking, since he was convinced fully of the legitimacy of what he was about to do.

He brought the 8 x 10 closer in and over to the left.

What he saw on the ground glass had a heavy element of hokum to it—the waterfall a column of dancing radiance filling the left of the frame, the smooth, regular wall behind in shadow, the supine naked man easily mistakable for some representation of the noble savage, especially since there was generality and even what could be construed as coyness in the fact of his face being covered up.

But Willie didn't care. He needed the shot. If he was going to remember everything there was to remember about Ernesto, he would certainly need a memory of how he slept, of the rounded contours of the raised leg and the strongly defined musculature in the thigh of the other.

Happening to look down into the shadows under the shroud, Willie was embarrassed to find his penis waving in front of him hard as could be. As the negative-holder slid into place, he saw how he would look from up on the hills, the diabolic figure humped under the black drapery up top, below three slender tripod legs, two hairy human ones and a bobbing phallus obviously in charge of the whole nefarious operation.

By the time Willie came out from underneath, Ernesto had moved. Raised now on his far elbow and gazing down into the water, so intent and secretive he was not aware yet of what Willie had been up to. The photograph was a bust most likely. The figure would probably come out blurred. Or at least something different from what Willie had intended, shot through with elements of chance, a comic scene which included the photographer in the cast along with the naked man.

"What did you take?"

"You."

Willie's erection had receded. Plate held before it, he came over to the pool and sat down across from Ernesto.

"Can I have it?"

"A copy? of course."

Ernesto reached over and yanked the plate from Willie's hand. "Not a *copy!*"

Willie wasn't sure whether they were joking now. He reached his arm out across the water to retrieve the plate, but Ernesto drew back. Willie didn't try it again.

"Do you know the story of Narcissus?"

"The man who looked in the water? Yes."

"Well," said Willie, "do you know then the legend of the Other Narcissus?"

"No."

"They say there was one. After three or four thousand years

loving himself, Narcissus finally came upon somebody he found equally as fantastic as himself. There was a grand outing in the country, a barbecue, and so he could take his new friend's picture the original Narcissus brought along his Kodak. You know what that is?"

Ernesto nodded. "The amateur camera."

"But what happened," Willie said, "was that, at the critical moment, our hero returned to his original great interest in himself and ruined the photograph. So in the end history has no record, no *proof* of the existence of the famous Other Narcissus of the legend. Now give me that, please."

Ernesto passed the slender box back. "There aren't any other photographs of me either, you know," he said.

"Fear that they'll capture your soul?"

"Like the Indians?" Ernesto laughed. "But in some ways, I suppose, yes. The only power people like me retain is the power to cover up our tracks. If we need to, we can deny we were ever here. So in the end you'll let me keep that picture, won't you? As friends?"

"Of course," Willie had to say, his voice tight, "as friends."

SEVEN

TWO WEEKS and a day after he arrived in Cuzco, there was mail for Willie. As he had not anticipated getting anything at all so soon, even the small weight of the envelope delivered into his hand sent a warm sensation coursing through his long body, as though he had received an unforeseen kiss or an unexpected blessing.

For just a moment he thought the letter from Sara would contain an answer to his urgent request for whatever advice she could give him about Ernesto. But no, of course not. The plea itself would still be somewhere in a canvas bag on some ship steaming northward. What he had here was written not long after he set out from San Francisco.

Sara never seemed to have much concern for the distance Willie's travels took him away from her and the boys. She wrote as though he had only moved across the room, giving her no cause to raise her voice. So it was that, after bits about how the studio was running in his continued absence and details of his little nephews' new passion for baseball, Willie was presented with the news that he might not be able to stay as long as he had hoped.

'As if as soon as they notice you are gone, the powers external to your powers poise themselves to yank you back, recall you to your former self,' he thought as he climbed the Central's grand staircase.

"Yesterday just as I was about to close up shop, who should come in but Mr. Edward Curtis himself," Sara wrote. "He was in such a hustle and a bustle I assume he must have stopped off between trains, though he never really said as much. He was surprised not to find you. His idea being, as he said, that you would have finished up on the Sioux and Cheyenne and would have run out of cash by now and so would be here. Your letter about going off down there with Professor Bingham must not have caught up with him yet, so I got the task of breaking *that* news to him.

"I can't say he acted pleased, especially when I came back at him with my own not-so-humble opinion. I said straight out not him or anybody should think they could *own* your time unless they were paying for it, and with no employment what had he expected you to do through the summer, sit home and cool your heels? Well, then Mr. Curtis calmed down a bit and admitted what I said was only justice and asked to see your most recent productions. Luckily your boxes had arrived express the day before so I had something to show him, though I hadn't had a minute to open them up and sort what was in there (or really the inclination, since that time you mailed the boys the rattlesnake skin from New Mexico Territory without giving me warning about what I should expect in the parcel). Mr. Curtis was condescending as ever but I noted too that more than once he also mumbled, 'Wish *I'd* done that,' highest accolade that man has to offer. He wanted to take the negatives of several portraits away with him (2 chiefs and the young girl in the doeskin with all the fancy beads on it). I told him not on his life. I would print up for him and send them on to wherever he liked, but I wasn't about to let him have your negatives without your specific say-so.

"Mr. Curtis said he would write you, but I should pass along what he said as well. He insists that you go back on his payroll September 1 and that you be present in New York City the 15th of the month, because that evening Mr. J. Pierpont Morgan is giving a big powwow and exhibit at his house, purpose being to satisfy those who have already invested in *The North American Indian* volumes with the progress of the series to date and to get new subscribers interested. Curtis says, 'We are expecting the President to be there as well,' by which I'm sure he means not Mr. Taft, but his old friend Teddy.

"One thing more. Running through your Nebraska work, Mr. Curtis mentioned that the sponsors always appreciate the ones of the Indian bigwigs more than the scenics or the ethnological ones, since, as he put it, 'like likes to regard the likeness of like.' I don't know what you'll be taking while you're off down there, or if you care, but if the Indians of Peru have chiefs or whatnot, you might want to get their photographs."

Finishing Sara's letter on the landing at the top of the stairs, Willie started along toward his room.

"Willie? Mr. Hickler?"

Avery Hillman was bounding up the stairs after him. Willie turned back.

Avery's youth stood out not only because of his endless enthusiasm for everything, but also because, facing adulthood, he seemed to cling resolutely to the *idea* of himself as being still a boy. A student of physiology at Yale, he proposed, with the usual vagueness of the rich about the future, someday to become a medical doctor. In the current endeavor he was formally attached to Alvin Bumstead, the physiologist, and to Nelson, the surgeon. His father had, as Willie understood it, underwritten a fairly significant portion of the Expedition cost.

"Sorry to trouble you, Willie, but I wondered could you come down to the street with me for a minute. I've got myself in a swell pickle down there."

"How's that?" Willie tucked Sara's letter away in a side pocket as they started back down the stairs.

"Oh well, you see Dr. Bumstead's not feeling at all too well this morning—he's had to take to his bed, in fact—and today's the day Professor Bingham's got it all arranged for taking the Quechuas' pictures for the gross cephalic measurements and all. Even the chief of police of Cuzco is out front. And in principle I'm supposed to know all there is about operating Dr. B's camera, but somehow the damned thing has gotten itself jammed."

"Couldn't Dr. Nelson be of some help to you, then?"

"Oh, he *could*—" Avery snorted and wrinkled his nose, though he didn't really have the resources yet to convey serious contempt "—but Dr. Nelson isn't speaking to Dr. Bumstead right at the moment. Sore at me too, I think, by association."

"I see," Willie said.

Dissension in the ranks. The news of it came from all sides. Bickering and backbiting. Several of the gentlemen claimed they had been led into taking part in the Expedition by false promises. Clearly Hiram had undercapitalized his whole venture. Supposedly at least two of them, no names given, were determined to pack up and go home.

For more than two weeks now, Hiram had been refusing to attend to these bleatings. Drinking every day with different ones from the group, an activity which Willie knew had at least some strategic purpose, but which also enraged the ones who didn't drink or hadn't been invited or who had learned through bitter experience not to engage in toping with Hiram Bingham. A general meeting had finally been scheduled for this morning at eleven.

Willie and Avery went out through the glass-paneled main doors. In the street, Indians were crowded all around, well over a hundred men and women and numerous children. There were also enough police, most of them carrying firearms, to give the scene an ominous, military cast. Bumstead's camera, a cumbersome older German thing Willie knew and dreaded at a glance, stood to the side on a tripod, guarded by two uniformed men with their rifles out to keep the crowd from jostling it.

A sleek man with gold epaulets on his uniform made a way for himself through the onlookers, dividing them before him with the gold head of a *batón.* He announced to Willie that he was the prefect of police of this place. Willie clicked his heels and, mumbling his own name, shook the man's hand.

"These circumstances are very much outside the normal, *señor,*" the policeman said. His tone made it clear he was personally insulted by this. "I do not tolerate disorder in my district for anyone's sake. I do not permit circuses in the street."

Willie said he understood, he understood fully. Then he asked Avery in English where Hiram was.

"I haven't been able to locate him. Miss Long says he went

out early without telling her where he was going. With that Mena fellow."

Typical of the great organizer to set up a shindig like this one and then, when things began to fall apart, to disappear, leaving his unwitting, and in this case unsalaried, seconds to pick up the pieces.

Willie was about to suggest to the police chief that he go ahead and disperse the people and they could all serve the cause of science another day. But then he spotted Ernesto coming up on the outer edge of the crowd, craning his neck to see what was going on. His big mustache was spread wide from smiling. 'Delight,' Willie thought, 'the sort of person who delights in certain kinds of confusion. Those not his own.'

He motioned to Ernesto. Ernesto shook his head, no. At first Willie couldn't figure that. Then he recalled the complaint Ernesto's in-laws had drawn with the police to keep him away from his children. Willie motioned again, more emphatic, with a determined look trying to convey to Ernesto that it would be all right. Ernesto shrugged and pushed his way through the onlookers to the steps.

"*Señor*, this is *Señor* Mena, a citizen of Cuzco who is working with us. Perhaps you are acquainted," Willie said.

"Of course, of course," the police chief said, too busy to offer his hand, "I know everyone here." Then he turned from regarding the crowd and squinted at Ernesto. "But I *do* know you in some way, don't I?"

"In some way," Ernesto repeated, "in some way. What's the problem here?"

"Money," the officer said. "My people were told to go into the market and bring here one hundred *pure* Indians for a test the scientists wanted to make that wouldn't hurt anybody, no blood-letting, no injections, and worth a silver coin for a man's time. So now everybody in the world has heard about this and the whole multitude—*this* riffraff—wants their money, of course."

Ernesto drew Willie aside and showed him a sagging brown

envelope with a bank insignia on the front. It was full of small change. "He's wrong, by the way. All we have to do is start giving out the pay and the problem will go away."

"All right," Willie said, "if you say so."

Ernesto went down and started speaking to individuals in Quechua and trying to force coins into their hands. The one he got to accept he moved over into the beginnings of a line against the wall of the hotel. What was surprising was the number of people who, once the money was actually proffered, grew shy or even suspicious. So many ducked away from Ernesto that soon an empty circle of paving surrounded him.

"Well, I'll be darned!" Avery laughed. "Works exactly like the prof said it would. *I* should have remembered that, somehow."

"Hmm?"

"Professor Bingham was expanding just last evening on how upset it'll get these Indian folks when you press money on them. Because that's the way the Spanish people have always done by them, historically and all, getting them to take the pay and *then* telling them what the job is, always a good deal more work than the Indian would have bargained for, but he feels *obligated* because he believes that's what having the money in your hand means. That Mena is a smart one, all right."

"Well, he's on his own territory," Willie said. Secretly, though, the boy's open-hearted praise of Ernesto pleased him more than praise of himself would have.

The bells in the plaza two streets away had rung eleven. Willie got down to addressing the camera problem. He hardly had to take off the back to make his diagnosis, but for his own sake he supposed it better to show Avery once, because the machine was bound to jam again. It had been built in the days of the large wet-plate glass negatives, but was for the purpose of small keepsake-size photographs, so a single plate rotated through four turns, exposing a different quadrant at each stop. The modern celluloid negative, unless perfectly squared off in the cutting and rightly centered, tended to go to one side in the rotation process, to tear and get stuck.

Willie had to run the smallest blade of his pocket knife around the frame groove to make sure the last little pieces of film were removed. "Foolish thing for Alvin to bring all this way," he said.

"It was a practical consideration," Avery said, "I think. Dr. B needs the whole front and the left and right profiles and the full-faces for his measurements. And he's told me that since he's reached eighty he finds himself still capable of every aspect of his investigations except that he *loses* things. Four separate photographs of anything would get away from him. So he chose this camera because he can have all the data on a single individual on just one negative."

"I had no notion Alvin was so old."

"He surely does keep *in corpore sano,* doesn't he?"

Once the camera was back in working order, Ernesto could explain to the Indians how to stand and Avery could take their pictures. No further need for Willie, to his relief. He admitted photography's usefulness for the cause of correct description in science, but he couldn't help growing nervous and getting a sick feeling in his chest whenever people became the subject of measurement. Whatever his faults, Edward Curtis had a profound respect for native people. Though he might 'arrange' a photograph, Curtis had never, to Willie's knowledge, allowed a single picture to be taken which discomfited anyone, or which compromised anyone's sense of dignity.

"I'm going in to see how the meeting's progressing," Willie said.

"When you're through, there is something I want you to see," Ernesto said.

"What's that?"

"It will wait."

"All right."

Willie's hope had been to get to Hiram before the gathering got under way. He had in mind a simple question: could the Expedition support him on into the fall so Willie wouldn't have to go back to work for Curtis so soon? But the chance of even a brief private conference now seemed slim. The doors to the men's lounge off the lobby, usually open, had been pulled shut. Willie stuck his head in. Except for Avery and Alvin Bumstead, all of the gentlemen were on hand. Though it was only eleven thirty, several of them had already ordered up a drink or two. The atmosphere was blue with tobacco smoke and in human coloring as well. The unpleasantness of forced confinement with one another was evident on all sides. Percival Nelson, the surgeon, sat sideways all by himself in a chair in the center of the room, legs crossed, elbows folded, smoking. Clement Bailey, his half-silver beard big enough to obscure the top portion of his mammoth chest, paced back and forth before Nelson, engaged in an argument with a man named Jack Something Willie hadn't yet actually met. Involved as Clement was in his disagreement, every time he passed Nelson his beard seemed to bristle and Nelson would cringe and appear to draw further into himself. They reminded Willie of times when nature's enemies are thrown together—cats and dogs afloat on the same log in a spring flood, forced to endure what must seem an eternity of wet necessity together.

"Hickler? Come sit, come."

Edmund Foote was hailing him from across the room, vigorously patting the armchair next to him. Willie had been about to duck out. But old Foote was, in his way, impossible to refuse. He had left South Carolina for New Haven so long ago that people said his endless, unflappable cordiality was a rather self-conscious one-man attempt to heal up the wounds of war. Whatever its antecedents, the quality had taken him over completely. Of the university people Willie knew, Foote was the only one he had never felt condescended to him at one time or another.

Plunking down in the seat indicated for him, Willie said loudly into Foote's good ear, "How's it go, Professor?"

"Baltimore, my boy. Waiting for Hiram Bingham is precisely what they say about Baltimore: a *fortuitous* stage from which to forsake the mortal condition, because one is so unlikely to notice the *transition,* don't you see!" Foote laughed his basso laugh, so incommensurate with his fragile, small frame, and tapped the back of Willie's hand. "I mean, death *or* Baltimore would either be preferable to *this* god-awful hesitation!"

The old fellow's delight was contagious and Willie caught it. Irritated looks from the gentlemen around them. Foote had to pull out his handkerchief to dab at his eyes. "Please, sir, try and be serious now," he said. "Have you made your entry on the list for Mr. Claus yet?"

"I don't know what you mean," Willie said.

"Half-hour ago that charming Miss Long was sent in to tell us for our homework we were each to *list* all of the projects we wish to accomplish here before the end of the year. Mine is number three there on the slate." Foote pointed toward a large-sized chalkboard set on an easel at one side of the room. "A simple wish, mine: to take home with me a pair each of all the inventory of little winged things these mountains contain." Foote laughed again and half covered his mouth with his hand. "Some of the others have put up at least four projects of the same or greater scope. *Mine* the least could be accomplished if I were given just one boy to set snares for me. *These* fellows have plenty enough things they want done so we would have to engage the services of the entire Peruvian army. Now that's a force we know can be bought outright, but who knows whether it can be *rented* or not?"

All of a sudden Surgeon Nelson uncoiled himself from his solitary chair and, getting up, announced, "*I* will not stand for this. This is an insult. Worse than insulting. *This* is a waste of my time."

Almost as though on signal of some sort, Hiram came in quietly at the other side of the room carrying a paper sack. He went directly across to the easel, where he began to read the items listed there. Nelson stood by the lobby door, hand on the brass knob.

Hiram's ears were red and his face was flushed and somehow looked pushed out of shape. Drunk, sleepless. Willie was surprised Hiram would try to go ahead with the meeting. In the past, no matter how important the occasion, when he got like this

Hiram would have been unable to face the crowd and would have canceled out.

"Gentlemen: My apologies for the delay, which by now has cost you in the aggregate something like eight—no, I see our friend Willie Hickler has joined us as well—about nine hours." Some of Hiram's words slurred together. "Which I shall make up to you all somehow. I have no excuse. Though for those of you concerned about the state of Dr. Bumstead's health, I will announce that I have at last located for Alvin the most trustworthy of the local physicians."

None of the gentlemen took notice, as Willie did, of Dr. Nelson sneaking into a chair by the door and lighting up another of his nervous cigarettes.

"Your contributions to this listing are in themselves indication enough of the seriousness of those here present. Before we set off, I sustained a certain amount of guff, especially from your more rough-and-ready sort of explorer. 'Peru's a fairly civilized place, as I hear it. Not any sort of *expedition*, is it, Mr. Bingham, when you sleep nights between sheets?' Even some of our National Geographic backers begin to lose sight of the reason for purely scientific investigations. More than once 'those in the know' have informed me of where the 'smart money' is going nowadays in the exploration business. And you know where that is? The 'smart money,' my friends, has gone into *pandering* to the popular addiction to what is marvelous, what is quaint and exotic, what is—" Hiram made a sour face "—what is supposedly *new* under the sun."

The members of the group waited. Willie had long since discovered that your university sort of people share with actors a remarkable ability at the art of pretending to listen. As though their own years on the platform had taught them all the tricks of their students' trade, they knew how to mime interest, enthusiasm, attention. Above all, they knew how to appear at least minimally *awake* while their brains went on much-needed sabbatical.

In a low voice, Hiram said, "I suppose there really is no reason for the rather intense embarrassment I feel, gentlemen. You are, each and every one, a leader in his own field of inquiry. Intellectually, we need have no one mentor. But I took the initiative, made the plan and so forth, and hence am fully culpable when it comes to admitting that we *are* a bit over-extended."

There was some movement. The men settled in their chairs, some nodded to one another, others got out cigarettes or refired their cigars. Willie didn't quite know what to make of it all. He fended off any feelings of calamity, was not ready to believe his own question was really connected to the weighty issues of the Expedition's finances. Surely it was only a matter of his having been waylaid and having missed the opportunity of getting a short reassuring chat with Hiram before all this began.

Edmund Foote murmured, "Sounds like the moment's at hand when the vicar asks us to each ask our individual consciences just *how much* can we dip into our personal resources to help with the rebuilding of the belfry."

"Bit short these days myself," Willie whispered, "market being what it is. Think all I can offer is, once the wretched thing's finished, to provide new bats."

Foote tittered and tapped the back of Willie's hand again, and then got his handkerchief from his breast pocket once more and laughed into that.

Hiram had written "lost cities" in small, crabbed letters at the bottom of the blackboard. Then, at the top, he wrote largely the word "MASTODON" and punctuated it with a big question mark.

"Now, young man, what is it you've got there?" Foote demanded. He had had Hiram as a student fifteen years ago and always patronized him in exactly the same fond but diligent way. For his part, Hiram would turn coy and even a bit juvenile and 'oh gee' when Foote examined him.

"My item," Hiram said softly, "is meant to summarize virtually all of the remaining archaeological exploration I have planned for this season. The rains are over. There now exists, I'm happy to learn, a passable road constructed down the lower Urubamba Valley beyond, say, Ollantaytambo and Piri and, though the territory remains virtually unmapped, I have the Calancha text on Uitcos, or Vitcos, and the information about the 'well over the white stone' which I've explained, and I expect those of us who like our hiking a bit warmer and a lot more uncomfortable than what we've had to date shall have a pleasant enough time of it down there."

"Yes, yes, we *know* all *that*. But now what's this about dinosaurs you've got up there?"

From the bag he had brought in, Hiram produced a very large chunk of bone, yellowish in some places, still burnished with red clay in others, and set it on the table. "Three days ago Dr. Bumstead went up to the spot where the road crosses out of the Cuzco Valley and starts down toward Pisac. He had heard the rains had brought on a large landslide, and for his troubles he did come up with a certain number of human remnants, probably a hundred or so years old. And then this, which he went over with his usual painstaking carefulness, even though he had already begun to experience the lethargy which goes with his disease. At first Alvin thought it might be simply most of the hip of a large cow. But it's *too* large for that. Besides, on the basis of appearance alone, it's obviously too old. Every schoolboy knows the Spanish brought the cattle. The indication, then, is that we should deepen the excavation and be on the lookout for something prehistoric, Glacial probably, and not previously reported for the region. A *major* find would be my humble prediction, something of the elephant or mastodon sort, or human remains in the range of twenty to forty thousand years. Bumstead is *very* keen for it, I should tell you, though of course now he won't be able to oversee any more excavations. I'm for it myself. Just before I came here I made a personal pledge of my own time to carrying out what he's begun. That should be a matter of two weeks at most and will, of course, demand some further unanticipated expense for a work crew. All subject, of course, to the consent of those here present. My belief is that 'Cuzco Man' would be the perfect thing for us to have discovered this season—contributing both to science and also, through the stir it would cause, to our being back in business with another year's worth of funds for 1912."

It occurred to Willie that very few people hold out to us the possibility that they could be completely pleased. Hiram was one of the few, and it was not surprising so many others ran to do his bidding.

"Question, Hiram," Clement Bailey said.

"How's that?"

"You haven't said yet what was the matter with Alvin. Are we to worry? Will he be coming back to work?"

"I think not. As I was leaving his room just now, this Dr. Álvarez was sniffing at a sample of urine Alvin had produced for him. '*Bien cargado,*' the doctor said, '*bien BIEN cargado.*' "

"Please, Hiram, not all of us speak the patois, you know."

"Oh. 'Heavy-laden,' it means. The medical fellows hereabouts see so much infective hepatitis they can diagnose it with certainty fairly quick."

Dr. Nelson said to no one in particular, "*Not* a certainty. *And* not a diagnosis."

"Perhaps I needn't mention any of this, gentlemen," Hiram said, "but it means among other things that the rest of us need to introduce into our daily routines measures of extreme care as to our diets. Simply stated, no uncooked vegetables, no unboiled water. Where possible, we should oversee the preparation of our own food. The transmission, as I'm sure you know, can be from any unwashed hand. I do not mean to frighten you."

"And Dr. B? is he out now?"

"We have an expert," Hiram said, holding out his hand in Nelson's direction, "and I for one would appreciate an expert opinion."

The surgeon got to his feet. "I haven't *seen* the patient yet," he complained, "and I wouldn't take the sudden judgment of a provincial *Peruvian* doctor at much value anyway. But if it *is* in fact Weil's disease, and *if* at his advanced age Dr. Bumstead can make it through the crisis or attack period, then he will need *months* of complete bed rest and recuperation. It is a most debilitating sort of thing, causing as well unpleasant mental effects—peevishness, doldrums, lack of the so-called will to go on, et cetera. I would recommend provisionally that once he is better we see to it Alvin gets moved to the British Hospital in Lima for proper care. A certain forbearance and tolerance with the patient will be necessary, as he will not be at all in his usual rosy frame of mind. I should also add that there is no *direct* evidence that the transmission of the spirochete is only through the feces of human beings."

Nelson sat down.

Again a pause while the gentlemen took in the news.

Then Isaiah Mather cleared his throat and, appraising the palms of his hands, said, "Well, I'd propose we go on and do it. Under your direction of course, Hiram. You actually seem to *like* moiling in the earth. It's the least we can do for Alvin, and I for one—" he glanced up at the board "—well, I've always asked for more than I needed just to make sure I got at least what was crucial. My father taught me that."

There was a kind of general nodding agreement in the room. Hiram was sitting on the edge of a red leather armchair, staring at Bumstead's find, not even looking at the others. "Well, are we concluded?" someone asked. "Hiram? Drink?" Hiram nodded. People began to stand up, to stretch, to come forward to get a closer look at the alleged mastodon bone. Clement Bailey loped to the lobby doors, swung them open and called out for a waiter.

"Masterful," Edmund Foote said. "Of course it only goes to prove: it takes a gentleman to know how to manipulate the gentlemen."

"I'm afraid I'm not a member of the club."

Foote laughed and squeezed Willie's hand. "Not? Hmm. I thought for sure I had seen you down at the Uranians, Willie."

"I don't even know what that is."

"A club too, of sorts. One of mine."

"I mean I don't understand what you said because I'm not a gentleman."

"By nature, my boy, by nature you surely are. What I was saying is nothing complicated. It is only that a gentleman is raised—weaned, I should say—on the principle of self-sacrifice.

A little giving up of his own desires braces him and makes him jolly. It's like the old practice of letting blood. Whatever harm it does the body, it can be a wonderful tonic to the spirit. Just look around you. Relief. We few, we *happy* few. We've managed to give of ourselves in Alvin's memory and the poor fellow didn't even have to kick the bucket to get us to do it."

Ernesto, Willie saw, was waiting for him just inside the lounge doors.

Hiram had come through those standing around him. Dr. Foote said, "You were excellent, Hiram. An uncontestable straight *A* in Leadership. Young Bingham's horrendously overdue presentation proved, *en fin*, well worth the wait."

Hiram blushed out to his ears and shook his head.

So he hadn't been drunk when he first came into the room. This made Willie think Foote must be right. Hiram had arrived planning to pull the gentlemen around to his own purposes. The signs, even the slurring of his words, had come from guiltiness the missionaries' son had felt for what he was about to attempt.

"Come and have luncheon with us, Willie," Hiram said.

"After your warnings about food? I'm giving up eating for the rest of the time I'm in the land of the Incas."

"It's on me."

"Thanks. But I have some errands to do before the shops shut down."

Hiram glanced up at Ernesto, who now seemed thoroughly impatient. "Do what you must, old friend. I think you'll find you're in for a happy surprise right now—also on me."

In the street, the line of Indians waiting to stand up before the black box and allow it to work its worst on them had diminished. Avery was under the drape and did not see Willie and Ernesto go by.

EIGHT

TIMES I can't find some subterfuge or legitimate reason to be with him," Willie wrote Sara, "my mind keeps busy trying to frame in Spanish ways to tell Ernesto I love him without using the precise terms, which embarrass me and seem to make him nervous. Often I feel we are like two men locked in a toolshed together in the dark trying not to bump into one another. What we say to one another most frequently is '*Disculpame,*' forgive me, excuse me.

"Often too I can't understand things he tells me. Nearly as often I won't stop to ask for an explanation because I so hate to remind him of any of the number of differences and distances between us. Regularly I am also stricken with fear that Ernesto completely misapprehends *me.*

"Then it will happen—it did again yesterday—that in a moment, in the twinkling of an eye, the viscous obscurity we bumble along through will resolve and clarify itself and I will believe again, as I have from the first, that he can read my mind.

"Example: I do not recall telling him how unhappy I have been living at close quarters with the company at the Central. Daily encounter with some of Hiram's associates, with all that *blutlust* for 'discovery' and 'the cause of science' they carry in their patent-leather hearts, had me down. Then yesterday afternoon without warning Ernesto brought me to where I write you from now. A place of my own. It is on a street called Las Minas and belongs to Ernesto's mother, the only thing of value she has been able to get and hold on to in a life of servitude. I am her renter, though Hiram pays the bill.

"It has only one real room, my little house, together with a sort of half-enclosed roofed shed for cooking and, like a miracle especially tailored to a photographer, fresh clean running water. I am up on a hill. The one large window gives a view of the mountains across the valley, snow-peaked in the mornings now, what with the lower hemisphere's winter coming on, the center of Cuzco and, nearer by below though still far enough away that its sounds come in to me only distantly, the railroad depot. Two red chairs and a table, a lamp, two pots and three cups, one of them chipped. Ernesto wanted to clean the previous tenants' fleas out before he brought me here, so at the moment the floorboards smell mightily of kerosene. He also whitewashed the walls and, on one of them, copied out a Quechua song translated into Spanish. I translate it for you. You need only one fact: the *quipu* (KEY-poo) mentioned was the Incas' only form of writing, strings they tied knots in as a device for remembering accounts, especially taxes and tributes.

A LLAMA WISHED

A llama *wished*
He had a coat
Brilliant as the sun,
Like love strong,
Yet soft as a cloud
The dawn could shred;
So he could make himself a quipu
On which to mark
The moons that go by,
The flowers that die.

"(The men whose job it was in the old days to remember the information on the strings, the accountants, were called *quipucamayos.* In a more recent era, Ernesto was for a while an accountant and bill collector.)

"Last night when we had brought all of my things over from the hotel and were consuming a bottle I bought to celebrate the acquisition of a soft *alpaca* blanket for my new bed, Ernesto said he had been thinking, staying with his mother it was not easy for him to come and go, the gates at *Doña* Laura's establishment are locked up by nine o'clock at night and to get in after that you have to ring and wake someone, usually his mother with her arthritis since his sister would refuse to come, and, the long and short of it, would it be possible for him to stay here some nights, sleep on the floor, so we would have more time for talk?"

Night had come while Willie was writing. He pulled the lamp a little closer and held out his hands to it slightly cupped for the warmth. Time to shut the clacking shutters. The lights of the city far off were, tonight, aqueous, coming and going softly, as though Cuzco were an Atlantis or, he thought, as though some lens which provided tearful sentiments both joyous and maudlin instead of other sorts of distortions had been laid upon Willie's eyes. Downtown with its few outposts of electricity glowed stronger than the rest. Willie *thought* he could pick out the street where the moving-picture palace was located near what had once been the Coricancha, the Temple of the Sun, because it was at the moment the most brightly lit building in the city.

(He reminded himself: tell Sara how Ernesto loved the movies as she did. He claimed that in Arequipa whenever he wasn't out traveling he would go, as often as the bill changed. In one of the pictures they had seen together, Willie had been able to point out to Ernesto North American 'Indians.' Unfortunately they were all white fellows in make-up and the film had been shot on Long Island, so not even the ponies were authentic in any way.)

When he first got into bed, for just a second, faintly, between the cool cotton ticking and the new *alpaca* blanket, or maybe in the jacket from his brown suit wadded to serve as a pillow, Willie smelled Ernesto's slight tart smell. Then it was gone.

Lying in the dark on the diagonal so his feet wouldn't stick out off the end of the bed, Willie remained agitated, sleepless.

In a detached way he wished that he wasn't going to masturbate, though he knew he would. Now, before he started, it was still as though his actual flesh itself could remember the touch of Ernesto against it. That would begin to go. The new alertness of his body to itself would become a thing of his mind, subject to the corrosions fantasy brings on. "A *llama* wished . . ." *Willie* wished there were a way he could gather up all of last night's sensations, treasures on earth, and hoard them, fix them forever as they had been.

Behind his own eyelids he saw himself moving with extreme care, a thief lifting tiny curls of gold leaf from a wall or a manuscript.

Last night.

They had finished off Willie's pack of cigarettes with the Pisco. But then, when they got in bed, Ernesto had asked wasn't it possible that God might be good and that there might be *one* left overlooked somewhere? and Willie had gotten up and chosen the biggest butt from the saucer they had been using for an ashtray and got back under the blanket and they smoked it.

He thought of his arm under Ernesto's head, Ernesto's thick dark hair, of how the few threads of white hovering at Ernesto's forehead had made him think of ghosts.

Willie had turned out the lamp and they had lain together, Ernesto's short legs pressed against Willie's longer ones. "*Contento,*" Willie had said. Thinking more, though, he remembered, *thinking:* 'If I should die before I wake, *this*, this *contentment* would be enough.'

Him stroking lightly along Ernesto's heavy thigh. Ernesto's hand in the collar of Willie's cotton-flannel undershirt, exploring, warm, over Willie's shoulders, plucking up his skin, pinching him until it hurt some.

Willie remembered tugging Ernesto's shirt up out of the drawers he was wearing and touching the strong vertical muscles of his belly. Holding Ernesto's hip, his hand curved to the bone.

"Your body is soft and hard at the same time," Willie said, "like stones under water."

How his beard had brushed the stubble on Ernesto's cheek.

How he'd touched his lips to the soft skin at Ernesto's temple where age was beginning, and then to the mouth hidden under the smooth fur of Ernesto's mustache.

He remembered feeling laziness, ease in the midst of fire.

Ernesto lightly cupping his genitals. Willie moving his hand aside and beginning to undo the buttons of his drawers when Ernesto had stopped him. "*Pisi pisi yamanta,*" go slowly, slowly.

"All right."

"Mine's only a little one anyway."

"Same as mine."

"No, under the water I saw—yours is bigger."

"It was erect then."

"And you wouldn't feel ashamed in the morning?"

"Not I. You?"

"No," Ernesto had said, "I told you, I've had all the experiences you can have."

"With that fellow, the singer, what was it he liked?"

"To sing. He was a fantastic singer."

"I meant at night, in bed."

A laugh, Ernesto's belly bucked under Willie's hand. "All *he* wanted was to be my little woman. To turn around and bend over. And blows, he wanted me to hit him."

"But you did love him, you said."

"I said he loved me."

"Oh. And with me? does my saying I love you offend you?"

Ernesto laughing again. "How could anything a person who speaks as sweetly as you do offend anybody? No, of course you don't 'offend' me."

Next Willie remembered sleeping. Then waking up in the blackness, his throat scarred from the cigarettes, smelling kerosene and chalky whitewash and not knowing where he was. He had gone out into the little courtyard, bright with a patina of moonlight, and gotten fresh water. When he came back in, Ernesto stirred. Willie had fed him water, putting the cup to his lips for him.

They had slept again, Willie now allowed to cradle Ernesto's genitals in his hand. And woken to find the pouch enlarged some, his thumb stroking along the cloth, Ernesto's penis hard, then in the dawn soft again.

Tonight, however, tired as he was in body and relaxed now that he'd spent, Willie still could not sleep. So he relit the lamp and put on clothes and sat down again to his red table and the unfinished letter to Sara.

"He has brought me along into certain habits of his. One of the few generalizations I would broach about Peruvians, at least the denizens of these mountains, is that they are all hell on *soup.* They speak of it as though soup possessed mysterious powers, often referring to it simply as 'sustenance.' Soups of all sorts appear at odd times, e.g. in a fiesta at four in the morning where the drunks slop it up to provide them with the requisite strength for one final assault on the topmost pinnacles of drunkenness. When we have been as badly used by Pisco as Ernesto and I found ourselves this morning, he drags me off to a hole-in-the-wall where they serve penance and rejuvenation in the same bowl. The great stunning question always before the watery eyes of the acutely drink-ravaged individual is, of course, 'Will I survive?' I think there is no better way to dramatize the question than to set in front of the poor soul a plate containing, in addition to a potato and a minty broth, an entire sheep's jaw with the teeth and the tongue intact. One feels pity. One feels revulsion. One's more rational side notes that much-needed nourishment is here present, should one be able to 'stomach' it. And if one finds he can, then, spoonful by tentative spoonful, one begins to address the larger matter of whether he can continue residence on the mortal plane.

"Often I ask myself, 'Where are we now?' and the answer comes back in Spanish, *Bien metido,* 'Well in' or, as I prefer to think of it, 'In the soup.'

"Your news about the date Mr. Curtis wants me to return is of course very poor. On that timetable I would have to leave Cuzco before the end of July, and even then would be counting on great good fortune in connections, departures and so forth, to get me to New York, and for what? For foolishness, for nothing at all connected with *my* part in Mr. Curtis's estimable work.

"It seems this is to be a time when there will never be enough time.

"This morning while we were eating our soup, me the brain and he the jaw, as though he knew the contents of your letter riding in my side pocket, Ernesto asked first how long I would be staying in Peru and then whether I would remember him and write to him when I was gone."

Willie paused. In the afternoon he had climbed the hill up behind the Jesuit College on his way to the site where Hiram was supposed to start today clearing away to begin excavating for dinosaur bones, and where Ernesto had said he would be working his mules. More than halfway to the top Willie had stopped to catch his breath and, gazing down on the city, had seen a plume of white-blue smoke rise, and a few seconds later had heard the tooting, and then had watched the green train thread its way through the switchings and begin to pick up speed for the long journey down to the Pacific. The machine he saw as being in some way himself, since it seemed possible now that some afternoon very much like this one some eight or nine weeks hence *he* would be aboard the same train, going away from Ernesto, back toward another life, possibly not ever having eased his tongue into that gap where part of Ernesto's tooth was missing and not having convinced Ernesto of how he loved him.

Willie wrote, "I spoke to Hiram about staying on. At first he was highly enthusiastic. A thousand projects requiring my services sprang to mind (including, by the way, a volume of photographs on the Quechua suspiciously similar in style to Mr. Curtis's project, which in Hiram's always fecund imagination soon grew into a *series* of volumes, larger in number and more comprehensive in scope than even *The North American Indian*). I do not speak to Hiram about my feelings for Ernesto in terms of 'love,' but rather in terms of the developing 'friendship,' although I think Hiram understands me better than that. In the effort to convince Ernesto to visit the States at the end of the year, I report my progress to Hiram. Yesterday when I said I felt with more time in Peru I could *make* Ernesto want to come to New Haven, Hiram asked me how'd I do that, and I said, 'By making him care.' Hiram replied, 'What makes you think he doesn't already?'

"But in the matter of keeping me here, Hiram then was evasive. He promised an answer for me tomorrow, 'after a look at the books.' I know for a fact he has no 'books' at all, that the management of the Expedition funds goes on solely in his chaotic head, that he has no real idea of what funds there are remaining. (Christina may have a better idea, since being overdrawn is frightening to her and she tries to keep some tally of what Hiram has spent.) Toward the end of our conversation (we drank a certain amount of beer as well), Hiram began to treat at length the question of what would be the quickest possible way for someone to get home from here, whether overland through Panama, or the long way by sea around the Horn, or back to San Diego or San Francisco and then across by train. At some point I grew very upset, feeling as I did that I was being toyed with, that my oldest friend had finally after twelve years gotten a handle on me, that it was a profound mistake on my part to let him know my desires because, even if in the end he should come to my aid, in the meanwhile he meant to run me as hard and as fast as he could, make it hot just to see Willie dance.

"It is late now, and these I fear are thoughts of the dire hours of the night. In the morning I shall be more cheerful, as I was beginning this letter, and will set to work again on my question with whatever resources I have.

"I am sending separately a few shards with painting on them which Ernesto plucked from a place we visited called Tipon for the boys' collection. My love to them too,

"Willie."

PART II

1926

They seemed like virakochas, *which was our ancient name for the creator of the universe. . . . We also called them this because we had seen them expressing themselves onto white sheets, just as one person talks to another—this referred to their reading books and letters. We called them* virakochas *because of their magnificent appearance and physique; because of the great differences between them—some had black beards and others red ones. . . .*

—TITU CUSI YUPANQUI,
nephew of the Inca Atahualpa

NINE

JUST before he moved to California in 1921, Sara had presented Willie with a shoebox which had "W.H., South America" penciled on the lid. Inside in chronological order were all the letters he had sent from Peru. "Ah, treasure!" Willie had said, though at the time he had not been especially interested in them, and had packed the box away with other mementoes of his travels.

What he had been looking for now were photographs from the Yale–National Geographic Expedition. When at length he found them, he was surprised at how meager the file was. Strange to recall that the reason there were so few was *because* of his being a photographer and not the reverse. Any sort of normal tourist would have snaps by the hundred.

He had begun thinking again about the whole Peruvian business because of an essay on the conquest of the Aztecs in Mexico written by a medical doctor from New Jersey named William Carlos Williams, whom Willie had not previously heard of. He copied out the opening of the piece and tacked it to the wall above the long table where he mounted pictures and made out his bills, hoping that catching sight of the sentences over and over might cause them to slip effortlessly into his memory.

> Upon the orchidean beauty of the new world the old rushed inevitably to revenge itself after the Italian's return. Such things occur in secret. Though men may be possessed of beauty while they work that is all they know of it or of their own terrible hands; they do not fathom the forces which carry them.

Revenge against another civilization for its unattainable beauty—not a motive for conquest you'd find in the economic analysis of history Willie generally tried to hold with. The followers of Marx (though not always the old man himself, as far as Willie could tell) consistently made the mistake of turning vast human stories into exact, predictable events like the soundless knockings and skitterings of billiard balls off somewhere in frictionless, lifeless Newtonian space. The more traditional historians *tried* to deal with the effect of human feelings on the course of things, but they limited themselves to imagining that it is the desires of some few individuals, the princes and generals and heroes, which make the world go one way or another.

What Willie knew different was this: for every tale of conquest there must be a shadow history, *not* the story of heroes and seldom or only incompletely recorded. The story of at least some of the conquerors would be the story of being conquered. Revenge is a motive of lovers.

Two evenings in a row Willie searched the San Francisco Public Library for the account by the friar Carlos Zárate he had first read in Cuzco fifteen years ago. With no luck. But on a third visit he came across the Zárate *Relación*, occupying a hundred or so pages in the back of Volume XXVI of a seventy-one-volume compendium published in Madrid called *Library of Spanish Authors from the Formation of the Language Down to Our Time.*

An introduction pointed out that the first Indian interpreters had been a group of men who played an absolutely critical role in the history of Peru, but "such was the temper of the period that, with the singular exception of Zárate, not one of the early writers saw fit even to mention his native guides. Zárate, however, over and over will say that the customs and beliefs he recounts come 'not from my own vain imaginings,' but from a man given the name 'Martín' at his christening. This Martín is cited on some 94 occasions in the brief space of the *Relación.*"

It was the coincidence, Zárate's Martín and Martín being an older, more familiar name of Ernesto's, which had first sent Willie off into his own vain nocturnal imaginings about the Spanish scrivener and his informant.

He recalled now an afternoon, one of the rare occasions after his initial enthusiasm for mastodon bones had died off, that Hiram Bingham had gotten up to see how things were progressing at the gravelly site Dr. Bumstead had found. That would have been somewhere along in the month of June 1911. Willie was then spending most of his days at the dig, waiting and watching while Ernesto supervised the work. When the calciferous pieces which might be bone were brought up, Willie dutifully photographed them from several angles before they were submerged in petroleum jelly for safekeeping.

Almost from the minute he arrived, their great leader had been anxious to get away. Ernesto had more to do, so finally, reluctantly, Willie had left with Hiram. They chose to cross over through the round hills at the top of the valley and come down on town by way of the great guardian fortress of Sacsayhuaman and the narrow path beside the Tullumayu, the Incas' "Feeble Stream" which descended from there. A few women were still beating their wash against rocks at the water's edge, though the sun was already in rapid decline. The others were already gathering clothes from the grass where they had been spread to dry and warning their children to come out of the water before they caught "the airs."

As they sauntered on, Willie had asked if Hiram liked the proposition that "upon the stage of universal history, all great events and personalities reappear in one fashion or another."

"Well, I think it's *true,*" Hiram said. "Hegel was a clever fellow. Aren't *we* rediscovering Peru? Isn't Peru being rediscovered every day? Now whether I 'like' the idea or not is another matter." Hiram looked sideways at Willie. Then he grinned, a certain slyness. "What I *like* to chew on is Marx's fillip."

"What's that?"

"Karl Marx says, very gentlemanly of him, that the part Hegel 'forgot to add' is that on the first occasions these great events appear as tragedy, on the second as farce."

Willie pondered a bit. "Why that order?"

Hiram laughed. "Don't know—that's what *Herr* Marx himself 'forgot to add.' Though it seems immediately commensurate with our other guesses about history, doesn't it? that this old world is running down, that we begin life so serious and come in the end, if we've gained any wisdom at all, to see *ourselves* as the joke? What child ever laughs at himself?"

The path wound to the right here, parting company with the stream, and, framed by tall arches of cool trees, there was a sudden view of the pink-brown city below. It was from here Carlos Zárate and his soldier companions also would first have seen Cuzco, the gold glinting along the walls, the smoke seeping up through the roof thatch. And perhaps would first have noticed its soft hum, eerie, disquieting to people used to the city clopping of horses and the endless rumble of wagons.

"*KOS-ko* is how they would have heard the name."

Willie knew that. "Like Cos Cob, but with the accents reversed."

Off the left embankment then Willie and Hiram could peer down into the patios of the great old houses which clung to the hillside. From the street, many of them were still establishments of tremendous grandeur, regular-stoned Inca wall and figure-embossed Spanish gateways high enough for horsemen to get under without dismounting. But from up here you became party to their common secret—the dishonorable poverty the titled residents had slipped into in later centuries. The courtyards were strewn with rubbish and muddy with gray wash water and slops. One of these places belonged to the Ávilas and was where Ernesto had grown up. But Willie didn't know which one.

He said, "I keep thinking how there must have been a period when the chaos was of a euphoric sort. Everyone forgetting who they were, all the grim necessities, slipping out of the old legirons before the new ones were clanked in place. A moment of freedom."

"Freedom to do what?"

"I don't know. Fall in love, I guess."

"I doubt your Professor Marx would include 'falling in love' in his category of 'great events.' More slitting the throats of the lords and masters he had in mind, wasn't it?"

"I suppose."

Willie was losing courage. If what had happened to him was *not* a great event, and if Hiram, his pal, couldn't somehow tell it was going on, Willie could think of no way to argue the point.

They had come by then to the grassy level field next to the garden of Colcompata. Hiram pointed out the row of trapezoidal niches, wider at the base and narrowing to the lintel, which lined the upper wall of the ruined palace. They were not deep enough or tall enough to have been sentry boxes or to serve any purpose. Tremendous effort for decorative reasons, then, yet the 'decoration' was serene, even severe, so submerged in structure that it hardly seemed to exist.

" 'Poker facing,' you might say," Hiram said. "A style more like yours than mine, my boy."

"How's that?"

"Me, I'm *all* announcement," Hiram said. "Big schemes. Plans. My mother berated herself every single day of her life for not sailing all the way back to California to give birth to me."

"Why?"

"American soil. *Her* fault I could only grow up to be Secretary of State, never President. You, you have great goals too, but you mean to *slide on* to whatever it's going to be, and never get caught out *wanting* anything."

At the distance of fifteen years, Willie was struck by how much he had wanted Hiram's blessing. The desire surfaced even in the way in the night in his bed in Calle Las Minas Willie had constructed a first meeting between Carlos and Martín: Carlos Zárate's protector 'giving' him Martín, just as Hiram had 'given' Willie Ernesto to be his friend.

He had had a date to pin it on, the evening of February 14, 1533. In the hall at Cajamarca Don Francisco Pizarro had requisitioned for himself, the men gathered to wish godspeed and to lend courage to the three setting off in the morning for Cuzco.

Manuel Hierro, Pedro Bueno, Carlos Zárate. Torchlight, drinking, singing. Their grisly lame commandant in his famous buckskin hat booming out suddenly, 'Carlitos! Here, take this one with you for your eyes and ears.'

The native pointed out, as Willie thought of him, a youngish, slight man, his earlobes only slightly distended by small rings of wood. A 'string-counter,' as they called them, taken from a party of envoys bearing gifts back months ago when they were camped at the Inca port city of Tumbez. But previously assigned to Tomás Trujillo, one of the priests, so Zárate would know him only for the unusually bright blue of the tunic sort of garment he wore.

Carlos going off alone to get some hours' rest before tomorrow's march, stooping to enter the stone cubbyhole he had found himself. (In 1911, Willie had thought Zárate a bona-fide monk of some sort, a Franciscan maybe. From so many years of being locked in a solitary cell every night, even in this entirely new world he would have become a burrowing animal, would need to seek out the vacant small chamber or crevice to sleep in.) Startled by sound behind him, by the discovery the new fellow given him had understood he was to keep to Carlos now.

In the darkness, or in and out of a slit of moonlight, Zárate pulling his robe up off over his head and spreading it on the straw for them. The Indian man taking off the blue cloth with the neckhole and laying it over the Spaniard's habit. Then Martín, the smaller of the two, placing hands on Carlos's ribs and holding him so, as though Carlos were a simple keg or cask of some sort and Martín was going to lift him up.

Dread tugging at Carlos, the thought that the man here might be feeling for the advantageous slot between the bones to slip in the blade of his round knife.

But his body would know the touch as something different. As curiosity, old in memory, and welcome. The Indian plucking at the thin flesh along his sides, pinching him enough so it hurt. Carlos slipping his arms around the other man and drawing him close. The top of Martín's head only brushed the ends of

Carlos's beard. Carlos sighing and then inhaling. No smell at all he could pick out, except perhaps the slight acid tang of woodsmoke.

Some of it not so strange to him, acts he had performed as a boy with other boys, penises in one another's mouths, things he had refused then but had watched, 'Turn around, Juanito, and get on your knees' (or in Willie's case, 'Turn over, Johnny, won't you?' in the dark dusty back of a stable off Teele Square in Somerville), he and his little comrades always furtive, mischievous and quick, laughing as they went about jabbing at each other (though Willie also could bring to mind certain other moments, once in a disused warehouse an older kid pulled as deep as he could go into the ass of a towheaded boy who giggled and squirmed and pretended he loved it, the older kid's face pressed out of shape, stupid-looking against the other's shoulder, all at once lifting up and, like a cat, giving the pale skin there a long abrasive lick).

The wedge of moonlight had moved over onto Carlos's brown and Martín's blue thrown together. Carlos himself moving down, kissing, head swaying so his beard ran brushing across Martín's smooth chest, Carlos kissing the indentation of Martín's navel and saying into it softly, '*Pu-pu-ti,*' the playful-sounding explosions in their word for it. Him taking Martín's penis in his mouth. How it fit him, round like something of wood turned on a lathe and polished, like some hardwood as well in its weightiness. Carlos bringing it out far enough so he could pull on just the head of it with his lips, then slowly sliding it down again until the penis touched back against his throat. How still Martín lay through this, his solid thighs still, his little chest rising and falling slow, a soft-voiced wordless croon coming from him, and then how he shivered, once, and the second time harder, trembling moving through his body like the rumbling ire-of-God motion of these mountains and, flowing simply, Martín's sweet milk spilling into Carlos's mouth and out onto his beard.

As THE days and nights of Spring 1911 (southern Fall) ticked by, Willie had discerned a change in the atmosphere of his little house on Calle Las Minas. The mixture of the kerosene and the whitewash from Ernesto's original fixing-up had gone faint and then no longer existed. Willie tried for some weeks to believe he could still find the smell of Ernesto's body in his blanket, but that was mind over facts. The house had become marked: just another of the places W. Hickler, Photographer, had parked his mukluks under the bed for a time. Nicotine and caffeine in the room, and the courtyard, even though it was open to the air, foul as a tannery from his chemicals.

One lightly raining afternoon while he was waiting for Ernesto, who had promised to come by, there was a tentative knock at the gate and, when Willie opened up, Christina Long stood before him. Willie brewed coffee in the Mexican way with a sock-shaped flannel filter he had sewn up. At one point Christina wondered was he keeping a rifle. She thought she could detect gunpowder. Thus it was that Willie discovered mice had eaten through the cardboard canister in the corner where he stored fuses for flashpowder shots. The paraffin on the paper wrappings would have attracted them. But though they had sampled widely, the gunpowder inside must not have been to their rodenty taste.

Willie had in those days a chronic fear of women happening in on him. In waking life nothing so drastic as in his dreams, where the nuns still often caught little Willie with his fingers inside a convenient hole he had dug himself in his pants pocket. More a dread that, unlike a man, a woman friend let into his life would pick out the scent of loneliness there.

Christina had asked was it all right for her to copy the poem about the *quipu* and the *llama* Ernesto had put up on the wall. When she was through, she wrote out something else, tore the sheet from her address book and gave it to Willie. It was a quotation from John Keats:

> *I am certain of nothing but the holiness of the*
> *heart's affections and the truth of imagination.*

Willie had never been sure of the reason for Christina's visit. She was increasingly forlorn-looking and at loose ends, and probably had just wanted his company. The moment she was gone, he became convinced that she had sniffed out what he still did not like admitting to himself—that it wasn't going straight ahead with Ernesto, that more often than not these days, even when he said he would, Ernesto did not come by in the evening for a drink or to give him a Quechua lesson. He stared at the bed, its neatly tucked blanket. He would not put it beyond Christina's powers of intuition for her to know also somehow about his thumping away there in the night, nose cold in the cold air, body warm under the *alpaca*.

Now, sitting in the Library reading room with the Zárate open before him, Willie wished he knew some way to get in touch with Christina. After the War, as Willie had heard it, in preparation for his entry into Connecticut politics Hiram had married her off to another of his graduate students and found them both work at a college somewhere in Illinois. The marriage seemed not to have lasted, and Willie didn't even know Christina's new name. If he could find her after all these years, what Willie would tell her was that he had hung on to faith in the heart. And that, about the imagination, he had discovered a paradox: its truth is only limited by its experience.

If he were conjuring up the first meeting of Carlos and Martín today—'knowing what I know now,' Willie thought, lifting his brow a little—how would it be different?

For one thing, all more various. Though, paradoxically, the hungers of the two men would be more alike. Feed one another. The fantasy now would tell how just the novelty of the other body soft and depleted against your own kindles desire all over again.

Them lying together, Martín on his side with his head on Carlos's heart. Martín rousing to comb his fingers through the strange hair on Carlos's chest, and to suck his nipples, one and then the other, his mouth wide, then small, near biting. Laughing, Martín getting to his knees and presenting Carlos his buttocks.

Carlos pulled up to kiss there, one side and then the other. '*Manan,*' Martín's whisper, him spreading his cheeks with his fingers. The moon gone by then and the dark so thick Carlos could not see the place. Feeling for it instead, up slowly from the leathery underside of Martín's scrotum to the soft pucker, then, remembering the older boys, letting a gob of spit onto his fingertips and applying it. When Carlos pushed his penis in, a little sigh escaping Martín.

And the trapezoidal window in the wall of the cramped chamber glowing above them as they made love, nine or ten frames for as many different colors, deep blues to violet to grays and then iridescences graded and various as the bands of hummingbird feathers which made the cloak the lord Atahualpa would wear today and then, like his celestial equal and parent the Sun, discard forever with no further thought.

Zárate getting to his feet, pulling his robe back on over his head, picking straw from it, brushing straw distractedly from his hair. 'I did not sleep,' all he would have time to whisper to Martín before they stumbled out into the waiting morning.

THE SOLDIER Manuel Hierro had insisted on bringing his horse along on the journey, even though the Indians provided litters as not only the easiest way to convey the Spaniards to Cuzco, but also the fastest. "When we were passing through centers of population such as their great city at Jauja," the *Relación* said, "our companion Hierro would get out and mount for a time in order to further astonish and frighten the natives."

Zárate noted that through such a densely inhabited territory no march could be made without the knowledge of the entire citizenry. Seeing the rainbow bands of Atahualpa's standard, they would flock to the road in advance of the little procession and sweep and pluck the way so clean not a blade of grass remained between the stones. They screeched and howled their blessings, which Zárate transcribed (*Ancha hatun apu, intipchari, canqui zapallapu tucay parcha ocampa uyau sullull*—'greatest and mightiest lord, Son of the Sun, our only lord, let the entire world harken to Thee'), and, as the party passed, threw themselves to the ground and put their foreheads to the dirt.

That none of the three litters proved actually to contain their Atahualpa seemed not to lessen the people's joy and enthusiasm one bit. "For though the person of their lord was sacred to them," Zárate wrote, "so also was *any* thought of him. As the sun blesses the world with light and warmth from which follow all growth and abundance, so their prince, to their glad eyes, endows all life with its variety. The higher sort of warriors, Atahualpa's lieutenants, are more like us, capable of dissembling, their faces slateboards of contrary and battling emotion. But in the features of the common man one finds no such dissension. They appear simple, not in the way of fools and dotards, but as any people who have not the war of good and evil raging inside them, who are not from moment to moment thrown about in their loyalties, worshipping money or drink six days a week and hastening on the Seventh to make amends to their neglected Master."

They would stop every few hours, either at the inns provided for travelers called '*tambos*,' or at some pretty spot, usually where there was water. The new relay of bearers would be there waiting for them and the men would squat together to wad what Zárate called their '*kuka*' into their mouths to give them strength. The soldiers, Manuel and Pedro, became more fretful with each additional league they moved away from the protection of the other Spanish still at Cajamarca. Every moment's delay was "an arrow in their flesh."

But Zárate, Willie thought, would enjoy the pauses, the opportunities to speak a moment with Martín or to write down a few new words Martín would give him.

Willie imagined them at the first resting place, Carlos going off a bit by himself along a stream to wash. Coming back. Martín there, Carlos saying, 'I had some blood,' which first would make Martín frown and then, when Carlos shrugged it off and laughed, would cause Martín to laugh out loud too.

In the higher mountain passes, Zárate reported, they had all suffered tremendously from attacks of dizziness, the "seasick" feeling, headaches and retching. Martín prepared him teas made with the leaf *kuka* and Zárate felt better. His companions were convinced the stuff was poison and remained sick. They were pleased, however, with the natives' sweet beer and consumed large quantities of it at every stop.

Willie wondered how Zárate would come to appear during those twenty-some days of travel with everything about him swelling to new dimension, new fullness and plasticity. He thought of alpinists, how for some time after they come down their faces remain as though turned to the dazzling glare of the icefields and the skin around their eyes retains a purplish, papery texture.

IT WAS late, near midnight, and Willie was at home. He had always kept notebooks—not the formidable ledgers a writer likely would favor, but little pads that fit inner pockets—which he used mostly for jotting down exposures. Sometimes, though, there were also notions. Without much rummaging, he came up now with one from 1912, the year after he had been to Peru.

"Hap?" he called into the next room.

"Hmm?"

"Know the first thought I had about myself after I met you?"

"Hmm?"

"Several days actually, as I recall, before my mind started going again." Willie then read out from the notebook, " 'Once more, yet again, I have become a stranger to myself. When I can sleep, which is not enough, I wander through the place called me knocking into walls and hitting doorways, a sleepwalker in the corridors of a dark, unknown, yet hospitable-enough house.' "

From the bedroom one more soft "Hmm."

"Oh. And here's the first thing I ever wrote down about *you:* 'His belly warm and round as a melon picked at noon.' "

Nothing. Willie had thought Hap was reading, and expected a mildly contemptuous snort. But when he got up and went in, the bedroom was dark and Hap breathing as regularly as a sleeping man with a cold in his nose can. What forbearance.

In Willie's case, when he finally joined their enterprise, he thought at first that he had discovered an entire other half of life, the night part the rest of the world had been living all along without him. The ordinary daytime movements of people suddenly would tell him how they, men and women, would look lying together asleep, awake, stroking one another, in embrace, while they dreamed and snored. Willie had even imagined that all the others were calling out to him and welcoming him into their secret.

How would that have been for Zárate?

Nearly a whole morning climbing severe flights of steps leading up out of a dark gorge. Carlos reaching the top first, getting out to stretch his legs and have a look back down on the way they had made the ascent. Manuel Hierro coming up behind, foolishly forcing his poor hobbling gelding to bear him up the last of the stairways. Manuel sweating as he leaned forward against the horse's neck, the animal straining—Carlos thinking of himself astride Martín's heavy little legs, Martín bucking him, him reaching down to force fingers inside Martín's mouth, his other hand behind stroking, tugging at Martín's sack, at the testicles moving inside as though he, Carlos, could somehow pull all of Martín's genitals up into himself. And on the far side of the wall he was leaning against, a very old Indian woman, her mouth open, working. And from the way she returned his glance, brazenly, confidentially, Carlos at once convinced she knew his thoughts, and was pleased he shared the knowledge of what it is like having your body entered, how a penis can hurt as it goes in, the inevitable surprise when the juice pumps into you, the rue in the moment the thing withdraws.

He would have felt an urgent need for a confessor—just at the first point since coming into the communion the Church offered that he had left behind the last of any mortal souls who might hear him.

But what Carlos would have to confess were not the present

sins of the body. They were much older sins, of the spirit and of intention.

In the imperfect way they had of talking, he might try to explain all of this to Martín. How he had wasted himself, misspent. How in the hope of glimpsing the face of God before he died, he had removed himself from the concerns of other men, had thought their struggles and their temptations not his. How, though clearly earthbound and fleshbound as he now proved to be, he had tried to extricate himself from the world.

Now Carlos would see, as Willie had come to, how through understanding the second text, the one which announces profane love, ubiquitous and holy, we lose our individual markings, including even the scars time cuts into our flesh. As we really are, we are each in every moment portraying the act of our own creation. From his gold-lined litter, Carlos would watch families digging in the terraced fields high above the road or in the tiers far below it, men going first, driving their bodies down on the twin poles joined together in a point they used for plowing, the tiny women behind, babies bobbing on their backs as they bent to smash apart the larger clods of earth, little children along in back snatching from the ground the things they called potatoes missed in the last harvest. Carlos would now see these little clusters as outbursts of a single casing, spillings of a single womb, the work the noisome moving part of making love, the rests to eat and joke and drink water from the gourd the same pauses as the quiet moments when Martín idly plucked at his nipples or buried his face in the soft hair on Carlos's chest.

THE *Relación* told how, the afternoon before their arrival at the Inca capital, their procession had stopped early. Ambassadors came out from Quisquis, Atahualpa's great general who was in residence in the city, bearing gifts of fruit and clean cotton clothing they offered the visitors to wear the next day.

Willie could imagine Carlos going in to explain the pause to his companions. (Without necessarily knowing why, they too would have begun treating him as they treated each other, putting their arms around his shoulders when they were laughing, at the way-stations where they rested leaning against him as though he were a pillow, after they'd eaten wiping gravy off their hands along his thighs—in short, admitting Carlos to their familiarity.) Carlos telling Manuel and Pedro how all members of their traveling party, the litter-bearers, standard-bearers and so forth, had to cleanse themselves before they came down into the valley of Cuzco. Martín and others certified as messengers could, on occasions of urgent business, go directly into the city. But there was a way of saying 'extremely luckless' or 'lacking fortune' which would translate as 'to come dirty into Cuzco.'

"Some of the pools to be found all about for bathing were reserved to the Inca's personal use," Zárate wrote, "but many could be enjoyed by functionaries who had the sorts of religious duty which demanded ablutions."

Martín leading him up a steep hill to a lookout on a ledge. Behind them in the cleft between the red rocks a square cistern fed by the small regular outpouring of a spring. When they had washed, lying out together like lizards in the sun on the ledge, far above everything.

Maybe Martín, like Hap, shy about nothing else, would dislike having his body looked at, and now Carlos would have to persuade him not to cover himself.

Asking why was that.

Martín silent, which would bring Carlos to attention very quickly, since from the beginning their habit would have been to speak without hesitation, to be without secrets. The work of translation encourages this.

Martín finally saying he had begun to think maybe it was his color Carlos liked about him.

True, he did like Martín's brown skin.

The difference, then.

Difference. It is something needed in learning another person's language. Carlos wishing for a moment they did not have the word. Then admitting yes, he loved Martín's color, loved the 'difference' of their colors, stroking as he spoke with his fingertip along the line of his collarbone where his own changed so drastically. Asking, 'What about you?'

'The same.'

And then they would laugh, because the day they had hammered out 'difference' between them, they would have come at it finally by finding the words for 'similar' and 'equal.'

TEN

WILLIE had not been the only one in the 1911 Expedition trying to piece together an Eden from smashed, tantalizing bits. As he had written Sara in a letter dated 23 May, "Such thinking is bound to occupy people engaged on any archaeological endeavor. Only here we have developed a bit of a mania for speculation. Hiram is convinced the next advances in the reconstruction of Inca civilization will come from treating the well-worn chronicles as though they were infallible and it is only us latter-day mortals who have not yet understood the secrets they have to reveal to us. He thrusts the documents on anyone who will take them. A while back I noted one evening that among the six of us about the fire at the Central, no one was reading a book published later than 1635. We receive very little news of the outside world anyway, and it turns out the 1500's serve just as well as fodder for debate and raillery.

"Yesterday at lunch at one of the little *chifas* or Chinese restaurants on Plateros Street (the food is the best in town, the owners people who came to build the railroads in Peru after working on the U.S. and the Canadian lines), a dispute began over whether, as Garcilaso reports, there actually were houses of ill repute to be found in the suburbs of Cuzco in the days of the Inca. Hiram took a hard puritanical stance, citing Cieza on how the Inca detested and ruthlessly stamped out the 'abominations' practiced (and obviously widely enjoyed) by the people they subjugated.

"But old Dr. Foote, having read the relevant passages more recently than Hiram had, was of the opinion that the 'abominations' so-called were not dalliance with ladies of the evening, but the same thing as the well-known predilection of the Greek gentlemen for one another. 'Uranians, you know, are everywhere about us,' he said.

"Hiram's Incas are a god-awful prim lot. As he constructs it in air, their empire would please a Fabian Socialist. It is a kind of picturebook British India in which the masses were secured against hunger and privation and, in exchange, had to surrender every personal freedom to an implacably cool but reasonable administration. Punctilious, even pugnacious as he can be about guarding his *own* liberty, Hiram is entirely easy about signing away the individual rights of whole races of people for their own good.

"All of a sudden Hiram boomed out, '*Holy! The city of Cuzco was to them twice-over holy, being not only the principal residence of their living god, but also in itself venerated as a god.* Calancha says that.'

"And Foote said, mildly, 'But, my lad, didn't *I* or *someone* ever teach you anything? All cities are consecrated first and foremost to love. At the very least you forget your Lycurgus. Out in the countryside man may live like the animals, spending as he gets, in harmony with the famous profligacy of Nature. But once you think of walls, of hoarding, of saving, of "centers" of things, of moldering and smoldering, you have changed. You have discovered the principle of value, which has increase as its correlative, and which is also the principle of lust and the genesis of longing and romance. Goodbye to the things of Nature—except perhaps for the bees and the ants and the squirrels, who are so oddly like us.' "

BEFORE the Peruvian jaunt, whenever he was out at night in the streets of foreign towns, Willie had always been a little on guard, the hair on the back of his neck ready to stand up at a moment's notice. What was different about Cuzco, he had thought at first, was going everywhere with Ernesto Mena. Ernesto's knowledge of the city turned out to be even better than he himself had claimed, so good in fact that Willie took to tagging along a little behind his friend and stepping where he had stepped, because Ernesto seemed to know even which cobbles were missing from all of Cuzco's narrow walkways.

But then one humid though not warm evening, going home from the Central alone, Willie sighed and began to think it must be the *darkness* of Latin cities which had made him think them sinister. And if his queasiness was after all only economic—centers of light = centers of capital, the golden hives are where the buzzing must or can go on all night—then he could give it up.

In Cuzco too, the times Willie had alone with Ernesto were mostly after work, the nights. No wonder he came to find the city's darkness comfortable, even embracing.

A Saturday when Ernesto had just got his pay from Hiram. Ernesto and Willie hurried to the shoemaker's to pick up a new pair of short boots Ernesto had ordered, "quick," as he said, "before the place closes or I've spent all my money." Then, on the way to celebrate the purchase, they ran into an old friend of Ernesto's. His name was Carrasco and he was called 'Sergeant' because it seemed he had served long ago in someone's army. Or maybe, Willie thought, only because of his disreputable, dirty uniform and battered cap. The man smelled strongly of horses or mules, something Willie noticed particularly because Ernesto never did.

At the entrance to the bar they chose, Ernesto hung back a bit and whispered, "This is very lucky. The sergeant will be able to help our cause."

"What cause is that?"

But there wasn't time. Carrasco was holding the door for them.

Ernesto and the sergeant had worked together as peddlers at various points in their lives, had shared, Ernesto claimed, a "thousand nights of beds under the stars with no more than a rock for our common pillow." Carrasco, Ernesto said, knew the verses to eight hundred songs in Quechua and could play them all on the tiny sweet difficult guitar called the *charango. And* he was the kind of man who'd never burden you with his troubles unless he could find a way to make you laugh over them.

Eventually, some hours later, the talk turned to Carrasco's family. The sergeant's ancient father, Willie gathered, was some sort of functionary, Keeper of the Seals for the Department of Cuzco. The language of the two old pals was elaborate and elliptical, even for the bar talk of Peruvians, but through it Willie began to figure out that Carrasco's father was somehow capable of running up a bogus document which would attest to Ernesto's having done his military service. With that in his pocket, a passport should be easy enough to come by.

Ernesto was about to go out back to relieve himself. Carrasco took his hand. "But you had better come by my father's tomorrow evening," he said, "because Monday morning early I go back down to Pisac to my job."

Done.

When Ernesto left the room, Carrasco leaned confidentially toward Willie. "It makes me happy you from the north could see the *possibility* that exists in our mutual friend. Maybe up there—"

Willie was drunk by now. "I know. Here he's so weighed down with all his 'problems.' "

"Ah," Carrasco smiled, "so you've heard. Behind his back, we always said of our little Ernesto that if he didn't have his famous *problems* with him, you wouldn't be able to recognize him coming down the street."

The bar was closing. Ernesto insisted they take the sergeant wherever he wanted to go because it was their fault they had all gotten so drunk. A cab was summoned, and when they finally sailed into the street, Willie felt for an instant like a great full goblet and then the contents of him, beer undigested, poured forth into the gutter.

The place Carrasco asked to be let out was only a few streets beyond the bar where they had been. After the sergeant disappeared into the dark, Willie tugged open the sliding door in the roof of the cab so he could give the cabman up behind the directions to the little house in Calle Las Minas.

"What is it?" Ernesto said. "You're done for? Don't want to go on for another drink with me?"

"There's a bottle at my house. I thought—" The sensation of the bile rising in him was more physical than the beer coming up had been ten minutes before. "No." Willie shook his head. "You know me by now. I will go wherever you want. In order to be with you. Just that."

Ernesto gave new directions to the cabman and soon they left the paved streets and were rumbling out past town in the direction of San Sebastián. Around a great curve and up a deep-rutted road they came into the courtyard of what must have once been a country residence, surrounded by low outbuildings. A Pianola played somewhere and the courtyard was filled with hansom cabs like theirs.

When they got down, the cold of the night took Willie's breath away. Steam was rising from the flanks of some of the cab horses. Willie felt shaky. "Do you think this is it?" he said finally.

Ernesto was holding him by the elbow and trying to guide him forward. "They have soup. We'll have a bowl and then go home if you want."

Willie allowed himself to be led, then, to a small room away from the lights and music. Warmer here. Two men hunched in their coats at one end of a long table, two older women to ladle out the sustenance from a caldron over the fire. Willie sat a long time watching the bloated grains of rice and the little fans of coriander swirl and slow and at last come to a stop in his bowl and listening to Ernesto scrape away at his with a spoon.

"What made you think I was hungry?"

"I know you, don't I? By now?" Ernesto said.

'So badly,' Willie thought.

Anger was shifting and rolling in him now like loosened cargo, slamming the timbers, threatening the very continuance of the ship itself. Far off somewhere Willie could hear a sweet bell sounding. It repeated two notes. Either *hold on, hold on,* or maybe *let go, let go.*

'But it is my life we're speaking of,' he thought.

And then, though he couldn't do it, Willie could at least see how he might forgive Ernesto this one: mark it up to their blessed differences, find it 'sweet' somehow, 'touching' even, that Ernesto could understand Willie's heat, even if he wouldn't believe in himself as its cause.

"Well, if you're not going to eat, we should at least go have a drink."

Willie shook his head.

"Just one. Then we'll go home."

In the big room lit by the colored lanterns not one drink, as it turned out, but three or four. And pretty young women with faces whitened with powder daring one another to go up to the giant stranger and ask him to dance. The new liquor coursing through him caused Willie to lose the intimation he had had before of what it would be like if he could think generously of Ernesto now. He leaned against the bar and tossed his shots off like bad medicine, quick as they were poured. There was *coca* loose in his pocket and he made up a wad. Ernesto had taught him how the leaves could keep you at least afloat when you were drunk.

"Try not to let everyone see that."

Willie shrugged and said nothing.

It was five fifteen by Willie's watch when they got back to the little house. The sky was already showing promise of light over the eastern ridge. They drank what Pisco there was, about a cup and a half, neither of them even troubling to sit down. Ernesto spread the blanket to make up the place in the corner where he now slept when he stayed the night.

"Wouldn't you be more comfortable in the bed with me?"

"No. I came into life to be the *velador.*"

The servant, usually a kid, who sleeps on the pavement inside the front gate at night. Well, if that was how Ernesto wanted to think of himself— Willie let down his pants, kicked out of his shoes, got into the bed and blew out the light.

Ernesto stumbled and fell heavily against the foot of Willie's bed. So drunk. In the dark Willie couldn't quite tell what had happened. Ernesto must have found his place, though, because soon Willie heard laborious snoring, Ernesto's breath dragging in and out. Willie was falling. But then his heart began to beat very fast. A couple of weeks before they had gotten drunk one night here and had smoked up a lot of cigarettes and in the middle of a dream Willie had heard Ernesto fighting for breath and had leaped out of bed and dragged Ernesto coughing and resisting against him over to the window and had thrown open the shutters to revive him. It had been the combination of cigarette smoke, the closed room and the lack of circulation in the corners which had starved Ernesto of oxygen, they had figured, and with the window left cracked everything would be fine. But Willie could not forget Ernesto's face when he got him to the air, slack in the blue moonlight, his jaw hanging.

"Ernesto?"

No response.

Willie was standing over him holding his own blanket to him like a child's comforter. "If you won't sleep in the bed with me, then I'll sleep down here with you. Is that all right?"

Nothing.

Willie squatted and felt his way until he found Ernesto's feet and knew how he was lying, and got down beside him. The space between the bed and the wall was narrow. Willie was still. His own blanket was spread across them. He waited for his heart to slow, for the sense of at least a shred of well-being to cover him. But it did not.

His hand moved under Ernesto's blanket, found the hard shoulder.

"No." Muttered, like a reflex, a response from sleep. Then Ernesto said, "Go slow with me and maybe there will be time."

"When? I don't *have* time, Ernesto."

"Sometime soon. When my problems aren't on me so much."

Ernesto's 'sea of troubles,' Hiram had said. But so near the beginning Willie hadn't taken heed.

A song of the Indians he liked: "Enough love will smooth the wrinkles from my lover's brow." He had thought that, for sure. But now tonight Carrasco, who had known Ernesto so long—

"What a convenient cave our 'problems' are for whenever the weather turns bad or courage is lacking."

Silence. But somehow, from the shortness of his breathing, Willie knew Ernesto wasn't asleep.

"What are you doing?"

"Crying."

"And where do the tears come from?"

Again silence. Then, "From little pockets under my eyes. Or so the scientists tell us."

A movement in Willie's heart. That it could flood so with venom, and of all people for this man. A turn back. For the greatest of these is— "When I ask that, it's not from evil intentions, Ernesto, but from the desire to know everything I can about you, so we can walk the same road."

Ernesto sat up. Willie could see his face then, cut by bars of faint light coming through the shutters. "*You* think we can walk the same road. But that can't be done and it makes me laugh to watch people waste their lives in the attempt."

"And you and your friend the sergeant? your 'thousand nights under the stars' with 'only a rock' for your 'common pillow'?"

"A manner of speaking."

EVEN fifteen years later Willie was still sometimes puzzled recalling how after those storms, so terrible at least for him, the climate between him and Ernesto inevitably improved.

Willie was up first the next morning. While churchbells clanged far and near, he drenched his whole head in fresh cold water and stood in the sun combing his hair this way and that to dry it and waiting for the kettle.

At the altitude of Cuzco, water boils at such a low temperature, $\pm 186°$, that the ground beans didn't get hit with enough heat and the result, flannel bag or no, always somewhat lacked the bludgeoning WAKE O ISRAEL! quality Willie admired in coffee.

Going into the little outhouse, he discovered Ernesto had been there some hours before him. Willie got a cloth and some bleach and, with the door propped open, was rubbing vomit off from around the hole when Ernesto came in behind him.

"Give me that." Ernesto grabbed for the rag.

"It's all right."

"No. Since I was very small I have never permitted anyone to clean up my mess, not my mother or my sisters, not even my wife."

"Have you ever thought what false pride that is?" Willie went right on doing what he had been doing.

Sundays the place they usually went for sheep's-head soup was closed. So instead in the afternoon they climbed the hill to a *quinta* which had behind it a number of flagged terraces where you could eat and drink and play dice in the shade of ancient ruined fruit trees and arbors and look out over the city. Ernesto ordered roast *cuy*, which arrived at the table with their crackle skins still popping hot, bright red peppers wedged in their mouths like gags or Christmas gifts and their little front claws curled over the edges of the platters as though they had been hanging on for dear life when the other possibility had struck them.

After the sun had gone and the waiters had set lanterns, Ernesto began to tell about a girl. Willie couldn't figure quite where the episode fit in Ernesto's story. During his marriage, though, and in Arequipa. The woman married too, and there was a child, but she and her husband lived apart.

"We got along. You know," Ernesto said, "no problems. I became used to it, the situation. Just coming back at the end of the week or from a trading expedition I would feel everything was good. Then without any warning one day she tells me she's going back to her husband. I couldn't argue. Just looking in her face I could see it was finished. My wife was complaining, even without knowing about the other girl, so I came to Cuzco, handed myself back over to the authorities, as you'd say, to the life of the little father. That was the time I collected bills. And then one day I saw her on the street *here.* She had come to see her family. I found us a place. It wasn't much, but I do remember borrowing money and going to buy a bed and carrying it home on my back and we even had a set of dishes of our own if I remember. The feeling that everything was all right began coming back over me. And then, when exactly one month by the calendar had gone by, I came home one day and she was packing her things. Her husband had found her and convinced her to go back with him. I said, 'And what about me?' and she said, 'Well? what *about* you?' and that was it. The end."

They had forgotten their appointment with Sergeant Carrasco and his father. Willie paid up and they trotted down to the plaza to find a cab.

Then for several hours they chased in circles all through the dark city. It turned out Ernesto, knower of Cuzco, had only been to the Carrasco home once, and that was long ago and, he admitted finally, he had been completely drunk on that occasion too. For a long time they had the shade down so Ernesto could see the streets they were passing and the little door overhead open so he could tell the driver up above them where to turn. The night was smoky, cold, clouds near overhead blotting out the sharp colorful stars.

They kept returning to the little street which ran only the half-block from the cathedral to the convent church of Santa Catalina and setting out once more along the intersecting thoroughfare. The joke about these two streets, difficult to translate, was that the little way was the 'narrow passage' of Santa Catalina and the grander one her '*Ancha*' or 'Wide Place.' Before it became home to the wealthy Spanish celibate ladies, the convent had been the Incas' Temple of the Virgins. Both streets were as they had been, lined with old wall.

The durability of a jest. What harm, then, in imagining that in a city which was itself a god there would have been another laughter, sweeter and softer (and better), about the two accesses to the temple? Never out loud, only a wonder-filled sort of Lilliputian murmur more like a prayer, *Hush, for it is She Whose precious body we tread, on Whose skin we make our incidental paths, where we catch sight of one another, fall in, arrange to meet later to lie down a little while, in the secret folds of Her unchanging flesh.*

Ernesto had given up looking out and was slumped back in the seat. He was shivering, so Willie spread his *poncho* over onto his friend's legs, then glanced up. Their driver's cap was pulled down snug over his ears and tied under his chin. He was not watching. Willie placed his hand on Ernesto's thigh.

"What do you think you're doing?" Ernesto tried to lift Willie's hand away.

But Willie only clutched him tighter. "Don't say anything. I just feel we are in it right now."

Ernesto then reached over and grabbed big handfuls of Willie's beard and pulled his face close and kissed Willie hard on his mouth, then released him and whispered, "Oh, how I love the way you can be sometimes, William."

EVEN at the time Carlos Zárate and the two soldiers were leaving Cajamarca for the journey to Cuzco, prominent members of the Spanish expedition had begun complaining about Francisco Pizarro's keeping Atahualpa alive as long as he had. Everyone understood the ransom was a trick, but the dissidents said too dangerous a trick. The fact that Atahualpa was permitted to send out and receive messengers made them unhappy. They were sure he was organizing an army to come free him. Better to slit his throat and get the plunder honestly, fighting for every ounce of it if need be, they argued.

So the safety of the three so far from the main troop hung on the slender question of whether or not the Pizarro brothers would continue in their planned course.

At first, according to Zárate, he and his companions were shown great hospitality in Cuzco. On their arrival, they were given a triumphal parade with sweet rushes laid in their path and showers of pink *cantut* flowers hurled upon them by the citizens. Every time they went out to see the sights, they were accompanied by a large and solicitous group of 'big-ears' from the commanding general's household.

The soldiers failed to recognize that they were under the most cordial sort of house arrest. Atahualpa had promulgated a decree guaranteeing their safe passage anywhere in his empire. Though he was in chains himself and a usurper, such was the power of the office of the Inca that the order was obeyed by Quisquis in the capital city.

The *Relación* told how one day early on in their stay, despite the watchfulness of their noble guides, the visitors had gotten off alone and wandered through the tall, gold-faced entrance of one of the palaces or 'enclosures' of the Incas. There would have been no gate, no locks anywhere (if you could believe the reports), and the palaces of the deceased monarchs appeared no different from those of the living. A full staff was kept and the household proceeded as it had before, retainers padding about on fiber sandals through the large interior courtyards.

The strangers had entered a great chamber, so dark they could tell neither its height nor its extent. Once their eyes grew accustomed to the gloom, they could make out rows of votary lights glowing before a man and a woman asleep on gold stools with their arms folded on their breasts. A huge plumed fan swept languidly back and forth above, keeping flies away from the bodies of the Topa Inca Yupanqui and his wife. Before the Spaniards could venture even a step closer, the old woman in a gold mask whose lot in life it was to wield the fan ran to them and insisted they remove their boots before drawing near. "Which done, and with much laughter," Zárate said, "we were permitted to make account of the many treasures of gold and emerald and other precious stones which the hall contained, and without further incident our soldiers were allowed to carry away whatever struck their fancy."

Zárate must have tried to explain to the other two the actual precariousness of their situation, certain as he was that they were only tolerated in Cuzco, not in any sense welcome.

But they persisted. One day Hierro and Bueno announced that they intended to carry back to Pizarro the plaques of gold which were the paneling for both the interior and exterior walls of the Temple of the Sun. The lord general Quisquis deferred to them. However, none of the Indians would perform the work of the dismantling. So Manuel and Pedro, both gone a little soft from weeks of litter travel and generally easeful living, had to get out themselves and sweat to pry the tiles from the walls. For the three days it took them to complete the task, Zárate made himself scarce, spending his time (with Martín, Willie thought) cataloguing the contents of royal storehouses in other quarters of the city.

(In Cuzco, Willie had dreamed several times that he and Ernesto, Carlos and Martín, were at the business of relieving the Indians of the circlets they wore as earrings. Some of these were elaborate mosaic inlays in aquamarine or turquoise and soft mother-of-pearl, others were simple bits of cane stalk or cloth, or dangles of brilliant red feather from tropical birds. It did not matter. Everything was tossed into a reed basket on the Central steps—or sometimes the steps in front of the Temple of the Sun. If it was a Carlos dream, he wrote down each item in a great thick ledger. When it was Willie, once they had politely surrendered their jewelry, he got Ernesto to convince the people to stand up and be photographed. He, Willie, worked mechanically, without feeling, a machine-gun, heartless cameraman.)

Toward the end of April 1533, Pedro Bueno left for Cajamarca, taking with him a pack train of two hundred and twenty-five *llamas* and also an unmentioned number of Indian carriers. Each *llama* would have been able to bear a hundred pounds of gold or silver and each man almost that. Manuel and Pedro had concerned themselves almost exclusively with the solider stuff. There was one gold altar which they guessed to be over nine thousand pounds, but there was no way available to break it up. Also the Indians in Cuzco hadn't learned yet that the ransom was to be by weight and objected, mildly it was true, to some of the more elaborate pieces being crushed for shipment. In the central courtyard of the Temple of the Sun there was a garden of examples of every beast and bird and flower in the realm, life size and wrought wholly in gold. "My military companions greatly admired this garden," Zárate wrote, "and bemoaned the fact we had brought along no one who knew the smelting procedures, as the big-ears claimed there were no furnaces anywhere near the city."

Carlos must have been glad when Pedro left, and even more pleased by Manuel's sudden departure with a second train of sixty *llamas* two weeks later. As their days there went by, Cuzco would have more and more distracted the two soldiers, made them like children of unattainable, aloof parents. The Indians' lack of concern over their obvious thefts and open sacrileges would drive them into a rage—and of course to greater and greater attempts at giving offense. Unlacing themselves and pissing on things. Insisting on different women all the time. (At first, Willie thought, their noble keepers probably brought them 'women of the field,' as they were called, from the places on the edge of the city. Then women from the different neighborhoods where the people of the subject nations were quartered—including one night, Martín claimed, two young men who dressed as women and served in the Chimu temple—on the theory that it must be variety in forms of pleasure and appearance the white men wanted.)

Zárate had sent a message with either Bueno or, more likely, Hierro. He begged pardon for changing his plan, but said there remained "many more fabulous things to bring and still others to be catalogued." He promised to set out to rejoin the main army as soon as he could. In a kind of postscript addressed to the elder Pizarro, he mentioned he had begun putting together a "small collection" of items he thought would be of special interest to the leader of the expedition.

A footnote in the edition of the *Relación* Willie was reading gave a listing of a group of Peruvian objects no longer in existence thought at one point to have been owned by Francisco Pizarro, who was known for his taste for extraordinary workmanship in toys, trinkets and miniatures of all sorts:

"Entire herds of little long-trunked *llamas* and *alpacas* and *vicuñas* in both gold and silver, each group twenty or so animals in various attitudes" (grazing, moving, looking up, sniffing the wind—so Willie thought of them), "rendered so small they would all fit easily on a drumhead. A necklace of eighteen copper-bodied spiders with polished glinting gold eyes, joined in a ring by clasping their spindly wire legs to those on either side of them. All sorts of *tumis,* ceremonial knives topped with long-billed jungle toucans or crouching mountain lions. Perfect silver frogs, none bigger than the cubes from a set of Spanish dice. Three little monkeys drunk as lords, cups still in their unsteady hands."

Things chosen because, Willie imagined, they would make Carlos and Martín laugh. A man in turquoise on the head of a cane who was hunting deer with a long spear and a big gold erection, a sitting fellow in fine stone masturbating, eyes shut, mouth half open in the pleasure of the moment, figures of men and women lying on their side, the male penetrating the female from behind, a man crouched over a woman, his large penis disappearing into her mouth. Such things as these came from far away, the north coast. The lords in public were tolerantly amused at these jests of the artisans of the less-cultured nations—though it is thought that the reason so many of these objects found their way to Cuzco was that they were prized and collected by nearly all the hundreds of members of the royal family.

GIVEN the risks involved, including the likelihood he would incur Francisco Pizarro's notable wrath, why did Zárate stay on alone in Cuzco?

Hard as reconstructing now what it was that had kept Willie Hickler in Cuzco so long without pinning Hiram Bingham down on the question of supporting him on through the end of the year.

"*Blindness to the maintenance of own well-being.*" It was an item on a list of reasons his mother was kept at Waltham the people there had given Willie to read once.

Fear, like the fear of certain illnesses, so great you become incapable of your own distress, of asking for the doctor?

For Willie, yes. Fear of not getting what he wanted. One day he had a piece of time to kill in the plaza while waiting for Ernesto. So he set himself a task: to see if in exactly one hour by the cathedral clock there would pass by anyone—man, woman, child or dog—that he could conceive of wanting as much as he wanted Ernesto.

And who had gone by? and what had happened?

No one. *Nothing* of interest until the moment Ernesto came whistling around the corner from Loreto, the street next to the Church of La Compañía.

The same afternoon Willie had received at the Central desk the only response he ever got from his sister-in-law to the urgent plea for help about how to conduct himself with Ernesto. Her letters had never arrived in Peru, and this telegram, Willie could tell from the top coding, had come a roundabout way, via Chicago, Galveston, the new station in Panama and then, given that it was nearly two months old, probably by carrier tortoise down the Cordillera.

The last time he was home, Sara had been attending meetings of something newly sprung up in New Haven called the Vedanta Society. As much as Willie could understand it, she had become a follower of sorts of a little man from India named Vivekananda, who himself had been a disciple of a Hindoo holy man, now dead about twenty-five years, whose name had been Ramakrishna. The telegram concerned him: SRI RAMAKRISHNA SAID THE MAN SEEKING ENLIGHTENMENT DIFFERS FROM US ONE SIGNIFICANT WAY STOP PHYSICAL BODY ORDINARY THOUGHTS ARE MIGHTY WALLS IMPRISONING US STOP BUT THE SEEKER SAYS I WILL BEAT MY HEAD AGAINST THE WALLS UNTIL THE WALLS FALL DOWN STOP SO ALSO WITH LOVE WILLIE STOP LOVE SARA

(And so also, Willie had been pleased to learn years later, with revolution. In an article about V. I. Lenin he read that even as late as 1915 or 1916 a friend had told the Bolshevik leader that no revolution would come about in Russia in their lifetime, so he was only beating his head against the wall. Lenin had responded, 'Then I will beat my head against it until the wall crumbles.')

Willie had written Sara that same evening, recalling an afternoon some days following the coming of the news that his poor brother, Danny, had died in Manila. "You sat with your hands in your lap in the middle of the sofa and, it being cold and rainy, I stoked the fire. I especially remember bringing you coffee, because you had asked for it instead of tea. And eventually, with no more little tasks to perform and nothing I could think of to say, I came and sat beside you and put my hand over yours. You were very kind, but said you preferred not being touched just yet. And when I asked why, you said, 'Because my loneliness is all of Daniel I have left now, and when you touch me, Willie, I feel I am losing even that and I'm not willing to let it go quite yet.'

"The reasonable part of me begins to prophesy that I will never have my friend Ernesto at all, all in all. The other day Hiram said that whatever mechanism it was that kept Ernesto from learning the lessons the poor digest along with their daily bread—cynicism, close reckoning, survival at any price, including at the expense of joy (how wrong the well-off are always about this last)—is also a mechanism which will allow Ernesto to slip sideways through his life and never become bound to anyone.

"I thought I could make him love me by proving to him how much I loved him. To do this, I planned to take photographs of him. Simple strategy, my best foot forward. Except that, like all fiery people, Ernesto does not accept the idea that he might be even that slight bit less fast than the speed of light. That even his *image* could be captured by anyone else frightens him.

"So I came to another plan: to *remember everything* about him. (Isn't that it, somehow? I am always reminded of how much you love me when you recall some tiny quirk of mine I had thought a piece of the wholly incidental history of me which I would bear alone to my grave.) But this memory business makes me feel I understand now better about your not wanting to give up your loneliness for my brother. As soon as I begin to salt away things about Ernesto, he, the man in the room, begins to recede from me."

THE LAST twenty or so pages of the *Relación* convinced Willie that it was even more than the delight of being with Martín in Martín's place which had kept Carlos Zárate in Cuzco so far beyond the time he should have stayed. Zárate must have caught what Willie thought of as the ethnologist's disease, the feverish idea that you have about pieced it all together, that with only a few more facts or the money for one more season or some break, some stroke of luck—

Zárate was taken to the academies where young men from all over the empire were trained for the huge priestly bureaucracy (logical, Willie thought, to suppose the one described would have been Martín's school). "Delighted as the masters were to meet a soul as strange to them as I, they were uncurious about the place I had come from," Zárate wrote. The teachers had turned at once to displaying their knowledges to him. He found he had to be attentive because as soon as his eye wandered they would change the subject immediately, like mothers trying to please a finicky eater.

He described going at dusk to the top of the various stone towers in the hills around town. Up there he met the 'star-herders,' as they were called, who pointed out to him their markers and calibrations etched onto the stones. (All bundling up against the cold, Willie supposed, Carlos and Martín under the same *poncho*, Martín's smaller body nestled in against his, his hand spread and holding Martín's belly, Martín's feet curling against Carlos's legs in the funny way they did, and the sky wheels around overhead and at various times through the night someone comes and calls softly and everyone gets up and goes to the wall and, almost as though they themselves have willed it, the appropriate star or planet rises or sets or comes into alignment with one of the stone pillars on the other side of the valley.) When Zárate asked why, since they knew all these things were bound to happen, they continued to watch, he was told of a figure (a god or a principle? he was unsure) they stood in full awe of. "We in Spain might call this power 'Reversal,' or perhaps Fortune or Luck." At first, because it had such sway over the astrologers, he imagined it must be as great as their Virakocha, who created the Sun and the Moon. "But when, in all earnestness, I broached this opinion, the necromancers were firm to the contrary. Great as it was, their 'Reverser' had only the power to disrupt and turn things around, which is, they assured me, much inferior to the power of creation."

As the time of year approached when the sun neared its greatest withdrawal from them, rising from bed every morning farther and farther along the northern horizon, Cuzco entered a period of cleansing. There were no torches anywhere. All fires, even those for cooking, were put out. "Along the narrow lanes the sad prayers and lamentations poured from behind every wall." Zárate's thought at first had been that news must have arrived of Atahualpa's death. But no. "Deep in the night we went out to stand in the crowd along one of the great avenues which quarter the city. All about, the people shed their clothes and beat themselves with branches or scrubbed at their flesh with bare hands as though their bodies were covered with some especially odious substance. They were dredging up their sins. Noblemen, great-ears, came into the crowd brandishing lances to frighten the dregs of the evil from the natives.

"Before the sky even started to grow gray, people began straining along the avenues toward the two squares in the center of town. There we waited until at last we could see, far off, one of Atahualpa's children in his father's part hold aloft a golden goblet to drink the sun's health as it began to appear over the top of the mountain. Behind the boy on their knees were all the princelings and the ranks of the nobility and behind them the common people, all kissing the ground to 'drink up the first rays of the returning light,' as they say."

It was Zárate who first reported that at the height of the principal fiestas the two clear streams which crossed the main plazas ran yellow with urine and the strict laws against drunkenness were greatly stretched.

Then a messenger arriving asking for the foreigner. The date fixed by Pizarro was only twelve days off. Zárate had to abandon Cuzco in a matter of hours, taking with him only the few *llamas* he would need to carry the collection he had made for Don Francisco's personal enjoyment. He left an order with Quisquis to send after him the part of the general treasure he was responsible for.

(By the time of the return trip, Carlos would have become strong enough to go on foot at the jogging easy trot messengers used. Along that same road which, coming in the other direction, had carried him from joy to joy, did he ever think of *not* going back? Martín telling him how, in the folds of some of the greatest and holiest mountains, there existed small uninhabited valleys warmed by updrafts of hot country wind so constantly that jungle fruits grew there all year round. People chanced upon these small paradises from time to time, but were uncomfortable at such proximity to the spirits of the mountains and never stayed. The two of them could have—)

But no. By the second week in July of 1533, Carlos Zárate was in Cajamarca, where things had changed drastically. The Spanish garrison had been reinforced by a second contingent down from Panama. Pizarro had had the treasure collected so far assayed and the first distributions had been made. Everybody had gold but, after paying their debts to one another, nothing to spend it on. Many Indians had died of smallpox and their comrades would not come into the part of the town the Spanish occupied to take out the bodies, so they rotted where they lay. Did Carlos try to get in to see his commander, to open his baskets and set out the little objects? Not known. Only clear that he was ordered to hurry along down to the coast after Hernando Pizarro, who was accompanying the King's portion of the gold at least as far as Tumbez.

When Zárate reached the port, he reported they found "many of the people of the place hanging from doorposts or disemboweled in the streets." This was Wednesday, July 30. News had just arrived at Tumbez that on Saturday late in the afternoon Atahualpa had been garroted and then set afire in the public square at Cajamarca.

> Those among the natives who took their own lives did so hoping that they too would be drawn along to the other, richer world in the great whirlpool created by their lord and master's passing out of this poor dark one.

Such is the last sentence of the Zárate *Relación.*

THE END of his book is also nearly the last trace of Carlos Zárate himself.

He was listed as one of those arriving at the port of Sanlúcar December 5, 1533, on the galleon *Santa María del Campo* in the party of the younger Pizarro (a remarkably short passage, given that it included the land trek across Panama). They sailed up the Guadalquivir, or were towed by teams of mules if there was insufficient breeze, and landed at Seville.

When Hernando Pizarro forwarded the first half of his portion of the Inca's ransom to Carlos V—the whole of the King's fifth would amount to twenty-six hundred pounds of twenty-two-karat gold and five thousand pounds of high-grade silver—he sent with it a letter telling the King that he also had with him a series of "objects of merit crafted by the natives of the principality of Pirú" which he and his brother wished their sovereign to see, "so that you first of all may know of the excellent degree of the development of the arts in this new addition to your domain."

The King had no desire to see gewgaws made by the savages. In reply, he ordered Hernando to hand over the objects to the Council of the Indies for weighing and melting down.

At that point, perhaps as a delaying tactic, Hernando took the 'objects' to the office of the Council to be recorded. Willie found several descriptions of the outstanding items in the collection:

thirty-four large urns of precious metal, including one of silver in the form of an eagle which could contain eight gallons of water; a gold platter and one of silver, "each of which would serve to carry the entire edible portion of a cow"; an idol of gold the size of a four-year-old boy; gold masks, footstools, fine gold dust.

Ten days later the King reversed his original decision on the Peruvian treasures. At least for a time. He ordered the things to be put on display in the Council of the Indies chambers in Seville for a period of exactly two weeks and then for the process of melting them down to begin. He himself did not come to see.

But among those who did was a thirteen-year-old boy named Pedro Cieza de León. In the great comprehensive chronicle he began on his own return from seventeen long years' fighting, traveling and recording in the "Indies of the Ocean Sea" as he calls them, Cieza remembers how his lust for adventure was first fired by the "rich pieces of gold that I saw in Seville, brought from Cajamarca, where the treasure that Atahualpa promised the Spaniards was collected."

Thirteen. Old enough certainly to pass into the large rooms in front, dim chambers which would cause the great vessels and platters and the statues still to shed their own beguiling light and still to have their own beguiling life. Pressed through with the motley assortment of out-of-work soldiers and sailors, men who had known the ne'er-do-well Pizarro brothers before and were affronted each time now they saw Hernando parading through the streets in his new velvets. Very rarely did any of the men of influence whose imaginations Don Francisco had hoped to prick make a visit. Most of those who came were only passing time, waiting until the papers they needed in order to ship out for the Indies were completed at the Office of Contracts. But at thirteen would you be allowed to peek into the even darker little room toward the back where Hernando had posted guard over a small assortment of obscene objects, jewelry and little whatnots? Would you even notice the bearded man crouched on the low stool in the corner, eyes downcast, bleary, could you even engage his sad attention? Carlos over and over taking the little pieces from their careful straw and cloth wrappings and setting them on the floor—*but what has happened? is some of it missing?* digging through to the bottom of each of his baskets, trying not to let the smell of the straw, the same as what he and Martín had slept on together so many nights, make him cry, mumbling to himself, *No, all here,* the copper spiders in their ring, the clay figure of the two conjoined bodies, loose, legs folded over each other, slack and content in the aftermath of love, their smiles which had forced him and Martín to smile—maybe just by watching the way this strange fellow would lightly, absently run his fingers along the inside of his thigh, a smart boy of thirteen might know, for a moment at least, that in the Indies there awaited him things as yet so unimaginable that to lose them, as this man must have, would be somehow worse than the loss of all the gold and silver on earth.

PART III

1911

This kingdom has fallen into such disorder . . . it has passed from one extreme to another. There was no evil: now there is almost no good. . . .

—MANCIO SERRA DE LEGUIÇAMO,
the conquistador *who received the great golden disc from the Temple of the Sun as his share of the booty of Cuzco*

ELEVEN

ONE AFTERNOON two weeks into July, Christina Long read those having tea at the Central a letter Alvin Bumstead had written her from Lima. He had improved so much his doctor was allowing him to sail north in the company of a nurse on her way to San Diego, where his wife would come meet him and take him home to New Haven on the train.

He also offered Christina advice: Even in the very throes of lethargy at the beginning of his stay at the British Hospital he had noticed the other infirm gentlemen padding about the marble halls in a kind of pink sock with felt soles. Mayhap, he had conjectured, these booties were awarded to the swift or at least the ambulatory or (this through one period of fervid relapse) only to bona-fide subjects of the King. "At last," he wrote, "summoning all of the pitifully small amount of strength and courage left me by my disease, I did 'What a Man (and I do not exclude the distaff from my observation) Must Do.' I DEMANDED booties! *And* I got 'em! As you must do, my dear young lady, as we each must do. I think now to make this my testament to the generations and to have it inscribed as my epitaph. 'DEMAND BOOTIES!' It is the most important lesson I have learned in eighty years residence upon the planet."

"O fortunate Bumstead!" said Clement Bailey.

"Indeed," sighed Isaiah Mather. "All his life before him and Peru mercifully behind."

"I meant more the good fortune of being subject to a malaise which is treatable," Bailey said, pulling his bushy beard through the big cup of his hand, "without recourse to regicide or parricide or whichever damn thing it is. I always forget."

By now the Expedition members hardly tempered their discontent at all in Christina's honor. Their conceit was Shakespearean and self-serving, but also precise. Though not dead, their king *was* largely removed from them and, at least for the loyalists, Hiram's old friends, the roses appeared, but cankered in the bud. Even their dreams often would not unfold.

A few of the scientists were able to get on with their own work. Larry Bruner had the short-horned locusts of southern Peru all neatly pinned in battalions and sent off to the National Museum, his paper for the *Proceedings* in the mail and an addendum longer than the original already in the works. Surgeon Nelson and Chief Whelp Hillman had gone off to collect wax impressions of the insides of the mouths of a recondite and supposedly fierce tribe of Quechuas called the Q'eros. Back in June, Willie had photographed fifty-six separate pink ellipses full of craters for Nelson, who was lacking plaster of Paris and preoccupied with the possibility his specimens would melt during the tropical phase of their passage homeward. Though he had sat through the reading of an extensive article on the subject, Willie could not for the life of him remember anymore whether chewing so much *coca* as the Q'eros did gave them better or worse teeth. The result was, however, significant one way or the other.

(Himself, one night eating toasted, salted *ava* beans while drinking in a bar with Ernesto, had experienced the sensation of a caving-in somewhere in the back or business portion of his mouth. The sharp-edged new hole hurt Willie only when he had a headache. Dr. Nelson had looked in and said, "Nothing that can't wait till you get back.")

Sometimes their errant prince would slouch in on their tedious evening presentations in the lounge. In the question period he was likely to attack—the premise, the method by which the whole piece of research had been done, the style of the paper, anything. Afterward the scientists would slink off and the next day you would find them at work harder than ever, as though by sheer diligence they could forge some sort of fabric so tough that even Hiram Bingham couldn't pick holes in it.

The long-timers knew better than to try. Clement Bailey said, "It's because he doesn't have one of his own that Hiram so resents anyone who's got any sort of method at all. Makes you understand again the happiness of the boundaries of your own intelligence and the limits of your own little enterprise. H.B., he's *got* no profession, except pestering the living daylights out of us and letting the fun out of our little preoccupations. Down on the artists too, I'd bet. Hmm, Willie?"

He wouldn't know, Willie said. Then, slowly, well, yes. "Your scientist at least has to turn in his homework. So if you can't get at his result, at least you can get at how he got there. But the artist claiming not even to know how he does what he does, that when all's said and done there remains mystery—that infuriates Hiram. When he wants to get my goat the worst, he'll thunder at me, 'At random, Willie, shoot at random! Any damn thing! Who are *you* to decide one slice of life's any damn prettier, better, more uplifting than any other?' "

In the division of the forces, Ernesto was like the scientists in imagining that more and more effort on his part might somehow gladden his boss's heart. He had poured endless energy and ingenuity into his job at what the gentlemen had inelegantly taken to calling 'Hiram's Hole.' On the other hand, more like the loyalists, Ernesto seemed to understand that the gloom of the monarch would not be dispelled by any mortal's good works, and that all his subjects could do was attend upon the mournful scene. Also like the loyalists, Ernesto 'visited' Hiram as though he were a shut-in, poured his drinks for him, agreed with him and forgave him his tempers.

At times Willie plunged into intense jealousy. He even wished on himself some sort of illness, either of body or of spirit, so he could find out whether in the crunch Ernesto would lavish the same sort of attention on him. But he remembered himself saying once that eternally asking other people to choose was not the happiest way to conduct affairs and, besides, he was so tuned up by love that his health remained remarkably good. He was losing weight, daily becoming more goat, as he thought of it, less sheep. (But which were saved, which cast into outer dark? He could not recall, though he was rooting for the goats.) And, for the most part, Willie recognized that their common concern for Hiram bound him and Ernesto together. Like brothers justifying the ways of the father to one another.

The Hole drew no visitors anymore. Several thousand hours of laborers' time had produced nothing much for show except piles of mud and gravel and a timber-braced entrance like a mine-shaft opening for an excavation which ran some twenty feet horizontally into the hillside. Indians on their way across and down to the town of Pisac in the Yucay Valley inevitably stopped at a spot a little above the site to turn back and bow and say their Hail Mary's in Quechua as farewell to Cuzco. But the dig itself they hurried by with heads down. Travelers sometimes asked one another what might be going on here, and though Willie couldn't understand all of what they said, the Indians were always quite clear about who the workers were. *Huaqueros.* A '*huaca*' was any holy spot. The reports were that there had been some 342 of them within the city limits of Cuzco in Inca times. A '*huaquero*' was a grave robber.

July 19, Willie and Ernesto quit for the afternoon earlier than usual. Ernesto had "something to do in town"—an errand which must involve work, since he brought with him a case containing the original bone fragments Alvin Bumstead had come across. Willie was on his way to the telegraph office to wire the W. R. Grace Company in Callao for the sailing schedule of ships August 1 and after. He had determined that if he was going, the 26th or 27th would be the last day possible to depart Cuzco with any hope of being in New York by September 15.

"Let's look for Hiram as we go along," Willie said. "I have to face him with the question of whether I'll be leaving or not."

"We were talking about that the other evening."

"You were? And what was decided?"

"It was mentioned how sad we all would be. How for some of us there would be a terrible drunk to get through if you left—and tears in some eyes."

"Whose?"

"In Hiram's. *Doña* Christina's." Ernesto had stopped. "Mine."

They walked on, Willie whistling a song which in Quechua began, "Girl, girl, pretty red-skirt girl." A jagging route down the steep streets of the oldest quarter of the city took them past all the bars Ernesto knew in that end of town. No Hiram. On Plateros Street a certain Mr. Lee was standing out front of his restaurant in a white apron. They asked were there any '*yankis*' inside. Mr. Lee had under his arm a San Francisco newspaper dated March 17. The banner concerned the St. Patrick's Day Parade. Lee, whose English was not only good but a little ornate and sometimes too elegant, said he would be "tickled pink" to lend Willie the periodical and that, though Dr. Bingham was not present, his lady was, and wouldn't the gentlemen like to step in to gaze upon her?

Willie said they would.

Mr. Lee led them between the empty tables, past the drapery which curtained off the private dining room, then around the corner into the dark. He flicked aside something, a patch it must have been, and there through an opening which was a comfortable inch and a half wide Willie and Ernesto were treated to a sight: In a cubicle, Christina Long in gloves and a wide straw hat with a plum-colored ribbon sitting across a white-clothed table from Leo Ávila, he in full military tunic and regalia, *his* gloves nicely flattened and lying atop his hat on a chair.

'Proof,' Willie thought. He and Ernesto often puzzled over the question of whether there was or had been an affair between these two. But the proof here was not at all about the body, only confirmation of Hiram's notion that they had betrayed him in spirit.

As Willie and Ernesto hurried toward the front of the restaurant, Mr. Lee pursued them, waving his San Francisco paper at Willie.

Willie stepped into the street, then turned back. He refused the paper. Maybe later, thanks.

Mr. Lee's face was creased with pleasure.

"I hadn't known, Mr. Lee, that you too are an *artiste,*" Willie said. "And specializing in that most difficult form, *les tableaux vivantes.*"

Mr. Lee said, "Oh yes? What is that, please?"

"What they call 'living pictures.' "

A camera in every home, a photographer in every breast. What is a human being? The animal which creates scenes. What 'moral,' then, in Mr. Lee's little presentation? Something evolutionary maybe. At least strongly about race. The yellow man delights in showing the white man and the brown man the white woman giving herself to a brown man. Any number of conclusions could be drawn.

Willie and Ernesto went on through the streets with their heads down, not speaking, shamed by what they had witnessed as though they themselves had been the actors.

At the telegraph office, Ernesto departed for the market. Willie sent his wire, then went over to the Central. He checked the desk and then Hiram's room. No luck. Nearly six o'clock, beginning to grow dark. He was about to set out to hike across town to his own little house when he noted the doors to the gentlemen's lounge were closed. Willie peeked in and there was the man he sought, alone in the gloom, attended only by a waiter and his trusty police dog, Benito, lying by Hiram's feet.

Yes, Willie would have a beer.

On the table before Hiram was the first English edition of Bishop Las Casas's *Briefest Account of the Destruction of the Indies.* Published in 1654, the translation had been retitled in order to appeal to anti-Spanish sentiment:

> *THE TEARS OF THE INDIANS; Being an Historical and True Account of the Cruel Massacres and Slaughters of Above Twenty Million of Innocent People*

"Believe in the Devil still?"

"If you have secrets, I suppose devils could be of some use in excising them," Willie said.

Hiram smiled slowly. The reference was to a saying of Ernesto's: '*Para descubrir secretos, los diablos de Condoroma.*'

"Found out what that may mean, by the way." Willie tugged on his beer. "Condoroma was a place the Spanish were convinced the Inca had gold mines, but they couldn't get the natives to hand over the information. Finally, Ernesto says, two of the Christians disguised themselves as devils and made their way by night to the head man's little house. They accused him of having turned the mine over to the whites and so terrified him that the man then led them straight to the lode to show them it hadn't been worked. Hence 'For discovering secrets, the devils of Condoroma.' "

"Before I read up on the conquest of Peru, I never had any need for a literal Satan to explain to me the evil of the world," Hiram said. "But what Pizarro did, and Toledo after him, no theory of human greed or even a theory of maniacal lust for saving souls can account for. Something unhumanly pure and uncontradictory infected those men."

"Different in *kind* from your own desire to 'discover' things?" Willie asked.

Hiram sank his chin against the palm of his hand, which forced his mouth into a wide pout. At length he said, "No, not in kind. As one of my colleagues back home is given to announcing, archaeology is 'restoring the order of the ages which time has put asunder.' But me? what in the world am I if not a lord of *dis*order and *mis*rule? If I have a talent, one, it is for taking the big stick and stirring up everybody else's comfortably-arrived-at solutions. Were I the Peruvians, Willie, I'd never in a thousand years let Hiram Bingham get his hands on even one of my blasted old sites."

Big drunk's tears were running down Hiram's cheeks. "You know," he went on, "they're saying now twenty million is not so great an exaggeration. What with slavery, murder and disease, the new world's native population was reduced somewhere between thirty and fifty percent in the first hundred years after Columbus." Hiram gazed at the banks of frosted windows on the street side of the lounge, their light turning blue now. "And maybe it's age, or booze, Willie, but I can tell you, these hours between day and night ain't getting any easier for me to get through. Christie not back yet. You didn't happen to see her, did you?"

"No," Willie lied. "Where'd she go?"

"With Leo, to his aunt's to copy out Quechua lyrics." Hiram raised two fingers to the waiter for beer. "I only know one thing for sure anymore, Willie."

"What's that?"

"That I'm going to die."

"Same as the rest of us," Willie said. "Me, every morning these days I look in the little shaving mirror from my kit and I say to the tarnished little fellow in there, 'You are going to die.' It started as a joke, but it gets more serious every day."

Hiram nodded, but he didn't say anything.

Under the table, Benito stirred. He got to his feet, claws scrambling on the tile, and growled. The waiter had come in with more beer, but ordinarily that wouldn't have alerted the dog.

It was the deer. Willie and Hiram could see its head appearing above the tables and the backs of armchairs as though they were shrubs and outcroppings of rock in the wilderness.

"Lie back, Bennie, lie back."

The deer was allowed free roam of the hotel. It browsed cigarette and cigar butts out of the cuspidors, apparently to no ill effect on its innards, and the maids and porters cleared away the small piles of droppings it left discreetly in out-of-the-way corners. They were devoted to the little animal, calling it Inocente and believing it a *salvado* whose luck enhanced their own chances for luck in life.

The story was that the archbishop of Cuzco had come to the Central one day to order the menu for a banquet he was giving in honor of a visiting dignitary from Rome. Having decided on venison, he was led out to the back of the kitchen where a large number of deer were penned. Asked which ones he would like to have roasted, the prelate announced that, like his Savior, he would prefer them to suffer the little ones to come unto him. Then it was, amidst the polite laughter, that this smallest animal had come forward and forced its smooth head into the archbishop's hand. And at that even so hard a man as he had had to relent.

Inocente approached their table. Below, Benito beat his tail rapidly and edged his eager damp snout out from under the cloth. "Go slow, Benito," Hiram said softly.

Neck extended, head turned up so one of its large dark eyes was directly on Hiram, the deer licked at the ashtray between the two men. Frozen there, it looked like an animal on the block, this time Willie or Hiram the potential executioner.

"At first I took a great shine to Inocente," Willie said. "Kindred soul, fellow *salvado.* But now I begin to wonder if there isn't some real difference between being saved and simply being spared. Maybe the archbishop was wrong."

"As your confessor," Hiram said, "I need to know what is it that ever gave you the idea you might in fact be 'saved.' "

"Falling in love." Willie paused, then smiled. "Even in the end if it doesn't work out—"

The lounge doors opened. Hiram turned expectantly. But coming in was Edmund Foote, not Christina.

Hiram begged the good professor to come sit with them and ordered him a gin from the waiter.

"Saw *Señor* Mena in the market," Dr. Foote said, "and he has something most provocative for you to have a look at."

"What's that?"

"He'll be along directly, and it would take more time to tell." Dr. Foote was looking fondly and directly at Willie. "What an extraordinary fellow I find him to be."

Willie's impulse was to hide his face somehow. He was blushing.

"Best second man *I've* ever had," Hiram said. " 'Course we take to Ernesto partly because he is so like us."

Dr. Foote asked, "In what ways?"

Willie said, "His believing friendship is the most important thing in the world. The way he embraces sadness. How he understands life occurs mostly not in its doing but in its remembering."

"Very nice, Willie," Foote said. His glass was full of Dutch gin, yellow in color. As it floated in front of the blue windows toward the classicist's mouth, it turned briefly pale green, then back to yellow. "Though as to the reason why we come to 'love' a particular person, I tend to agree with Montaigne that this cannot be expressed." The old man laughed. "Not any better than Montaigne himself did: 'Because it was he, because it was I.' "

"And cruelty—" Hiram had, with effort, pulled himself back up into the conversation "—don't forget that one, Willie. Like you, Ernesto has not a mean bone in his body."

The lounge doors again eased open. By what appeared a feat of will, Hiram kept himself from turning. He reached down and dug his fingers into the fur at Benito's neck. "Now on the other hand, my Bennie here may just *be* developing a mean streak. Our fault, likely, bringing him along down here. They turn out to be mainly scent-and-sound dogs, these shepherds, quite weak in eyesight. Hotel's not a proper place for him, streets are too sensation-filled. Twice now, thinking they were other dogs, he's gone after little children. I won't keep any animal like that. If he does it again, the first time he breaks skin I'll have him taken out and shot!"

Willie's impulse was to laugh. Hiram must be convinced it was Christina who'd come in behind him this time. Except to upset her, there could be no reason for him to concoct such a threat about their beloved Benito.

When he saw it was Ernesto, Hiram got to his feet and called for more beer. He insisted Ernesto take his chair. "We have just been discussing you, *compadre,*" he said, "and in a manner which would have burned your ears had you been present."

This false too, Willie thought. Too large, what an actor might give you before he remembered he was at last offstage and could gesture small. What had happened? Jealousy because in nearly the same breath both Willie and Edmund Foote had spoken well of Ernesto? It was in Hiram's style to become overly polite to people right before he turned against them.

"Perhaps," Hiram said, "we would all like to adjourn to a more *alegre* locale now."

"I wonder are you up to reaping the benefits," Dr. Foote said.

"I'm up to—" Hiram turned and started for the lobby "—no good."

Halfway to the door he began to teeter. Ernesto got to him and grabbed his arm to keep him from going over.

"Have we lost him?"

"I don't think so," Willie said. "I think he had to relieve himself."

Dr. Foote finished off his gin. "Something else, Willie. I didn't put my two cents in to you earlier, so I'll do it now. When Hiram said your friend Ernesto lacks cruelty?"

"Yes?"

"Well, I probably should save my breath for my porridge, but I've had my eye on you of late, as you may well know, and I simply need to point out to you that there *can be* a sort of tyranny of the mind in some people which is *very like* cruelty. In the face of the overwhelming evidence we find even in supposedly grim nature if we look, certain people continue to insist on their own precious isolation. In the young—the undergraduates, I mean—we have to tolerate it. They *are* alone, on the brink, with life teeming so variously before them that an easeful death would in a way seem preferable to what they understand they will have to go through. But not by the time you've accounted for as many years as you have, Willie. And I assume you and Ernesto are of an age, approximately?"

"Forty-six days apart."

"Perfect almost." The old man smiled. "Must be."

All in a rush Willie said, "There're times I'm convinced we *are* the same person, Ernesto and I, and it's only I've had two kicks in the head, one coming to Peru and the other meeting him, which have jolted me ahead a step in my understanding."

"Understanding of what?"

"Of how fortunate I am. Of how the world rights itself and goes on with or without us, no matter whether we've fallen or broken our hearts or whatever."

"Ernesto has had one of the same advantages."

"Meeting me?" Willie shrugged. "Maybe you need both for it to work. It's why I'm so intent on getting him to make the journey, to see the States."

"Ah, the famous broadening effect of travel. But soft, our tragedians approach."

In the particular moment you would hardly have known them for tragedians, Ernesto and Hiram with their arms about each other's waists, laughing together, Hiram saying, "Are you convinced, *compadre?* sure as you are of your name?"

Ernesto wiped a tablecloth with the heel of his hand and laid out the box which contained the Alvin Bumstead mastodon bones. Next to it he put a package wrapped in newsprint. Inside this were two other bones from the market, still slightly bloody in several places. Marrow had been oozing from the end of one. The fresh pieces were of course much whiter and more sharply contoured, but to appearance at least there was no other difference.

"What animal?" Willie asked.

"An ox. From the hip. My mother served an ox stew the other night and something in it looked familiar to me."

"Peruvian oxen ñative?" Hiram asked.

"I'd have to read up on it, Hiram," Dr. Foote said, "but my memory says no—brought over on ships."

The waiter had come in with a tray, glasses and a bottle of brandy. Hiram poured drinks all around, including one for the waiter. He proposed a toast to "Ernesto the Liberator" which they drank off, then one to the "end of the search for the wild geese" which they also drank, and one to the "opening-up of the open road."

Then, bottle in hand, Hiram waltzed them all out into the lobby. Isaiah Mather and Jack Wingate, together with several of the other more scientific types, were just coming down the staircase. They were dressed in either tuxedos or tails, for tonight the gentlemen were celebrating Clement Bailey's birthday at a little formal dinner. Hiram poured brandy for as many as would have it into as many glasses as the waiter could rustle up on short notice, then bade them all go into the lounge to see what they could make of "a little exhibit our *Señor* Mena has put out for our edification."

When he returned from the lounge, Mather was shaking his head. He said to Willie in an undertone, "You fear for him when he has the blues, but when he changes gear you begin to long for the restful calm of the blue periods to return, don't you?"

Hiram was in the process of trying to convince Edmund Foote to accompany him down the so-called Sacred Valley of the Inca on Ernesto's mules, setting out bright and early tomorrow morning. Also that he repair with them *this minute* to continue their frivolity in more congenial circumstances.

The first offer Dr. Foote said he would be more than glad to take up. "As to the second, though, I'm afraid not, my boy. I'm terribly late now. I must hurry up to dress fast as a rabbit as it is."

Hiram made a face. "But *you're* to be counted on, aren't you, Willie?"

"Of course," Willie said, as soberly and as deadpan as he could manage, "I am certainly to be counted on. 'RELIABILITY,' it's on my card, even. What's the task now, my lord?"

"The photographic record of our researches in the valley of the Urubamba."

Hiram was swaying as he spoke. Ernesto stood solicitously at his elbow.

And at last Christina was coming in from the street in the buff-colored overcoat she had had on the evening she and Hiram met Willie at the train in Puno, and the straw hat with the plum ribbon. Leo Ávila was behind, a discreet dark-green shadow.

Hiram refixed his attention on Willie.

In a low voice Willie said, "I have eight days left here, Hiram. Count 'em, *eight.* That is the case unless there is something you could do to change things around so I could stay on."

"Is it dollars and cents we are talking now, old friend?"

Hiram's free hand went for his front pants pocket, where he usually kept a large wad of bills.

"It is," Willie said. His voice was tightening more each time he spoke.

'Not now,' the warning self said, 'when Hiram's fighting another, uglier battle on another front. Not when he's this charged and unreliable. Choose a better time.' But with a man who had never had to live at tempos set by anyone else, what chance was there any 'better' time might ever come along?

Hiram withdrew a handful of *soles* from his pocket. He was about to thrust them on Willie—Willie knew, it was an old scene between them—when something gave him pause. The coins and bills dropped back in his pocket. Hiram straightened. "I'm afraid there just aren't such resources at my command at the moment, old sport. Your passage down here and your lodgings, your replacement chemicals, the meals I've been able to get you to take in my company, your goddamn *cerveza!* These I've paid when I could, out of personal funds. But now there just *ain't* any more. Well's run dry."

Willie waited almost complacently for the change, the reprieve or the joke or whatever it was that was bound to follow. The desk clerk announced he had been unable to find a room key for Christina. Hiram went charging toward the street doors, brandy bottle tucked to his chest as though he were carrying a football. Christina ran after him. Stopping to fish the key out of his pocket for her, Hiram spilled all of the money he had been going to thrust on Willie. Ernesto and the waiter stooped at Hiram's feet to gather it up. The gentlemen stood still where they were, at the lounge door, on the stairs, watching with the placid diligence of supernumeraries in an opera.

"You will want me along tomorrow, I assume," Leo Ávila said, "for my knowledge of the Yucay at least."

"You?" Hiram swayed, his eyes coming up on Leo's face in a zigzag pattern which began with the view of Leo's shiny shoes. "Not 'want,' *señor*, I shall *require* your services. At six tomorrow morning, shall we say?"

Ernesto had darted into the lounge and now hurried back bearing Hiram's rumpled suit jacket. On his way by, he said softly to Willie, "Come with me, please."

"What for?"

Ernesto didn't answer. He held Hiram's jacket for him, but Hiram would not put his arms in the sleeves, so Ernesto reached up and draped it around his shoulders. As they were pushing out through the glass doors, Ernesto turned and beckoned Willie with an urgent downsweep of his hand.

Willie could not help but follow.

TWELVE

THEY did manage finally to get a start the following day, July 20, but so late the sun was setting as they passed Hiram's Hole, deserted now, the workers paid off and boards nailed across the opening to the shaft in an 'X,' as though the dig had been found not to be the solution to whatever the problem was.

At the brim of the valley, while the others began going down the steep farther side, Willie pulled up to have another look at Cuzco. Not the last, certainly, since he would be passing through again in a few days. Willie didn't have it in him at the moment to slip up an *Ave* as the Indians did as they passed, so he went on, and it was only a few minutes later he recalled Sara repeating what her little Hindoo teacher had told: that the shortest prayer he had found in English was 'Amen' and the second shortest 'I wonder.'

Not even that left in his heart to say.

There were only six of them, Hiram, Edmund Foote, Clement Bailey and all his tubes of charts, Ernesto, Willie and Leo Ávila. Ávila had refused to ride any of Ernesto's mules. At the last moment he had shown up with a roan mare of unusual size for this part of the world. Hiram's invitation to the present trek had galvanized all of the other gentlemen at the Central into sudden miraculous renewed concern for the state of their own half-forgotten knitting.

While they were cinching down the last of the gear in front of the hotel, Willie had asked if Ernesto could figure why in the world Hiram was bringing Leo.

"I put that question to him a half-hour ago," Ernesto said,

"and he told me, 'There are times, Ernesto, when there is nothing else to do but let the wolf gnaw at our own insides.' Is that a saying in English?"

It was, Willie said.

Christina had been there, watching from behind the lace curtains in her room as they mounted up, the dog Benito beside her. When they moved out, she had stepped onto the frail iron balcony, but she hadn't called or waved to any of them, so perhaps Willie had been the only one to see her.

After dark they reached the valley floor at the town called Pisac, where a bridge crossed the Urubamba, here in its lower reaches named the Vilcanota. Hiram was all for breaking out the tents and the canvas cots and camping on the river flats beyond town. But, small as it was, their party could not move unnoted through country as heavily populated as this. In the first street they were met by the Mayor of Pisac and a delegation, twenty or so grim men in large round felt hats carrying under their arms canes of office with heavily embossed silver heads. The officials spoke very little Spanish, but through Ernesto and Leo's interpreting the gringos learned that a place had already been prepared for them.

They were conducted along to the estate of a gentleman named Luis Dávila, who had been one of Hiram's hosts when he had come down the Sacred Valley two years ago. The whole mile from the gate up to the house was lined on both sides with formally shaped spires of cypress.

Pisac lies some two thousand feet below the Valley of Cuzco. Farther along they could expect to find rain forest, dense tropics at seven thousand feet. But even in Pisac the change is felt, the climate much less severe. To Willie, reminiscent of California in its mildness and fragrance. At supper he noticed he could no longer sense his blood thumping against his skin. He missed the pulsing, which he had come of course to associate with his being in love.

The Inca had treasured this valley, their host said, its year-round growing season, the river teeming with trout, the mountains alive with game, and so had dotted it all about with their country palaces.

"And then," Hiram said, "took their refuge here when the invaders came."

"Yes, fighting from place to place, holding one and then the other of what had been the seats of their merriment, youthful romance and joy, fortresses now, giving it all up slowly, at terrible cost, over years and years." Dávila's tone was descending, mournful. "Great civilizations, we must conclude, never die with grace."

Their hostess was a little woman with a head full of tight black ringlets. Her name was Marta and, over the custard, she mentioned that she had been brought up on an *estancia* a day and a half downriver at Pachar, and wondered could she be of any help with whatever the foreigners were looking for.

Hiram went to get his copy of Antonio de la Calancha's *Pious Account of the Augustinian Order in Peru.* Returning, he explained to the lady that there was reason to believe that at least one of the last citadels of the Inca had never been found by the Spanish.

"*Ay de mi, señor!*" The lady put her hand to her red cheek as though she had just developed an intolerable toothache. "Down there in *that* jungle there are places not even *God* has heard of yet!" And she crossed herself.

Hiram wanted to be more specific. " 'Close to Vitcos,' which might also be 'Uitcos,' " he read, " 'in a village called Chuquilpalpa, is a House of the Sun and in it a white rock over a spring of water where the Devil appears as a visible manifestation to be worshipped by the idolators. This was the principal *mochadero* of those forested mountains.' "

"*Mochadero?*" When she laughed, the little lady's ringlets bounced up and down and the filigree baskets of her earrings shook. "*Mochadero?*" she repeated.

"From the Quechua for 'kiss,' a kissing place," Hiram said earnestly, "where the Incas would have made homage to their deities by bending and kissing—"

"Oh, I know all that, *señor*. But you shouldn't even ask me such things. I was properly brought up. How should *I* know about kissing places out in the forest?" She gave her husband a bright, eyebrow-raised glance. "Certainly none where the Devil has ever been known to appear!"

Early the next morning Willie and Hiram were served coffee on a flagstone veranda overlooking the river, which here flowed wide and silver-gray. The sun came over the mountains, but the first rays could do little to take the chill off them. Hiram was casting about for things to say (had Willie slept well? were the cameras secured to his liking?), when Luis Dávila brought out to them a stumpy, unshaven man of fifty or so who looked somehow familiar to Willie. "The sergeant here knows the territory," their host claimed, "every rock, every pigsty from here to Quillabamba. If you think he'd be of help in your enterprise, I'd be pleased to lend him to you for as long as you'll agree to feed him, *Señor* Bingham."

Carrasco, Ernesto's fellow *arriero* they had gone drinking with one night in Cuzco. Willie started to say something, but the sergeant put his finger to his lips. Obviously he wanted to surprise Ernesto.

Hiram was telling their host he'd have to see. He didn't want any noses put out of joint among the guides he had already.

"I doubt you'll do that," Willie said confidently in English.

Carrasco came to them with his own surefooted little horse and an extra jenny he was willing to rent Hiram. This animal walked swinging her hips, not side to side precisely but in a kind of underslung sashay with a tiny hesitation like a bump at the end of each half-circle. At one point the sergeant, who played his tiny *charango* and sang as he rode, turned back to Willie and Ernesto and said, "Down in Quillabamba a woman who walks like my Carmen is said to be grinding her beans too fine."

Ernesto sat a mule as though it were the finest show horse, straight up even when he was resting. The way he laid his hand along his thigh, fingers in toward the crotch, heel forward, made Willie ache.

At length Willie said very softly, "How could I *not* love someone like you who makes me so happy?"

Ernesto didn't answer.

"Have you ever had anyone like that?"

"No."

"Not the girl with the husband who wouldn't stay with you?"

"No."

They made good time to Calca, and from there to Yucay, a town where the houses were lined up along the dusty main road like the desert towns of northern Mexico. Harvesting was nearly over. In the yellow fields teams of oxen and mules were being driven in counterclockwise circles over wheat thick on the stone threshing-floors. Women sat in large groups in whatever shade they could find, talking while they punched corn from dry cobs into baskets. On the road there were big shaggy piles of fodder running along like errant haystacks, the only visible part of the man underneath being his legs. In such a climate, no long fallow period would follow the harvest. All around, the branches of plums were already in naked pink blossom, and birds were carrying wisps of straw to new nests.

At twenty minutes to five by Willie's pocket watch the sun crossed the jagged western peaks and a curt wind began whipping dust all around them. They were at the town of Urubamba. Though Sergeant Carrasco said there was a decent inn a little way up the road, Hiram chose a campsite down by the river. Then, with very little assistance from anyone, he set up all three tents, gathered wood to start a fire and, after some rattling around in the food boxes, came forth with arms full of tins. Squatting by the largest of their cooking pots, Hiram began opening cans and dumping in the contents.

Willie industriously trundled his own stuff and then Ernesto's single striped bag into the tent Hiram had raised closest to the water. It was separated from the other two by a weeping willow tree. Leo Ávila sat smoking and watching him. At one point his eyebrows rounded up and he smiled. Willie didn't care. He no longer even remembered why he had ever cared what people like Ávila thought of him and his life. Waste of time.

In with the candles and the waterproof matches he found a single kerosene lamp and a pint of fuel. Thinking of himself and Ernesto long ago in their hotel room in Puno, he filled the lamp and squirreled it away under his cot. Likely all in vain anyway, since Carrasco would probably be put in with them for the night.

Clement Bailey and Dr. Foote returned from a brief scouting of town to announce there was a fiesta in progress. All during the time they were consuming Hiram's stew, skyrockets zipped up the sky, flared and gave loud gunshot reports over their heads. The echoes volleyed back and forth endlessly across the valley. After supper, they took a walk up to the plaza for a look-see, leaving Avila behind to guard camp. He had, he said, long ago satiated himself on whatever quaint amusements these villages had to offer.

On the steps before Urubamba's stolid brown church an Indian band played, flutes, drums, a guitar and harps. The harps here were held upside down, their fat bellies resting over the shoulders of the musicians. Both harpists, themselves fat gentlemen who bobbed and swayed in time to the heavy thumps of the drums, would peer over and again into the round holes in their instruments, like little boys shaking big piggybanks, surprised each time they looked that there were yet more sprinklings of silvery notes to be gotten out. As the Indian ladies danced, they turned side to side in generous half-circles and their wide skirts ballooned and rode up so you could count at least some of the many layers of old skirts underneath. Finesse, rectitude, even a certain solemnity to everything, the tiny steps, the way the men flourished their handkerchiefs and their partners grabbed hold, the way they then wove themselves together in the dance, parted, returned, made people seem less drunk than they were.

From the stands around the *parque* Sergeant Carrasco and Ernesto brought the gringos mugs of the various sorts of heated *ponche*, punch flavored with cherries or with cinnamon or almonds, all of it so sweet Willie was not aware of its alcohol content until he saw a grim little lady tilting a bottle of clear stuff down a whole row of cups without once righting the bottle, just like the more accomplished sort of bartenders in the more desperate sort of mining towns he had visited in the North American West.

They were, of course, the center of attention. Slowly, one by one, the more substantial *mestizos* of Urubamba put themselves forward to the sergeant or Ernesto to be introduced. Once they had braved the experience themselves, they brought over their somber wives and their children. Willie was pleased that one little fellow, who hadn't really got anything more grand than a press of the flesh with W. Hickler, Esq., Factotum (and that lightly enough, the touch of all of them so brief, so sweet), still was able to trade on the fact. In exchange for permission to inspect the hand which had shaken Willie's, another, less brave little boy had given him a piece of hard candy.

And then Clement Bailey fell in love. Or so he said when he came back huffing and puffing from dancing a *wayno* with a good-looking girl of nineteen or twenty. She was there with her mother and dressed in mourning for someone, but several of the young locals had been able to lead her out into the square previously. Though she hid it almost perfectly while she was dancing, she had a limp. It appeared only when she was returning to her mother's side.

"You try her now, Hiram," Clement said. "That way the old lady won't suspect anything." He handed him a cup of the *ponche.* "There, that's for courage. And tell her what a gallant chap yours truly can be when he wants." Clement gave Hiram a gentle push in the general direction of the girl. "Oh—and find out her name, will you?"

A man almost as tall as he was had approached Willie. He was wearing a black suit and had a rich liquidy cough he could do little to conceal. Probably tuberculosis, very advanced.

"I am Peruvian. What is your flag?"

"I come from the United States."

"Oh!" Water coming out of his eyes, saliva at the edge of his mouth, a spot of something on his lip. *Coca.* He grabbed Willie's hand and kissed it, which made Willie flinch. "There is the Father, the Son and the Holy Ghost," the man said. "The United States is the little father and we, the countries of South America, Peru, Colombia, Ecuador—what are the other names?—Chile, we are your children. Isn't that so?" And then, in a sort of English, "You *papacito,* no?"

Willie said well, if that was true, then why did the father treat his children so badly?

"Oh! Anarchist, eh?"

Clement was passing around more steaming cups of the *ponche.* The *pizoos,* as he called them, that Clement meant for the lady vendor fluttered to the ground all about him. He leaned to pick them up, but his great stomach kept him from reaching. "Oh, the hell with 'em," he said as he came upright. And then the redness drained out of his face. Willie and Dr. Foote started toward him. "'S'all right, 's'all right," Clement panted at them, "I'll get it back in a moment." He cupped his hand over his left breast and shook his arm several times. "Doesn't matter anyway. Anything for love, when the call's on you. That one's got the very goddamn *whiff* of it on her, gents."

What was the gentleman saying? Carrasco wanted to know.

Nothing, Willie said. Just that he liked a great deal the lady Hiram was dancing with.

Shouldn't be any problem, Carrasco said. A word with her mother, some little gift. Not that she was a whore yet—

"*Puta?*" Clement said. "Tell him not on his life. Not interested."

"No, no," Carrasco said. "Inform the gentleman, *please.* Nice girl from lower down. Sad story. She was to be married, decent young man, I knew him, who said he didn't care at all about her short leg. But there was an older man too, who thought he had a contract with the mother—she'd taken his money, they think—and at a dance the night before the wedding the old one walked right in and shot the husband dead. Before the girl ever even tasted the fruits, as they say. Now what? A widow. A limp. What else can she do?"

"What's all that about?" Clement said.

"Nothing," Willie replied. "Just that she's on the border—at 'the point,' as they say here."

"Good. Because you know I'm not the sort who makes a habit of doing in virgins either."

"No, of course not," Willie said.

The tubercular man was staring at him. When Willie dared look back, the charcoal counters in the man's head made him think some kind of hypnotism must be involved. Then of a vaudeville in Central Square. His mother had loved taking him and his brother. Matinees when great singers were on the bill. Sitting right down front one time in seats they couldn't really afford when a mesmerist had beckoned to him. Willie frozen to his seat. *Don't go.* Later dreams when the mesmerist's eyes became the portholes in the doors to the women's ward where his mother was kept at Waltham. *You won't come back.* (Though in life Danny *had* climbed up onto the stage and all that had happened was that after the mesmerist had put him under and ascertained the child didn't know the song, Danny had sung 'Believe Me If All Those Endearing Young Charms' straight through without pause.)

"Francisco Pizarro came here," the man said, "and conquered this place. He had a beard like you do. The conquered people didn't have any. Me, I'm not all Indian. Look!" He plucked at some little hairs on his chin. "Do you have a yankee dollar for me? for remembrance?"

"No," Willie said, "I'm sorry."

"A drink, then? Share a cup with me."

Willie thrust his *ponche* at the man and turned away.

Hiram was back from delivering the girl to her mother, a button dangling and his celluloid collar flapping up on one side. There were circles of sweat in the armpits of his shirt. "Nothing there, Clement," he said. "The old lady tried to pimp her to me.

Money. I tire of all this so much more quickly than I used to."

Clement was on tiptoe looking through the crowd for the girl. "Tire of what?"

"I didn't come these six thousand miles to be gulled and charmed and *led,*" Hiram said vehemently.

Dr. Foote laughed. "Then for what earthly reason *would* you have come, Hiram?"

Clement had her spotted again. A new mournful song was starting up, a favorite of Willie's. Ernesto had translated the beginning of the lyric for him once:

In the road I will leave by
They have set a stone to guard me.
So don't tell my mother,
Don't tell my father—

Clement was trying to tug Hiram back toward the dancing. "Come speak for me, old man. *Pizoos* or no, when it's real love, what's the g.d. diff?" Hiram asked Carrasco to come along and the three of them waded back into the crowd.

Willie said to Dr. Foote, "Love?"

"Well," the old man laughed, "at least the fatal attraction to difference. Most of us of northern European stock know only the pale excitement of attachment to what is most *like* ourselves."

"But you? You know about the other?"

Dr. Foote laughed again, mildly, deep. "Oh, I certainly do, my boy."

Willie glanced over, not knowing how to prompt him to go on. Foote was gazing up at the sky beyond the weighty towers of the church.

"An uncle of mine down home *owned* him—if you can believe anything so strange to the ear nowadays. But, far as I can tell, none of what there was between us ever went one jot against what you'd call his own free will. To the contrary. Jacob was very very black in color, but the opposite, sunny, of disposition. When the War began I was only fifteen and my uncle took him along to cook and do for him in camp, because he knew cooking, and then my uncle let him go and get himself shot."

After a moment Willie, now also gazing at the stars, said, "How much does he still come to mind?"

"Oh, by now not much oftener than once or twice a day. That's waking life. In the arms of Morpheus, where we have so much less of the say in what will make us happy, I'd guess he comes around a good deal more often."

The tubercular man was back, holding out the cup to Willie and insisting he take the last drops. Willie said no and the man began again to pluck more fervently at the hairs on his chin and to say that he wasn't *all* Indian, not *all* bad, and so, sick, Willie took the cup and, without letting its rim touch his lips, made a pretense of draining it.

"There."

"Oh, *papacito*, thank you, what an honor!" He had seen Willie's subterfuge. The voice was mocking. The man reached for Willie's hand again, but Willie was quicker this time and snatched it away. "Oh!" The hypnotizing black eyes very big. The man held his own palms up to his chin, like a minstrel, and then dove in, grabbing under Willie's coat, spreading his hands across the stranger's chest, his right feeling to the place, and then bending and planting a big kiss directly over Willie's hard-beating heart.

That was all. The man then made off, hooting and coughing.

Willie had had his hand kissed before (and had not liked it) by peasant people in Mexico so drunk they mistook you for a *patrón* or a priest of some sort, and by errant lady friends of his mother in Waltham. This on his breast, though, he had not previously experienced.

On their way back down to the river Hiram and Clement were stupidly drunk. They had lost the girl and, it seemed, Sergeant Carrasco in the process. They stumbled along behind like the undergraduates you overtook late at night in New Haven and Cambridge coming from their final club parties smelling of their own vomit and confiding to one another things like "But I have such a fucking *bone* for her, Hiram, don't you see?"

Dr. Foote kept pace with Willie. "They're not *your* sins, my boy."

"I know." Willie had been crying; he wiped his eyes with the back of his hand. "But sometimes it's still hard not to feel bad about them, especially when you're a little drunk."

"Neither the old ones of history, nor the present ones of our comrades," Dr. Foote assured him.

When they reached camp, Ernesto and Leo Ávila did a piece of Alphonse and Gaston about which of them would sleep out to guard the mules and horses against rustlers. Not the sort of argument Ernesto could afford to lose, Willie thought. His own unhappiness increased by the moment, thumping now in his chest exactly like something swallowed without being chewed. Ernesto went to get his blanket from the tent. Willie followed him.

"Would you do a favor for a friend? Just one?"

"Of course. What's that?"

"Stay with me right now."

"But—"

"No. Just as I asked for it."

Ernesto sighed and turned and sank heavily onto the cot across from Willie's.

"I have a lamp here."

"Don't bother," Ernesto said. "I'm going to sleep with my clothes on, like this bed was my grave."

The river's sound in the dark was a hushing roar. Willie got the kerosene lamp out. Matches from his pocket.

The flare, the flame, the reduced warm glow. Ernesto revealed finally lying with his arm cocked over his eyes, elbow a big beak in the shadow on the canvas wall, his twill pants, legs crossed, boots still on, his body not coming even close to the bottom of the army cot.

"Talk before we sleep? You said once it's what you like to do best."

"I don't remember that."

Willie standing, taking off his pants. "I remember everything you ever told me."

Nothing.

"It's quite a lot to carry around in my head. Perhaps why I have a headache all the time."

Ernesto said, "Maybe you should have devoted yourself to taking photographs instead."

Willie thought to say *Maybe so.* But instead he said, "Oh, it's not so bad anymore. In the beginning you told me so much. But then after you found out I love you, it became less and less until by now it's stopped, more or less."

He lifted the hot globe and blew out the flame, then lay down. Ernesto's steady breathing. Not really asleep, Willie was sure.

What came at once to mind: pictures of pictures, Ernesto as he was now but naked, the wet shiny planes of his shoulders, water in bright droplets on his skin, as he was in the beginning, at Puno, as he was by the waterfall at Tipon, but Willie close in, at leisure, almost languidly examining his skin, where the color deepened at the other man's neck and wrists, on the inside of his thighs where the muscles stood out, how yellow the skin there was, blue veins, Willie laughing, brushing with his beard across the small grayish scrotum, the real laughter of Carlos Zárate brushing the same gentle way below the hard upright phallus of his Martín, on a rock ledge somewhere far above the world, the crinkling of hair, fingertips soft on the underside of the other man's penis, touching the little cavities where the balls could go in cold weather, Martín grabbing the fringes of Carlos's beard and pulling his head down onto his cock and saying in Spanish, 'I love you.'

Willie going at it aggressively, not caring that his bang bang bang or his single long sigh might be heard by Ernesto, or by the others sleeping nearby. His stuff came out thick and he brought his hand up from under the blanket and licked it off.

Sometime in the night he dreamed he was the friar Zárate limping through the twilight streets in his habit. At a heavy wooden door a man with Ernesto's wide mustache (but not Ernesto?) would not admit him. He could hear the bolts on the other side ramming into their sockets, one, two, three. He went on home, to a dark place, overhead a dim flickery electric light ('not enough light,' the voice in the dream maintained, 'half-light for a half-life'), and took out, warm from lying over his heart, a wallet of sorts where he kept his accounts. Miserably then, again and again he added it up, hoping somehow to make the figures dance together to total something more, or even something less, than zero. But it would not happen. 'Because *they* were not that way,' the dream voice said, 'owed each other nothing. Why will you not learn? why go on limping to his door imagining you once had something to account?'

Then, well before dawn, a thin gray light filtering through the canvas, Willie was woken by sudden motion inside the tent. It was Ernesto, up out of the other cot. He grabbed Willie by the shoulders and fell on top of him. The rough stubble on his chin grazed Willie's cheek, and he gave Willie's mouth a big dry kiss. Then, as Willie was reaching up to put his arms around him, Ernesto pulled free and got to his feet.

"Come on. We should be able to get a good distance along today," Ernesto said, and he went out.

As soon as there was the smell of coffee in the air, Dr. Foote, wearing a cream-colored suit, issued forth from the tent he was sharing with Leo Ávila. And Hiram was up early, going about wheedling the rest of them into accepting large doses of Jamaican rum for their cups. But Clement, though he wouldn't refuse a drink, did reject all proposed forward motions. At last the jaunty, rumpled sergeant returned from town and solved the problem by suggesting he and Ernesto rig a hammock for the *señor*, which they slung on poles between two mules front and back.

With Bailey thus couched, they passed through the narrow breach between the mountains at Pachar, where the little lady Marta of the ringlets had come from, and before ten o'clock were at Ollantaytambo. There were extensive ruins, but they did not stop. Hiram had spent several days at the site on his previous trip.

Though the clouds which had covered the valley all morning were only now clearing off, it had grown quite warm. All except Dr. Foote were in shirtsleeves.

On principle Willie had no quarrel with being drunk in the daytime. And increasingly as they went along he felt lifted and made happy by the quality of the light. Here, as in canyons like the Colorado and deep valleys like Yosemite, people got a kind of sunburn from what was bounced off the stony walls. A glowing holy look, as though they admired themselves in a modest way but, by their sidelong glances, admitted their illumination was only borrowed from a much brighter source.

Clement required a halt in order to have a consultation with Hiram about something. Willie got off to look around. They had come through a still-narrower pass and glaciers had reared up on both sides far above the forsythia-colored broom and the octopus-tendriled cactus on the river plain.

Hiram took Willie on a little walk down by the rapids and gave him a drink. It was Pisco he was pouring now. They gazed at the churning water. People were often swept away, Hiram said, their bodies never recovered. He called Willie's attention to thin tracings etched along the cliffs on the other side. Possibly footpaths hacked out by the Inca. In the modern era, before this road was built along the river to bring rubber up from hot country, the only way into the grand canyon of the Urubamba had been through bad passes high up there, dangerous at all seasons and sealed off by snow and ice during the rains. Raimondi in 1865 had gone by one of these routes and Wiener in '75 by the other. Consequently, the territory they were entering now was still uncharted.

Hiram cleared his throat and spat and took a cigarette from the damp packet in Willie's pocket. They shared a match. Then in a lower voice Hiram said, "Seems without even having the lingo Clement's somehow gotten it out of that loudmouth Carrasco that *por casualidad* the lady of last evening lives at Piri, which is the place we'll come on just around the next big bend. Clement says if he doesn't get her to come with him he won't go another step. Exactly at the moment I finally need him to start making me some maps. Any chance you'd accompany me to the girl's house? Her name's Rosa. The mother doesn't take to Clement."

"Why not?"

"Because he's so fat. Because he doesn't speak Spanish. You know—because."

"What d'you want me to do?"

"I'm going to present it as an invitation to travel with *me* instead. She said last night she'd do that. And I need someone to convince them of what an honest, sincere, harmless, all-round *swell fellow* I am."

Piri was only a tiny cluster of buildings up against the canyon wall. Hiram put on his jacket and brushed his hair with his hands, then went and got a bottle of sweet vermouth from the food boxes. They found their way up an incline to a little house surrounded by adobe wall with briars growing on top of it.

At first when they called there was no answer. Then the door cracked a bit and a woman's voice called, "What do you want?" in Quechua.

Hiram stared at the thick dust on his shoes and ran his hand through his hair.

"Just to talk to you, *mamacita*, just a little chat," Willie sang out.

"Rosa!" they heard, an order.

Through the bushes Willie caught a glimpse of the girl starting out from behind the house in a cotton shift which came only to her knees. Her long hair was wet and she was carrying a towel. Younger than Willie had thought, maybe not more than sixteen and in the light of day much prettier than last night at the fiesta. A large face, breasts round and prominent beneath the shift. Then she disappeared again.

After another interval of silence the mother came out to the gate with an infant in her arms. Hiram managed to blurt out that they had brought a gift for her and held out the bottle of vermouth.

They were led into the house's single dark room and given little chairs to sit on. The last trails of a dying cooking-fire reached toward the half-open back door. A pole bed in the corner, but no other furniture. Several white *cuy* bobbed about on the packed dirt floor.

The mother said in Spanish her daughter was washing up, but would come soon. Hiram set the vermouth out in front of him. The mother called out the back and after a bit a boy of nine or so came in, screwing his shirttail into a water glass. Hiram poured red liquid up to the brim and took it over to the mother. "Oh, so much there!" she exclaimed. "You want to make me drunk, *señor!*"

After the woman, a glass for Willie and then one for Hiram and a taste for the boy who had brought the glass. Satisfaction on the mother's part that the strangers knew so much about how things should be done, laughing and showing a spinachy wad of *coca* in the near-toothless hole of her mouth. And where did the gentlemen come from? Oh, nodding, repeating, the United States, oh. So far you must be from your homeland, your families. How sad it must be for you. Lonely. Are these states you speak of on the other side of the ocean? Oh. And where were they bound? as far as Quillabamba? Oh. Yes, she had been that far, but only once, to visit her *compadres.*

Rosa came in and sat by her mother on the edge of the bed. Before it reached the top of the glass he was pouring her, Hiram's vermouth ran out. He gave the little boy the empty bottle and told him to run down to the river and get the other foreigners to send up another one just like that.

They sat in silence, Hiram rubbing earnestly at his palm with the thumb of his other hand. From time to time Rosa would look at him and then his head would sink farther toward his chest.

The vermouth had done something to Willie he couldn't quite name. Earlier today, coming through the second pass, he had felt both excitement and a chill, as though the granite cliffs formed a portal he was not meant by fate or decency or something to go beyond. Not yet. Now, like a child holding his breath and counting the seconds through a tunnel or past a graveyard, he tried over and over to count the days to September 15, as though there might be unaccounted-for, overlooked time in there somehow. A grace period. But it always came out the same. Tomorrow the 23rd. In the morning he should separate his belongings from the rest, borrow one of Ernesto's mules, if he could, and turn back toward Cuzco.

Señor Bingham here was a noted explorer, he announced, a writer of books and articles. A professor in the second greatest university in their country and a world traveler—

Ridiculous. Not a fact in the lot of import to his listeners. Like the little biography of Willie Hiram had delivered Ernesto the night of his arrival.

He was about to say, 'Not only the pal of senators and millionaires, but a millionaire himself—' when the little boy returned with a new bottle of vermouth. This one was green and had a note attached which said in Dr. Foote's graceful, skating thin hand, "Sorry. Other's out."

Hiram reached in his pocket and took out a five-*sol* note. Without looking at it, he gave it to the boy.

Willie placed his hand lightly over his heart and announced that Hiram and he had been fast friends for thirteen years and that Hiram *could be* a tremendously generous person.

"Would he beat her?" the mother asked, "that's what I need to know. I mean to say, there's nothing to be said against beating a woman when she needs to be set back on the right road. But you know, *señor*, there are men in this world who want to do it for no reason at all."

Hiram was not that kind, Willie said. And he wasn't the sort who went to a large *number* of women either, so there wasn't much risk of disease.

"Watch it, old sport," Hiram said.

"Only covering as many points as I can think of in a short time."

The mother had called the little boy and had made him open his hand to her. Hiram's largesse—equivalent to two dollars and fifty cents—was more convincing to both women than anything Willie could have promised. Still, the mother was concerned for her girl's reputation.

"Why not say you're sending her to Quillabamba to visit the *compadres?*" Willie suggested. "Maybe they have been taken sick."

It would take a half-hour to get her ready, the mother thought. Their party might have gone on a little way by then, Willie said. Then to Hiram in English, "You *do* want her right now, don't you?"

"I don't want her at all, Willie."

"*What?* finally as shamed by all this as I am?"

"It's more real than I could have imagined it."

"Other people's lives always are."

If the *señores* had moved, they would catch up, the mother said. They knew the way.

Good. So, with a minimum of handshakes and curtsies and then a bit of giggling while the mother screwed up the courage to ask could she perhaps keep both the red and the green bottles, Willie and Hiram were past the gate and careening back down the gullied path toward the river.

Sun already passed over the valley, though it was only three forty-five by Willie's watch.

"What did you mean at the end there about not wanting her?"

Hiram stopped. Sleepy-looking. "I don't want Clement to have her."

"Why not?"

"Can't you see? I've fallen in love with Rosa myself."

Willie laughed inadvertently, a single bark.

"I meant to double back alone sometime and speak to her on my own behalf. But you've now seen to that, old sport."

"I can't read your mind, Hiram."

Ernesto, Leo and Dr. Foote were lying snoozing, heads resting on various packs and saddlebags. The mules and horses had been let to graze on the thin margin of grass at the roadside. Clement, who at home belonged to a small group of men who went ocean swimming once a year on New Year's Day, had gotten Sergeant Carrasco to hold the other end of a rope he tied around his tremendous waist and was paddling in between the boulders in a kind of frothy backwater at the edge of the river. Seeing Hiram, he tugged on the rope for the sergeant to reel him in and came stumbling up the embankment, water streaming down from his beard onto the heavy black fur which covered his giant chest. Naked, he was surprising. The flesh was abundant, but none of it was fatty or loose. Under the overhang of his belly the member was thick, bulbous, even drawn up against the cold water, the ball sack large, swaying as Clement pulled himself up between the rocks. To a man, the others stared, complacently, like buyers at the auction of a prize bull.

"What cheer, Hiram? My little Rosita? Did you succeed?"

Hiram was already moving away.

"She's fixing herself up for you," Willie said, "and will be along soon."

Hiram mounted up quick and rode on ahead alone in the bright unearthly valley twilight. The others had to move smartly to catch up with him.

When they reached the next place the road widened enough for them to go side by side; Ernesto came up next to Willie. "Well? And what?"

"By any chance would you remember one time proclaiming to me that you were a whore?"

Ernesto opening his mouth to say no, then stopping himself. "Possible," he said. "That one is a possibility."

"Well, now I've become something a whole grade lower down."

"What's that?"

"A pimp."

"She's coming, then?"

Willie nodded.

He was still fuddled, but already coming down some onto the mean side of his liquor. He started worrying about what he would say when Edward Curtis asked him, as he inevitably would, 'How'd it go in Peru?' meaning he wanted to be shown photographs. There were some head-on shots of walls in Cuzco, Inca walls damp and textured at sunrise, Spanish walls with grass growing from the adobe where the plaster had fallen off. But they would be too 'modern' for Curtis's taste.

No, more complicated than that. Curtis would look through quickly and then ask, 'Were there no *people* in Peru?'

You could say, 'Only one. And he was camera shy.'

Or, 'Yes, but in that enchanted land I suddenly forgot everything you ever taught me, sir, about the photographer treading the thin edge of human decency and the rule of never asking other people to do for you anything you would hate to have to do yourself, either for love or money, and as a consequence I so humiliated myself and betrayed my craft there I could no longer look people in the face for even the little interval it takes to line up a shot.'

"Hear what Carrasco's got?" Ernesto asked.

Ahead the sergeant was thrumming the high, almost reedy chords from his little *charango* and singing. The verses to this one were in Quechua, something about a girl in a red skirt and a boy, but the chorus was in Spanish:

> "*The mystery is*
> *How love makes us able to bear*
> *The shame and the disgrace*
> *That come with falling in love*
> *La la la*—"

THIRTEEN

RIGHT after the tiny settlement at Torontoy, Clement insisted that they begin looking for a place to stop the night. The decision had to be taken without Hiram, who had been slumped dozing in his saddle for more than an hour. But then for the next several miles the road became only a slender shelf twenty or so yards above the torrent, much of it won from the granite by blasting. There were two brief tunnels, and in several places rockslides had reduced the road to an unsure, sometimes treacherous footpath.

The moon had not yet come up over the canyon, but it was imminent and in its strong heralding light the travelers were able to make out unlikely and extensive tiers of *andeno*, terracing, some of it a thousand, even fifteen hundred feet above them on the other side of the canyon. Many of the patches were under cultivation again. Or still. On the terraces lower down they could see tassels of corn peering over the walls at them like frowsy haloed souls. Once Willie heard a dog bark. Must be people up there too. Never leave their fields unwatched in the growing season.

In the time after the Spanish came and the right world the Incas had known went crazy and fell apart, when they lifted up their eyes, instead of *knowing* anymore, in the absence of their lord gods, they would have had to ask *themselves* where their strength was to come from. And the answer was that the great gift which had once made them masters of the earth—the knowledge of how to win margins of tillable soil from the sheer rocks and how to bring water to it—would now mean their survival. You might sit up there amid your level little fields forever, fearless, heart calm as the sighing of the wind as the world and the devils passed you by.

The moral was obvious to Willie: in adversity hunker down and use your gifts as skills.

Since you're so savvy about what to do in the bad times, Willie thought, why are you being sucked along down this thing exactly like the egg going into the neck of the milk bottle in the vacuum experiment?

No answer.

The spot they chose finally was not ideal. The mules and horses had to remain tethered, since there wasn't enough room for them and the men too to spread out. They lifted Hiram to the ground and laid him more or less gently under a great tall mimosa sort of tree. The night was so balmy they did not bother to set up the tents (although temperatures were subject to enormous variations, Sergeant Carrasco warned them—when the wind turned around and came swooping straight down off the snow peaks—*hijo!*) and those not too tired to eat rummaged their own cold suppers from the food boxes.

They shared the only can-opener they could find. In the midst of shoveling sardines in with his fingers, Willie noticed Ernesto get up and move himself back against the canyon wall. By the time Willie could hear whatever it was about to come around the last elbow in the road, Ernesto had a small pistol up out of his boot and hidden behind his back.

The gun surprised Willie. You think you've learned what there is to know about a person and then suddenly, at the last minute—

"Hold up there, hold up," Carrasco was calling, "it's only the Virgin and her escort."

In the blue light they did look like some odd version of the Flight into Egypt, the girl Rosa got up in a long white smock with lace or tatting at the neck and mounted on a small gray burro led along by her mother. The old lady had her hat clamped firmly to her head and was licking sweat from her upper lip.

Carrasco made a stirrup of his hands to help Rosa down,

meanwhile telling the mother in Quechua thanks very much for bringing them her daughter, but she had better hurry now to get back to someplace she would be safe for the night. Rosa craned her neck looking for Hiram, evidently not picking him out among the packs and boxes stashed under the great spreading tree. The mother was not so easily dismissed. She wanted money for herself now, for the journey. Ernesto and the sergeant took the line that *she* had been promised nothing.

But *papacito*—

Ernesto called out to Willie to come settle this business.

Willie stayed where he was, licking the fishy oil from his fingers. Clement poured cologne into his hands and splashed it on his face and went over.

Ernesto called again. Willie pretended he had not heard.

The mother was saying *she* had never been told her daughter was going to be expected to sleep out on the *ground*, on the bare earth, and *that* of course changed everything. Clement gallantly kissed Rosa's hand and then tried to insinuate his thick arm around her waist. She struggled against him. What was *this?* the mother said. *This* wasn't the *jefe*, not the one she'd talked to. Ernesto said oh no indeed, this was only one of the *sub-jefes* of the *yankis*, so rightly they could only pay her girl half the amount previously mentioned.

There had been no amount at all, the mother contended. But even from her voice (Willie not watching, trying not to have to hear) you could tell she knew she was now in the company of two traders much craftier than she was. All during the time Clement was rigging a piece of tent canvas to the limbs of the tree to provide himself and the girl a little privacy, the mother stood her ground, complaining to them from time to time, complaining then to the night and the granite walls of the canyon. When Hiram came careening forth and made for the box with the booze in it, she started in again. Willie thought they could probably expect to find her with them in the morning. But just about the same time those of them who were still awake began to hear Clement thrashing on Rosa's body behind the canvas, Willie also heard the little burro's lonesome clop-clop, and when he looked, the little lady was gone.

Hiram had come up from his fishing with a bottle of Daniel's. They drank it out of tin cups.

"It seems our friend here may be a little embarrassed by the sounds of lovemaking so close by."

Willie thought first it was Hiram, head hanging low over his bourbon, that Carrasco was talking about. When he understood it was himself, he said, "Oh, to the contrary. In the future whenever I think of my last night out with this party, I shall remember the sweet music of their coming and going over there."

"Your last night?"

"Tomorrow I'll need to turn back."

"Ooh—" the sergeant drew out his surprise "—what's this 'necessity'? What *is* necessity, after all?"

Hiram said, "Willie has friends at home richer and much more powerful than we are he has to go see."

Willie said in English, "Be honest for once, Hiram."

"All right," with a nod. Then in Spanish to Carrasco, "People more *decent* than us."

Ernesto was gazing on Willie with a cocked, half-warm smile. He raised his cup and said, "Well, perhaps sometime long after you've returned to that country with so many more marvels than we poor Peruvians could ever claim for ours, it may come about that *one* of us, you there or one of us here, will remember the times like this when we were happy together."

Hiram and Carrasco raised their cups to join the toast. They waited for Willie.

Well, he decided, not good. But maybe the best that could be wrung from this particular moment.

"*Salud.*"

They drained their cups.

When Hiram had poured out more, Sergeant Carrasco said, "Of course it is the case that we human beings have a *tendency* to remember what is good in our lives and to overlook the painful parts. That is how—or, better said, that is *why*—we can survive at all."

Ernesto said, "Not in my case. And I think wrong, that it makes for a wrong assessment of our condition if we try to scratch out all memory of the worst moments. Survival's not worth it, survival is only survival if that's how you have to be to get by."

"There were times in my childhood, my boy," Carrasco said, "so unhappy if I ever got the feeling they were coming back, I would—" and Carrasco made a pistol of his hand, pointed his index finger to his temple and said, "Pow!"

Willie touched Ernesto's shoulder. "Recall what you said about our friend here?"

"No."

"A man who wouldn't tell you his troubles unless he could find a way to make jokes about them, you said."

Ernesto turned to the sergeant. "Then don't let me die a liar. Can you find us the joker in this deck?"

(*'Comodín'* was his word. Before, Willie had only known it to mean a jack-of-all-trades, a supplier. But sensible here too, in whatever your jam, a card of general utility.)

While Carrasco puzzled there was silence, except for the warm wind and the endlessly echoed roar of the Urubamba surging down its gorge. The pumping and groaning from under the tree seemed to be done with. No, only the tune had changed. Now what came to them was a high-voiced song, wordless, certainly it could only be coming from the girl's throat. Carrasco's yellow-edged eyes were alight. He held a finger up to them and mouthed the word *'Espera,'* wait.

"Ouch!" Clement's voice. "Ouch! Goddamn!" A slap, a giggle, then the singing continued.

"Pincher, once she gets going," Carrasco confided to them. "Devil's own fingers up and down you." He pulled up his sleeve to show them faint bruises on the inside of his arm just above the elbow. "Look there. And when you're least expecting it, all finished yourself and having those first thoughts about a beer or maybe a cigarette, pinch pinch pinch on the flesh of your very ass to bring you back up deeper in where she wants you."

Hiram stared at the marks on Carrasco's skin. Then he jerked his head away and, hiding the action by turning his shoulder, gulped what bourbon was in his cup. Holding the bottle unsteadily by the neck, he poured himself another.

They slept more or less wherever they fell. At some point Willie was woken by movement. Ernesto had gotten up and brought light blankets. He spread one over Hiram and one over the sergeant and was about to let the third down onto Willie's body when Willie whispered, "You take it. I'm warm enough."

"I thought you were asleep."

"No, not in this light."

Willie closed his eyes and at once began to dream in that vivid, realistic style where things are not speeded up, the details take about the time they take in ordinary waking life. The dream was that he had gotten up, unpacked his view camera and the tripod and prepared a time exposure. The moon had invaded whatever the unknown territory was around the next turn in the road, but had not yet come upon the sleepers on this strand. The moonlight beyond the portal appeared as a thick silver-white stripe right down the center of the frame. It was made so jagged at its edges by the rocky canyon walls that it looked like a mistake, as though the emulsion had been ripped right off the paper. The members of the Expedition slept in the foreground, the rounded forms of the men under their covers like sheep or rocks, the shadowy forms of the pack animals spectral and calm—all unknowing, all unaware of the great rending just beyond. Willie dreamed the exposure took an hour and that at the end of that time he got up and went to put the lens cap, sweaty in his hand, back onto the camera. Then he woke again.

Ernesto was lying near him. The air whistled through the gap between his teeth when he breathed.

"Martín?"

Without opening his eyes, "What is it?"

"Do you ever think about what comes next?"

"I try not to."

"For me, then. My life. Can you help me out?"

"What? You'll go back and take more pictures of your *retskinis*. Or of that street you live on."

"But not with you. For a while at least. What'll I do to survive?"

"What you've always done. Men have their work to keep them. Then you'll get married some day and then you'll have all *those* problems to keep you dancing."

Ernesto propped himself up on his elbow and reached two fingers toward Willie. Willie got his cigarette pack from his jacket folded on the ground on the far side of him, lit two and handed one to Ernesto.

Ernesto inhaled and blew smoke up into the air. "Will you promise me something?"

"What's that?"

"No, just promise." Ernesto touched Willie's wrist right on the pulse.

"All right. What?"

"It doesn't have to be the first—the first can be *your* namesake—but somewhere along the line name one of your children after me. That way you'll always remember me."

Willie didn't say anything. Now, almost like an electric switch being flipped in its suddenness, the top of the moon came across the cliffs right above them and they were caught directly in its light. The 'element of mystery' or whatever you'd call what had made Willie's sleeping self desire a photograph here had vanished. Willie put out his cigarette and turned over on his side to try sleeping again.

It's over here. Pack up and go, just as you've always done. Sufficient unto the day—

He tried reciting these things to himself. But underneath he was seeing again the sweet giggling girls the night Ernesto had insisted on taking him to the gay place beyond San Sebastián and something was towing him down so fast he felt dizzy and had to open his eyes to stop and steady himself.

Yes, he imagined himself saying, I *will* go back to making pictures of my goddamn front stoop, since that is what it pleases me to do. And you? what'll you do? go back to what? cadging beers in bars by doing your little tricks?

And Ernesto he imagined responding, Yes, for certain. My little tricks. Because *that* is what it pleases me to do with *my* life.

IN THE morning, clouds forced down into the chasm rolled billowing to and fro, sometimes glinting like sheets on the line, for long moments making it impossible to see more than a few feet ahead. Smoky wisps got caught in the foliage of the blue-green jungle trees which grew now everywhere their tangled feet could grab a hold in the rocks.

Down splashing icy river water on his face, Willie could hear them discussing how to reassign mounts. Clement thought the easiest would be for him just to take the mare, since she was their largest animal, and put the girl on up behind him. When Hiram translated this plan, Leo Ávila said if such was Hiram's wish, though his own opinion was that it was foolishness to mount two riders, one of them grossly overweight, on a perfectly decent horse, given what they had seen so far about the conditions of the road in some places.

"But then you don't *have* a right to an opinion in this matter, do you now?"

"I beg your pardon? You asked me, I think," Leo said.

"An action." Hiram shrugged and made a sour face. "Better said, a *re*action. Memory of other times. In *Cuzco* you will recall I sent you off with rather specific orders to buy or hire me two or more sturdy mules for this journey. And what do I get for my good money? Elegant, yes, and you do look extremely elegant on the mare, I'll admit. But parade-ground *elegance* was not what was called for in this situation."

"I told you I would pay you back from my salary. Please," Leo said, "I would prefer not to discuss this in front of these others."

"Why not? They are all friends, companions. I'd like them all to know everything. About the various 'loans' to you, all your 'promissory notes' and your attempts to sell me jewels from the Ávila family that don't even belong to you. When is repayment day, hmm? Judgment Day? I won't be here."

Willie went over under the tree to separate out his own belongings from the rest. His heart was beating fast and he was somewhat dizzy. He had never had any brief for Ávila, and he thought he had none now. But there was something terrible about watching Hiram bully the man, and also a feeling that everything was now breaking apart at such a rate and with such violence that none of it would ever be mended.

Willie was sweating, so, instead of putting his jacket on, he took the cigarettes and matches, his notebook and his watch from the pockets and strapped the jacket itself to the outside of his bigger camera case.

Ernesto came to him leading the mule he himself preferred riding, a fine gray animal named Primavera. "Here," he said, holding out the reins, "you may as well make your escape on this one."

Willie held out his hand, closed. "And you may as well have this," he said. He turned his hand over. In the palm was his pocket watch.

Ernesto shook his head. "What would I do with something like that? The first time I hauled it out in the square in Cuzco the police would figure I had pinched it and would have me in jail before I could even turn around."

"I bought it for this trip. Only the chain's of any real value, and that's more sentimental than anything. It's the only thing that belonged to my father I still have."

"Well, if that's the case—" Ernesto put the watch in his pocket. "Still, *señor*, you know there's one other thing."

"What's that?"

"The photograph you took of me that time by the waterfall. You promised it to me."

"It's in Cuzco," Willie said coldly. "I'll remember to leave it for you."

"The negative too, remember."

"Yes, of course. Not an example of my best work anyway."

"Willie?" Hiram was sitting on one of the unit-food-boxes, beckoning him with the little downward-brushing wave of his fingers you used to get a waiter's attention in Mexico. A habit Willie thought he had broken Hiram of several years ago. "Here," Hiram handed him a tin cup, "taste that one for me. Some of the bottles lost their labels somehow, and I can't tell my medicines apart anymore."

The liquid looked like coffee. But it had a strong alcohol kick and that particular oil consistency. "That's Pisco," Willie said. "And this is Peru."

"Finish it. There's more."

"I'd guess." Willie drank and then gave the cup back to Hiram.

"Go a little way with us? Old times' sake? Our pal Carrasco assures me an hour or so further on there's plenty of *incaica.* Maybe a picture in it for you."

Willie considered. "I—"

Hiram was dangling his cup by the handle between his legs, worrying a spot on the hard earth bare with the toe of his boot. "Yesterday," he said, "most of it, I thought for sure I was finally going out of my mind."

Willie said, "So did I."

Hiram looked up at him briefly. There were tears forming under his eyes. "And whenever I'd imagine maybe *I* wasn't, I'd think instead I was probably driving *you* crazy."

"Well, we both know that one or the other of us is going to have to pay, don't we?"

"I suppose. I'll call out to you from Protestant Hell and

maybe you'll be able to hear me over there in the Catholic one, if the flames' licking at us ain't too noisy."

Ernesto had Primavera all packed up. Willie shook Hiram's hand lightly, Indian style, and Hiram got to his feet and gave Willie a powerful hug.

Willie said, "I told you once long time ago I'd go to the ends of the earth with you—"

"And this time you nearly did, didn't you?"

When he faced Ernesto, Willie's impulse was to cup his hand to the deep hollow between the tendons at the back of his neck. But he couldn't do it. Instead, he stood patiently while Ernesto told him the location of the stable in Cuzco where he wanted Primavera left and then Willie mounted up.

After he rounded the curve and was out of sight of the great lacy tree, he allowed himself a big sigh. And then, what the hell? he allowed himself to think, 'Wrong this way.' He reined up and cried a bit with his eyes open. He thought of the green locomotive chugging southward through the empty *puna* and himself standing on the platform outside the second-class coach rubbing his foot across an already shining brass plaque which read

THE BIRMINGHAM RAILWAY CARRIAGE
& WAGON CO. LTD. SMETHWICH.

A little farther on something in the dust beside the road track made him stop again. Bits of twig lying in the shape of an 'M' and a 'W,' one above the other, thus: M/W. Willie didn't dismount to see were the pieces broken, formed to this configuration, or only some whim of nature. It hardly seemed to matter. Wheeling the gray mule around so fast the camera boxes up behind swayed dangerously, he started trotting back.

Past the outcropping of rock that had been in the photograph he had dreamed of last night, the road took on an uncertain quality. Willie crossed a bridge made of two rusty metal girders overlaid with wood strips and cane only about two feet wide, came around a bend on a narrow blasted-out path under a dripping overhang and found in twenty yards more the way jumped back across to the other side of the Urubamba and ducked into a tunnel. Coming out of the tunnel, he found himself in a patch of brilliant sunlight. A hundred salmon-colored giant bromeliads flared like signal fires in the trees around him and he could hear hollow voices quite nearby, Dr. Foote saying he imagined it was highly reminiscent of the Sandwiches, and Hiram saying yes, particularly of spots on the island of Maui. The mist ahead was lit from behind by the sun and so brilliant it hurt Willie's eyes to try looking into it. He paused and then the white lifted as silently as a theater curtain during an intermezzo and Willie could see Leo Ávila floating through the air above the river. An odd sort of vision, Leo, severely erect and buttoned to the neck in his green military tunic and wearing his *kepi* at an angle, an *hidalgo* in every way he could manage, given that it was Carrasco's lewd-walking jenny he had drawn to ride.

Dr. Foote was next to float out miraculously across the river. "Ah! a Hickler, a very palpable Hickler!" he called. "You *are* palpable, aren't you, no ghost?"

Willie plucked at his sweat-soaked shirt to prove his reality.

"Not yet ascended, eh? Always a difficult period. The Touch-Me-Not Phase."

No one else even commented on Willie's return.

It was better in silence, just in the onrush of the river and the chorus of the birds. Commenting some years later about this day spent in the Grand Canyon of the Urubamba, Hiram, who in writing would cross the street to borrow a cliché, said, "We found ourselves unexpectedly in a veritable wonderland. Emotions came thick and fast." The sun had now burned great gaping holes in the mist. Bits of scenery—the recognizable profile of a man in granite topped by an umbrella of trees, a waterfall—would become isolated in the white, stay for a few strokes of the brush and then disappear. Where the sunlight struck the trees they became hung all over with tiny jewels of moisture. There were many parrots, especially a small green variety which seemed to like falling from its perch and at the last moment unfurling and turning into a giant green peony with a yellow tailfeather center and then landing on the ground or a low branch and chortling so with pleasure that its throat puffed up.

At times someone would say something. "Dr. Johnson thought change of mood due to a change in weather was a sign of weak character. What would he think of *me* if he knew the heights to which scenery can lift my soul? or that I chose my life's work so I could look at it and get paid too?" That was Clement. Then in a while Willie overheard a conversation in Quechua he thought must be between Ernesto and Rosa and about how much she usually got for a single and how much for the whole evening, only to discover when he caught up that Ernesto had been bartering for oranges with some people they had met coming up from hot country.

A little after one o'clock they stopped to get some water, eat the oranges and some canned meat and a goose-liver paté on crackers. Then they set up Willie's tripod and mounted binoculars on it and gazed at the opposing canyon wall. There was a long waterfall and at its base clearly the remains of walls and at least a one-room structure lacking only its roof. A troop of monkeys seemed to be the only occupants. There was no way to cross the rapids here and get up for closer investigation.

"The best way to catch monkeys," Sergeant Carrasco said, "is to throw a straw doll up in the tree to the mother. They love new things, and usually she'll let her real baby drop right down to you."

An hour later they reached La Máquina, called that because a great 'machine' had its final resting place here. Giant rusting iron wheels lay in mud and rubble down by the river boulders. A milling or pressing device, the machine had been bound for one of the sugar plantations lower down and had gone off the road at this point. The beginning of a settlement, two huts, had grown up around it. The inhabitants appeared to be the machine's first devotees.

Clement was for staying. The canyon was nearly a mile deep

here, and the sun was already gone. But that was impossible. Not enough space for the horses and mules in the clearing and no fodder to be had.

They went on a way and came to another hut. This place was called Mandor Pampa after a sandy shore and some grass down through the trees by the river. On the other side of the water rose a nearly vertical expanse of thin jungle almost two thousand feet high, like an emerald felt-covered ledger God had pigeonholed here and then forgotten.

Clement told Hiram that last night he had been able to make do because it was the first, but the girl, it turned out, was extremely energetic and for tonight he was going to take her back to La Máquina and locate a bed in order to see what she could *really* do. So they needed to pitch only two tents. Dr. Foote at once made ready to go out and snare birds. Leo offered to accompany him. Probably, Willie thought, as a way to escape having to occupy the same slim margin of earth where Hiram Bingham was. He had never seen Leo volunteer for anything before.

In a while, Willie and Sergeant Carrasco walked up to the shack by the road. The lady there had been hanging out wash so white Willie suspected she probably had bleach in some form. She did, in granules, which was all right for his purposes. For the tiny amount Willie needed she wouldn't take any money. Her husband, a *Señor* Arteaga, agreed with the sergeant that he had far too many roosters for the number of hens about and finally agreed to selling the party one.

While they were out chasing them, *Señor* Arteaga trying to get his hands on the older birds and Carrasco pursuing the younger, the woman got up the courage to ask perhaps could Willie tell her what the gentlemen were seeking here.

Ruins—you know, terraces and things, Willie said.

Well, she said, her husband had land he rented to some Indians up on the other side there and that was "ooh, pure terrace, you know." Her husband had been up to the top, but she never had.

Carrasco claimed to know all about there being *andeno* up the other side. On their way back down to the river, he tried to point out pieces of it to Willie. But what Willie could make out was way near the top, and from here it was impossible to tell whether the work of men or not.

He took the bleach from the little folded packet the woman had given him, mixed it with water into a milky substance and got out a pen.

He had lied. The negative of Ernesto at Tipon was right here in a slot of its own in the case where he kept his unexposed film. He had never made a print of it for himself and had meant, despite Ernesto, to strike himself just one before he left Cuzco. But now he took the negative and wrote across the bottom of it "*Tu sueño—lo tomé,* Willie."

Carrasco had been looking over his shoulder. He asked could he see. When the bleach had sunk in enough, Willie held the celluloid up to the sky for the sergeant.

"Can you read it to me?"

"Oh, of course. It says, 'Your dream—I took it,' and it's signed by me."

"That's very good, you know. I remember whenever our little Ernesto would get drunk he'd admit the dream he had over and over was that they caught him without his clothes on."

Willie collected wood. By the time he had a fire going the little rooster's plumage was spread out like a shed cloak all around Carrasco and the bird was ready to have its pinfeathers singed.

"See the star?" Carrasco said, himself not looking up from his work.

Venus had appeared alone high in the darkening lustrous sky above the gorge, and had begun to trail toward the ridge almost directly in the path taken by the long-gone sun.

"Yes?"

"Last night when Ernesto asked what was the joker in the deck? If the girl hadn't started pinching the fat gentleman about that time as I was sure she would, I had it up my sleeve to tell about the Evening Star. Because the people down on the coast I used to work with call it 'the Trickster.' Had you ever heard that?"

"No."

"It's peculiar to them, I think. They say there was once long ago a chief of theirs rich enough to have two wives. But while he was at sea fishing, this Trickster got in and slept with both of them. The chief came home at sunrise and caught them all still at it. So at sunset he bound the Trickster and his wives together, as was their custom with adulterers, and threw them into the sea to drown. Which is why Venus sometimes sinks straight down after the sun like she's doing these days."

DR. FOOTE and Lieutenant Avila still had not returned by morning, which concerned no one very much except Willie, who would have to wait. Leo had taken Primavera bird-catching and Ernesto didn't want to make a substitution. Hiram had determined to go up the other side, if he could get across the Urubamba. Ernesto was going and *Señor* Arteaga, who had been paid for leading them. Carrasco, who was not on salary, said fairly vaguely he needed to do some work on the animals' hoofs.

The valley was closed in so completely you couldn't even see across to what the climbers were planning to attempt. There was a steady drizzling cool rain. Hiram had dressed himself up with a pack, a bandanna around his neck, hiking boots and a slouch hat. He and Willie shook hands. "See you," Hiram said. Ernesto then took Willie's hand firmly and said, "First you were leaving us and now we're leaving you."

The morning dragged by. Willie had no appetite, no feeling of any kind he could find in himself, very little sense of time.

Carrasco retreated to a boulder squared off like a monolithic slug of printer's type. He sat on top of it staring at the clouds slowly rising to reveal the shimmering wall of trees and tangle across the river. At one point he suddenly jumped up and began to wave his arms. Willie could see them too, Hiram, Ernesto and

Señor Arteaga little black marks getting close to the down-sloping ridge at the top.

Thoughts of Edward Curtis again. Some of Curtis's pictures had always made Willie so envious he couldn't look at them more than a second or two without being flooded with a dark, bodily sensation, very much like the markedness of lust. At this juncture what Willie wished specifically for was Edward Curtis's sense for the motion of the world. People in a Curtis photograph were always going somewhere. In his portraits, no matter how many hours he may have spent throwing blankets about on the roof of a hogan to cover the light on that area or expose it on this, Curtis inevitably caught his chief or medicine man looking as though he had only a moment ago and obviously in the midst of other things decided to sit down to this business, and that in another moment he would be off again to something else. Or, if the subject was settled and serene, it was the headdress or the hair or the wrinkles on the forehead which after a second would begin to flow and run and send your mind on its own mysterious way.

(Willie's Cheyenne girl in the doeskin Sara said Curtis had stopped to admire? Of course, because it was a Curtis-style photograph. The night he'd printed it up, bleary from trying to get everything sent off before he left for Peru, Willie had felt his heart stop. In the developer the broad swatch of beadwork on the girl's breast appeared for some reason to be polarizing. A moment later, like a motif in music which creeps in so tenuously it seems at first a mistake, that portion of the print began asserting itself in pulses, as though there was inside the young woman a second picture emergent, available, prairie riffled by sweet engaging winds, or something.)

Once, apropos of nothing Willie could decipher at the time, Curtis had said to him with absolutely bitter contempt, "The reason they all trip and fall down is the *hubris* they have of thinking they can cram the whole story into a single frame. Only dead things'll lie down like that. And even then— If once it breathed, Willie, it's never finished. Hit on their curiosity or your own, but don't ever let me catch you trying to *satisfy* either one.

Do that and you're doing nothing more than running a soup kitchen for the sons of bitches."

Willie remembered how he'd paused to look back on Cuzco at the outset of this little jaunt. A long time ago it seemed. And how he had wanted to say a Hail Mary as the Indians did, and couldn't. If, after so many years' absence, he could drag himself to Confession, he would first have to repent that he had somehow let himself put his curiosity on the shelf.

Afternoon had come and the sun was gone off their camp before Dr. Foote and Leo Ávila reappeared. They had with them a large ethery-smelling sack full of the carcasses of birds. They had stayed the night at a farmer's, where they had gotten a good supper and breakfast to boot. Next along, Dr. Foote said, the river did a full three-quarter turn to the left, making its way around a high solitary granite sugarloaf the people hereabouts called Huayna Picchu, the Young Man Mountain.

The sergeant had seen a light way up on the opposite side, a repeating signal from a mirror off the sun, beamed onto the rock where he had been sitting in the morning. None of them could read it except Dr. Foote. "Oh," he said, "that just means they'd like to send a message."

Because they were already in the shade, they couldn't use a mirror to respond. Carrasco went and got out the bull's-eye acetylene lamp that had its own sparking attachment and Willie got water for the carbide. They hoisted Dr. Foote up onto the slug-shaped boulder and handed him up the lamp. He'd call out the letters, the old man said, and somebody had better write them down as they came.

Willie took his notebook and a pencil stub from his back pocket and turned to a clean page. What came out was

VAST CITY WHITE GRANITE UNTOUCHED NEED HICKLER AND CAMERA FIRST UP BAILEY AM

There was silence. Then from Dr. Foote a heavy "umf" but no words.

The glint of the mirror came again.

"He's asking for reply," Dr. Foote said.

Willie stared at the green confronting mountain wall. Most likely, Hiram had taken his serviceable snapshot camera along with him. If he wanted the 8 x 10, tripod, film box and all lugged up there as well, it must mean big vistas of some sort.

"Can you tell him I'll be along before dark?"

Dr. Foote seemed surprised. "Of course. I'll do just that."

Willie grinned. "No need to say not because of any faith in him."

Dr. Foote was already covering and uncovering the front of the hissing lantern with his hat. Four shorts, two shorts, three, long-short-long. H-I-C-K. Willie could read just that much. "Good for you," Dr. Foote said, "good for you, my boy," as he went on.

The little sergeant thought he knew where they'd crossed the river this morning. He led Willie upstream along the road for about half an hour and then dove down into the wet jungle on a trail so faint that it was only the branches broken earlier in the day and a few of Hiram's large corrugated bootprints which gave Willie any reason to believe this really was the path. They came out onto the riverbank at a place where the Urubamba forced its way crashing and foaming between two mammoth rounded granite pieces. The bridge was only six or so saplings strung between these boulders, some of them not long enough to reach and so spliced with extensions by a ragged wrapping of vines. Carrasco went barefoot straight across, using the tripod as a balancing pole like a tightrope-walker. Willie got on his hands and knees and inched out onto the bridge. The saplings were slick with mud and wet, and the white freezing water was only a foot and a half below him. He got one knee up and over the thick knot of vines and then the second and was looking up to see how much farther when his foot caught and he was thrown off balance, mostly by the weight of the 8 x 10 in his pack. He clutched the wood and gulped air wet and very cold deep into his throat. His scalp prickled at the hairline as though he'd just taken off a hat he'd been wearing all day in the sun.

On the far side, Sergeant Carrasco passed Willie a handful of *coca* leaves from a figured kerchief. "To give us strength," he said, folding one leaf into his mouth, contemplating those left in his own palm as he chewed and before taking another.

"You needn't come for my sake."

"What?" the sergeant said, "of course not. I'm going up to see for myself."

Carrasco took the camera in addition to the tripod, leaving Willie only the satchel with his film, a few small cans of food and the negative for Ernesto he had put in at the last moment.

In the rhythm of climbing, no opportunity or inclination really for Willie to lift his head and have much of a look around. He began over and over estimating the general angle of ascent—forty-five degrees, sixty, somewhere between. When he started getting winded he remembered he was now the goat, prepared for this moment by all the other moments. Carrasco said the place was bound to be full of snakes, so Willie tried not to grab at strange vines or at rocks. Once when he did put his hand down inadvertently, there was a sizzling in the grass and a whipping motion right nearby and he saw the orangy tail, three or four inches of it, going away from him into the greenery. They got to places so steep that whoever used this path had had to set up logs notched with steps against the hillside.

What seemed like well over an hour up, there was a spot where a tiny trickle of water exuded from the rocks. They took turns drinking from it and then letting the water play over their heads. All about them was a kind of plant with a wide leaf like a banana and a flower like a thinner, more emphatic and exuberant all-scarlet bird of paradise.

Willie's companion was ready to push on. Another forty-five minutes or so's climb, two thousand feet above the Urubamba, they came up without warning out of the brush at a clearing with a thatched hut. At first they thought there were no people present, but the frenzied barking of a small dog soon brought an old Quechua man out of the hut. He had lain down, he apologized, but had not meant to sleep. His name was Álvarez. Their friends were looking at the terraces "over there"—the man nodded in the direction of the sugarloaf of Huayna Picchu. There was a well-tramped trail through the dense undergrowth which disappeared around an outcropping of rock. At about that point Willie could tell some tiers of terracing began. Intact and fairly much cleared off. The gentlemen, this polite Álvarez and the partner named Richarte he spoke of, had corn planted there. Probably the *andeno* Sergeant Carrasco had been trying to point out to Willie yesterday afternoon from below.

Without their asking for it, Álvarez brought them a gourd full of very cold water. They'd been working up here four years, he said, the two of them, and only got down to the valley about once a month. They'd never yet had a visitor, except Melchor Arteaga, who sometimes came to collect rent, and now they'd had *four* all in one day. Álvarez seemed surprisingly at ease and even happy with this tremendous unexpected turn of things, as though their coming was a piece of good fortune rather than an imposition.

They left the packs and the tripod leaning by the front door to the hut and went along the trail. Just before they got to the rocks, Ernesto came around from behind them. He raised his arms as though he was going to catch both Willie and the sergeant up in one big embrace, but when Carrasco started to say something, Ernesto put his finger to his mouth as a sign not to. They picked their way on the narrowed path past the outcropping. The sergeant whistled softly. What they had seen before proved to be only a tiny corner of a long flight of terraces, maybe a hundred giant steps up the side of the mountain, each of them several hundred feet long. The farmers had cut tall trees to get use of the terraces, but had had to leave the stumps and plant around them.

Ernesto led Willie and the sergeant across the expanse of steps on a wider tier which had an indented stone conduit for water running down its middle. The newcomers could see now finally that they were on a saddle of land running down from the high mountain Alvarez had said was named Machu Picchu and over to Huayna Picchu, which made a giant pommel for the saddle. The drop-off to the river on the other side must be just as precipitate as the one they had come up, so, through its sitting portion, the saddle was only about a half-mile wide. And this all untouched, heavily tangled with undergrowth and covered with tall trees. No vast city Willie could see. Only the wind quickening and the lush, comforting views—grand swoops of steep mountains all around, disorderly, nearly numberless ranks of them, those farther off glaciered, their white summits going lavender in the sun's decline, the myriad jungle gorges running here and there, all of it as uncharted as the peaks and folds of the brain. *Hush,* something in him said, *for it is on the convolutions of the mind of God we are making our tiny unmindful ways.*

When they reached the end of the terrace, Ernesto drew his machete and led them into the brush. A path had been beaten here very recently, bamboo stalks broken or hacked through, as though some big urgent beast had come thrashing into this gloom to find itself a place to lick its wounds. It was damp underfoot and to keep from slipping Willie reached up to steady himself. Under coarse rust-colored moss he felt the slight straight indentation between stones. His eyes were only now adjusting to the dark. To his left an old wall, fine, smooth white granite rising ten feet over his head. Then they were going down a bit and he could feel the regular edges of steps buried under the green, brushing his foot off them as he had learned to do as a child acolyte when he couldn't see his way beneath the cassock. Something cooler beside him, and darker. A cave, he thought. But then, forgetting the fer-de-lance and the other deadly vipers he had been warned of, Willie began to pat at the darkness like a blind man. The unbroken straightness of the doorstones and then of the lintel emerged. A room. He couldn't tell how deep. They climbed up some more and made their way along a ledge with another ledge overhanging it. Here the vines hung down in thick cords and between them, frames, you could see down into the gorge.

Accustomed now to the great silence of the place, Willie had begun as well to hear its constant chatter, the skitterish birds flushing from the trees, the lizards and whatever other *animalitos* there were scurrying along the wall. Far off, unless he was wrong and it was only the wind, he was sure there was someone singing—in Quechua, he thought, but whether a man or a woman he couldn't tell. And the sound of metal striking stone.

They inched to the left eight feet along the smooth regular circumference of a rounding piece of stonework and came into more light, a horseshoe-shaped room open to the sky and attached to a straight wall with three trapezoidal portals. Hiram was there alone, back to them, gazing out. He turned and opened his mouth, but nothing came.

Hiram's eyes clouded and the tears welled and flowed down his flushed grimy cheeks. Ernesto wet-eyed too. Willie, thinking he should say something and not knowing what it should be, didn't realize quite at first that he was crying as well.

How long they stood like that, looking from one to another, Willie never knew. Something occurred to him about this being as it was in the beginning in Peru, in the land where men cry. Something he remembered then about the great Virakocha being portrayed only by His absence, by the empty place left on the emblem of gold in the temple, as though in His hurry to perfect the world He had forgotten to leave the time to create Himself.

Ernesto said, "*Fantástico, no?*"

Willie's turn. He nodded to Hiram. "Just as the man says, *fantástico.*"

"Changes everything, doesn't it?" Hiram said, almost apologetically.

"Yes, of course," Willie agreed. "Everything."

PART IV

1926

Men make their own history, but they do not make it just as they please; they do not make it under circumstances chosen by themselves but under circumstances directly encountered, given and transmitted from the past.

—KARL MARX

So then because thou art lukewarm, and neither cold nor hot, I will spue thee out of my mouth.

—REVELATION 3:16

FOURTEEN

IN AFTER years with some regularity customers or visitors, taking notice of a *National Geographic* photograph Willie kept on his wall or hearing him mention the Yale Peruvian Expedition, would put two and two together and say, "But then you must have been there for the discovery of that Machu Picchu." And when Willie admitted it, or had said, "Nearly" as he sometimes did, they'd look at him more intently or would glance about the studio or his apartment in mild wonderment, perhaps at the notion that anyone who had once stood so near to glory should be reduced to taking passport photos to earn his living. Then Willie would add, "Only a spear-carrier in that particular drama." Or, if his mood was right, "I can assure you I did everything in my power to keep it from happening."

On a few occasions his guests posed the right question: *Was it luck?*

Well, Willie'd say, Hiram Bingham *was* a lucky man. Fortune, it had been noted, seems to smile on the fortunate. For whosoever hath, to him shall be given. (Willie then thinking what for the man Álvarez who had brought them cold water when they needed it, and for his friend Richarte? Some seasons of work, probably, clearing jungle, building the new trail up the mountain, putting stone back on stone. When the Peruvian government named the site national ground, probably nothing was paid either them or *Señor* Arteaga with his more dubious claim on the precious arable terraces. The hath-nots, as predicted, had had taken away from them even what they had. Not so lucky for them, the discovery of Machu Picchu.) But who knows what luck is anyway? There were also what Willie called the elements: the road, primarily, giving the Bingham party easy access to the unexplored Urubamba canyon, and to getting up to the heights (although later, Willie found from reading, they had come upon the remains of an elaborate Inca highway which ran along just under the peaks of the great majesties, the original connection of Machu Picchu to the rest of the world); and Hiram's willingness to climb to the top that day, and his being young enough still to do it; and his restlessness, you could call it, his *wanting* to find something. That too an 'element.'

The day after the discovery, July 25 that would have been, he had agreed to give Hiram a morning's work to get some photos. It turned out to be the hectic sort of shooting where he spent so much of his time under the shroud looking at the ground glass that Willie didn't afterward retain much sense of what had been going on. Hiram ran Carrasco, Ernesto and Álvarez and Richarte like roustabouts, getting them to hack away at the undergrowth to reveal as much building as possible in short order. (Arteaga, as the owner of the land, would only stand by and watch.) The machetes ringing on the tough trunks of the monstrous vines set Willie's cracked tooth to aching, and Hiram kept calling to him, "Did you get that? did you get that?" Finally, when the men couldn't clear enough off a set of giant ashlars to expose all of what Hiram wanted shown, he ganged them together to pull the greenery back with ropes and then had them get out of frame so a picture could be taken.

By midafternoon Willie was ready to begin the descent. He asked Ernesto to come with him as far as the farmers' hut. When they reached the ledge with the overhang and the curtains of vines, Willie sat down in the damp shade and dangled his feet over the edge. He lit two cigarettes and handed Ernesto one. The view here included the rocky envelope of the gorge with the sandbar and their little camp in the bottom seam of it.

Willie got out the negative from Tipon he had written on with bleach and gave it to Ernesto. Turning to look directly at him, so Ernesto would be sure he had been lying before, Willie said he had found it by chance.

Ernesto held the picture up and looked at it a while. Then he said, "I only asked for it to see if I had the power to get it from you."

Way below, figures moved about. Clement obviously, the biggest. Probably wise to disobey Hiram's summons to come up today. The girl Rosa. Going about their lives. Then, like a child at the zoo, Willie suddenly grew disappointed in them, their limitation.

And for some reason he was remembering Harvard Square, the crush of traffic, trolleys and wagons and the clanging of bells, and how Saturday evenings and right before Christmas and Easter the Square took on the aspect of a battlefield: the Protestants out in force to harangue the mick mackerel-snappers like himself amidst the blare of the martial bands of the followers of General William Booth. And what all this was going toward was the single memory of a pallid girl in a blue uniform much too big for her reaching out and touching Willie's sleeve, fixing him with her eye and saying, 'In your *heart* do you know you must be born again?' Willie had stopped cold and then, in his best stage Irishman, an imitation of the best of his Danaher uncles, had said, '*Again,* is it? *Again* and again? Well' (this to the steamy night sky), 'how long, O God, how long?' And the girl in the job far too big for her had kept up that fixed stare, as she had probably been taught to do, but Willie had seen the change in her eye: she had become indifferent, no longer cared anything for his soul.

It was indifference he had been fighting all along with Ernesto, he thought, and indifference he now wished he could stop struggling against. Ah, just to let it roll out over him too.

Willie managed to get down alone and, in the dark, back across the pole bridge with both the 8 x 10 and the tripod. At camp he set up and developed his most likely negatives. There was no time to provide positives, because Hiram was coming down early in the morning to choose a couple to send out to the world with Willie.

He remembered the 26th, their going into the tent together, how pristine his negatives had looked clothes-pinned to a line and lit from behind by the sun shining against the white tent canvas. Hiram examined the first five or six carefully, one by one. Then straightened, glanced down the row at the others and remarked, "Proof yet once again, as though we needed it."

"Proof of what?"

"Of what an artist you are, Willie."

"How's that?"

"The artist gives us the shape of things but never, God forbid, their structure, the how-it-works."

"Camera's a device, Hiram, a tool. By definition that means it performs a limited repertoire of actions. *Show what is* is all a photograph is meant to do."

"You know I don't give a tinker's dam for your holy *what is*, Willie."

Willie reached for the nearest negative and unpinned it. He put one piece of flimsy beneath it and another over and reached for the next closest, working quickly like a cookie putting butter between flapjacks as they came off the griddle. "I know you don't," he said.

About twenty minutes later, Willie just about done packing, Hiram poked his head into the tent again and asked was it all right to smoke in here. Willie said sure, all the chemicals were put away. Stepping inside, Hiram brought a cigarette out from behind his back. "Undergraduates maybe," he said, "but grown men, you know, don't go their separate ways because they disagree about *ideas*, for God's sake."

Willie said, "No, it's more about such things as how they treat their dogs, isn't it?"

Ernesto held Primavera's bridle while Willie got on board. His face was smudged with mild tears and emotions Willie couldn't decipher. In an attempt at jauntiness, Willie said he'd expect to see Ernesto after the turn of the year. Ernesto said *possibly*, although it seemed now Hiram would want him to stay here to head a work crew up on the mountain.

"What's that mean?" Willie asked Hiram in English.

"Ernesto would be the best man for that job. We'd agree on that, I think."

"And about New Haven?"

"I'm thinking maybe I should bring Leo up instead. Frankly, I wouldn't trust him with what needs to be done here. Rather have him where I could keep my eye on him."

"And all we agreed about our friend here's education? the 'armor' against the vagaries of his situation in Peru? the peril you've forced him into?"

Hiram had drawn himself up then, like an ancient nobleman, some Quixote fingering the last button into the worn hole of the tattered vestment called his honor, and said, "I'm not going to pimp him to you, Willie, if that's what you thought."

WILLIE missed his deadline for getting to New York, but only by a few days, so Curtis was still able to cart him along to the homes of the prominent for the actual signing of checks for the North American Indian project promised him at the September 15 to-do.

Not much required of Willie. Mostly a matter of his presence as proof that there really was an enterprise. Edward Curtis's eyes unfortunately told you here was a man perfectly capable of *dreaming* great things into existence. Willie's only duties were to be polite and to speak when asked questions. But, given his shaky belief in his own reality right then, the visits proved very hard on him. His face would begin to twitch and he would have to cover part of his mouth and his cheek with his hand. In the past he had found there might be for him a certain problem getting past the entrance—Irish parlormaids had an almost absolute sense for recognizing their own, 'Tradesmen's round the back' and the door shut in your face before you could pull out your invite—but once inside you could always count on the lords, their interest in you brightening for at least as long as you were under their roof. Now, however, Willie was noticing things he would not have noticed before: how the great lady, a Du Pont, had under her big beak a considerable mustache she bleached out with peroxide; how when actual dollar amounts came into the conversation her husband began to describe rapid circles on his vest around what must be underneath the crater of his navel. Willie kept thinking over and over how, if Curtis ever asked him what Hiram Bingham was like, he would say, 'An indecent man.'

By the end of the first week in October he was back in Kearney. There had been disturbances in the heavens all day, and by midafternoon when Willie got down from the train the wind was so cold and whipped up the dust in the street and blew it back and forth so, he thought at first it must be snowing. The silver clouds raced against a sky the blue going to the purple and black of Italian plums. So near dark Willie inadvertently reached for his watch. Not there, of course.

He secured his boxes with the telegraph operator and went over to a store across from the depot. It had the grand name of The Emporium, but was in fact a trading post very much like a number of others Willie knew. The whites in town didn't often shop there. The interior was gloomy and smelled fatty and somehow luxurious from the pelts the customers brought in.

"What'll it be for you today, mister?" the trader asked.

"Railroad watch. That twenty-dollar one there." Willie pointed to the row of gold and silver disks lying on red felt under the glass.

The trader fished one out and handed it over for Willie to inspect. "If I recall, you bought one of these here couple months ago."

"In February." Willie nodded.

"Something happen to it?"

"I gave it away."

"That was generous of you."

"Not especially," Willie said.

Then he thought how at least at the time he hadn't thought so.

And then, for some reason, he was remembering the bones of Ernesto's face, how resilient they were, yet light, like the bones of a bird, his own hand tracing them, his own flushed cheek brushing them.

Willie went back to living where he had been when Hiram's telegram arrived, a shed behind a tiny Baptist missionary school twenty miles outside of town. The teacher was his friend, a woman born in the Oglala tribe named Mary Louise Morgan. She was a year or so younger than Willie, and whenever there came a time they were both free, they would go on long walks or take horses out into the prairie together.

Late along in one Sunday ramble, Mary Louise all at once said, "You must have left something down there."

"Twenty-five pounds," Willie replied. In spite of the food being extremely good on the homeward voyage, he hadn't yet regained any of what he had lost in his months in Peru.

Mary Louise would not let him off so easy. "Something more?"

"Well, I miss the mountains."

Then Willie told her the dream he had had in Peru where the clouds beyond Lake Titicaca parted to reveal not the snow-capped mountains of Bolivia, but old gods. It occurred to him now the vision was at least partly derived from things Mary Louise had said about her people's spirit world. He described getting in the little boat and zigzagging east, which led to the necessity of saying something about Ernesto. This he did with some care: not the story of Willie falling in love, but the story of discovering in Peru a man his own age who had a real liveliness and inquisitiveness of mind, and about how they had often joined in a harmony of thought and talk which had given Willie pleasure.

Careful as he had been for himself, as they walked on Willie became nauseated and heated and felt badly hurt all through his chest, as though he had been kicked.

That evening after supper he retired to his shed, lit the lamp and poured himself a good drink before beginning a letter to Ernesto. It being not his own language helped him to write lovingly, even provocatively when he could concoct the phrases: "There is a furry little black kitten here named John Henry. When I let him he sleeps on my bed, and in the dawn, long before I am ready, he begins to run his motor right by my ear to get me started on my day. If I do not respond in time, he gives me a little bite on the nose. Tonight he asked whether when you come here you also will want little bites on the nose, and I had to answer that it is not yet completely clear where E.M. likes his little bites."

An hour and a half and maybe a pint of whiskey later, Willie was writing, "Figure—how is a man when he has been almost half a world away from what he loves for three months (or maybe it is more by now, he does not number anymore, it hurts him to count days as it hurts a dying man to hear the carpenter next door pounding the nails for his coffin)? He strums badly, without rhythm or hope, through the verses he can recall of songs his lover once loved. In the street, in the current of life, he catches sight of a light in the eye, an arm, a thick-wristed hand, a style of turning (whatever his actual employment, this longing, this long time, has made him more like the sculptors or the painters in his way of seeing), and this friend we speak of feels something enormous, uncomfortable, like an emotion we know is too big for the poor human satchel meant to contain it. It begins in the center of him at his belly and seems to descend even as it rises, a fire with two tongues, pain and desire. And the man's balls and his little thing say 'Touch me' and his poor frayed mind says 'But *he* is not here, *he* has not come yet.' And then the heart, the blind beggar, asks: 'How exactly is it when the loved one is not there?' And answers itself: 'Then we are like a plain, an unfencible expanse of grassland in the drought, ready to receive, ready for fire from heaven, ready to take on whatever it is that will burn.' "

THE WEEK of Christmas, Willie's mother died. The particular way she chose to go was kept from him until he had come back East to provide her some sort of funeral. A doctor named Winslow who had become director of the hospital at Waltham gave Willie the story. There had been an upright piano donated to the hospital. Even when it fell badly out of tune, Willie's mother would go in and play it and sing to herself. At some point, they did not know when, she had stolen a pair of pliers somewhere and used them to dislodge a string from the treble side of the piano. She had managed to fashion a loop-and-slipknot arrangement in each end of the wire. Then, early the morning of December 23, Willie's mother had snuck from her bed, attached one end of the piano wire to the post of a radiator by a window in a closet, got the window open (it was hardly above ground level and not barred), put the other end over her head and jumped. The cut through her neck was, Dr. Winslow said, cleaner than what a guillotine could have done.

There was an additional story. The woman who found Willie's mother was an employee of the hospital coming to work. She had first seen the bare feet sticking out of the bushes by the entrance. Then, turning, she had seen the head, which had rolled some. The poor woman had now been in one of the hospital's own detention cells for six days and showed no signs of improvement. He himself, the doctor said, had ordered the chief custodian to do something with the piano.

Waiting down at the road in the cold for the horse trolley which would take him to the depot for the train into Cambridge, Willie saw what had become of the piano. It was stacked in pieces on a rubbish heap by the far corner of the fence. He went closer to inspect. The remaining wires curled and bobbed in the wind like gross hairs, under the veneer the fresh-torn look of the wood. They must have gone at it with axes. This sight allowed Willie at last to cry. The vehemence of the attack, the stupidity or cruelty even, if you could say that. It augured somehow very badly for the possibility of any better world coming, men treating their sweetest machines this way.

The entire ability at connivance of his mother's family, which was considerable, even awesome, was brought to bear on the question of getting Helen buried in consecrated ground. His uncles and aunts left Willie free to mourn. Which he still could not find it in himself to do.

Sara left her boys in New Haven and Willie met her at the

Back Bay Station. They went directly to the funeral home, where Willie was required again to look. They had put a thick choker of dark blue velvet around his mother's neck and had set her dark hair in a fashionable pompadour. The effect, including the fixity of her face, reminded him of nights when he was quite small, his mother standing in the hall with her music sheets tucked under her arm before she went out to sing in someone or another's musicale. Willie had not even a shred of belief that for taking her own life she would end up in Hell. More likely just another hospital, the one where God is the keeper.

Sara asked was it all right for her to pin to the velvet the cameo brooch which his mother had given her at her wedding. In flushed, pinkish bone two girls, nereids with veils. It lay just over where his mother's vocal cords would be. Willie thought of the night he was taught to chew *coca*, of how maybe these wind sprites could help his mother finally propel her necessary prayers out into the air. He felt sad he himself had nothing more to give her. But that had been true for a long time now.

Willie carried Sara's carpetbag as they walked down Magazine Street. Two days ago in a shop, she told him, she had begun taking note of a young woman with long golden hair. At first because of the woman's being unusually sun-browned for the time of year. But then what had intrigued Sara even more was how completely lost in the contemplation of the things on display the woman was. Drifting from aisle to aisle like a sleepwalking princess, restless under her spell. Sara had thought perhaps laudanum and was out and down the street before remembering the woman was Christina Long.

"So you didn't speak?"

"No. All I can report to you is that they are back."

Curtis conferred a leave-of-absence without salary on Willie. He stayed in New Haven. He did the business of the studio and was unaware of how miserable he looked. Only Sara knew what it was really about.

He dreamed he had Ernesto's thigh in his hand and woke to find it was only that his own palm had brushed down into his groin and set him off again. Absolute self-absorption. He ate, but often only in token amounts, as though nothing good to eat could help him in his deprivation.

The first person from the Expedition he met up with was Dr. Foote, from whom he learned two things: that Ernesto had not come; and that at some point in the fall up on the site at Machu Picchu, Leo Ávila had thrown a small archaeological pick at Hiram, grazing his scalp at the right temple.

Willie caught sight of Hiram one day, charging like a bull into one of the various gray gates to the university, followed by a pack of undergraduates. He had a hat on, pulled all the way down to the ear on one side.

Then one afternoon at the end of February Willie saw Christina Long sitting alone by the window in a tea shop. He went in.

When he could, he inquired about Ernesto. Christina said they had asked him to go as far as Arequipa with them and Ernesto had demurred because of something to do with stabilizing a bridge across the river at Mandor Pampa, though he had told Hiram he would come if ordered, of course. Hiram had refused to issue an *order* on the subject. But when they arrived at the station the afternoon of their departure, there he was, ready to go. Christina also said that though she knew Ernesto had the watch Willie had given him, all through September and October she had not seen him use it once. Then, on that last trip down on the train, he had begun hauling it out regularly and checking it against the timetable.

About Hiram, she said it was because he was so *single-minded* that he often forgot the consequences to others of the intensity of his own desires. He was good of heart, finally. "And he loves *you*, Willie," she said.

"Hiram thinks there is a very limited amount of love in the world," Willie said. "He thinks that if he doesn't get it all, he will die. Which is wrong, of course."

"How so?"

"Because we die anyway."

He asked about Leo. Christina rotated her cup and said a few things and in a little while Willie, who had become distracted, realized that she had been telling him that she *had* been Ávila's lover, though she now repented it and was sorry for all the trouble she had caused. Willie was startled, momentarily excited. The thought? To tell this to Ernesto. They had worried this bone together so many nights in *huecos*. Then the sensation of utter desolation we get when we have an observation, a fact, a little joke only one other person in the world will appreciate, and we recall there's no pigeonhole at all for it. What death comes down to for us, the quick.

"Hope your next attempt at escape comes off better," Willie said.

"Escape?" Christina said, "I can't escape Hiram. What I found out in Peru was that without Hiram I don't *have* any life."

Willie gazed at her some moments, too furious, too full of words to speak at all. Finally he said, "I suppose that's where we go apart, then. Because I found out that I do—necessarily *do* have some sort of life I must claim as being all my very own."

There was a silence. Willie surprised, embarrassed even. (He could have laughed and pointed out that just-turned-thirty-three was a fairly advanced age for a person to make such a discovery about himself, but he did not.) Surprised really because up to this very moment all thoughts of a new life for Willie had been shaped to the belief that such a change was possible only because of and with Ernesto Mena.

"Come and see us when you can, won't you, Willie? I brought the spices back so I can cook up a real Cuzco-style *adobo*. And Hiram would be real pleased."

"No, I'm sorry."

"What did he do?"

"Played me on things I had let out to him about my heart, and I won't be able to forgive him that."

Christina didn't respond. She reached across the table and took his teacup and brought it over to her side.

"What do you see?"

"Dreams. The past, of course, and—look over here—Leo's

Aunt Laura taught me this—the future. Look how symmetrical, how nearly exactly alike they are!"

"So what would you predict?"

"Nothing so simple as what you've dreamed is going to come true. More likely for you the past as you imagine it will *become* the future somehow. I don't know. Hiram says it's superstition."

They agreed to meet again, just the two of them, but did not.

MARY LOUISE MORGAN wrote from Nebraska that she had seen Willie taking part in a sundance. (He couldn't be sure whether she meant a dream of hers or a waking vision. She rarely distinguished the two.) "You had been inside the tipi four or five days with the other men, fasting, singing, praying along with them. As you know, women are supposedly ignorant of what the men do in there, and of course aren't. Sitting outside, I grew concerned for you, not because I thought you would fail at bravery, not at all, but because of a piece of understanding the Indian men had not given you beforehand. The young men sought courage for deeds to make them worthy of becoming husbands. The older men were seeking the return of health, of the game, or the return of the time before the railroad. Our spirits drew near you with questioning faces, but even they could not read your desires. You suffered with the others, but you alone had not chosen any purpose for your sacrifice."

In March, Willie was laid up for several days with inflamed tonsils. Coming in to bring him some lunch one afternoon, Sara found him propped up in bed smiling. What was that about? she wondered.

"Nothing much," Willie said. "Only that all morning I kept dozing and waking up asking myself what would make me happy right now. And finally I decided two things—Ernesto and a cigarette. Neither of which I'm likely to get."

"Think not?"

"Oh no," he laughed again. "A cigarette right now would kill me."

"And Ernesto?"

"He begins to leave me, to go. Not at the pace I'd like, not even at the pace I sometimes think. Every time I reach what I think must be the death agony it turns out just to be more of the agony."

" 'Behold! I tell you a mystery.' "

"Is it that" (Willie here tried in his raspy half-voice to imitate the bass in *The Messiah*) " 'we shall not all see God'?"

" 'But we shall all be changed'? No, stranger even than that. The mystery is that love is vouchsafed us all."

"Oh yes?" Willie was rueful, but not cut off from the idea. "I hadn't known."

"I don't really know why, Willie, but I have a strong intimation. That it comes from the mother, from having *been* loved when we were small, even before we were born, in the carrying, in our conception. Also, that we *in turn* love is a demand on us, redeemable in time."

"In the hockshop of the heart?"

Now Sara laughed. "More or less. Some people think they can step aside, avoid it, let the whole thing blow over."

"Me," Willie said. (*Ernesto*, he thought.)

"You for an awfully long time. Certainly for longer than this sadness you're having to endure now for a while."

As soon as he got better, Willie wrote Mary Louise Morgan a short letter. Then he got out a list he had drawn up a month before:

ERNESTO'S SMELLS

1. Faintly the salty smell of his urine when we pissed together into the hole at my house; and again the time with Hiram and the waiter at the house at La Curva
2. The smell of his body left in the bed in the morning when he had gone to work
3. The smell of his vomit I cleaned up
4. The smell of his hair, pomade that must have had lavender in it, and of his clean mouth and his mustache against mine

5. The smell of him in mine after the *many times* of an evening we traded caps
6. The undershirt he left at my house—his sweat very slight in it

(None of which even began to account for all the smells and tastes he *associated* with Ernesto: Pisco, the black tobacco of his cigarettes, yellow tallowy laundry soap, Agua de Jesús in bottles with its limestone-well taste. Just yesterday Willie had stopped in at a spa for a tonic and forgetfully had ordered a Coca-Cola. Once you know the slight alkaline flavor of *coca*, forever after, cocaine or no cocaine, it'll come to you even through the sweet wall of the syrup. Willie had started crying and the poor waitress hadn't known what she had done.)

When he had read it over, Willie got out a match and touched the flame to the corner of the page. It writhed as it burned and, after he'd dropped it on the blotter, continued smoking and moving an unusually long time. Willie swept the ashes into the envelope and sealed it. In the note to Mary Louise he had thanked her for what she said about sacrifice without an end. *His* purpose now for a time, he wrote, would be to *forget* certain things.

Unclear whether this little piece of magic had any effect. The weather finally began to change toward the middle of April and Willie went in to New York on the train one day. He was intent on visiting again the saloons on the waterfront where men danced together. He set out and walked and walked, but at each of the possible doorways he experienced fright and dread wrapped together and could not make himself go in. At a little hotel on Sixteenth Street that night in sleep Willie heard a bell, one stroke of clear sound from the docks before the beating became, instead of the bell, insistent hope telling him to go ahead and hope his other self had returned. And as he barged his way through the dusty town, the doorways and people's faces he searched seemed to burn away to ragged holes. He did not care. He ran past the spice warehouses toward the wharf with tears flowing from his eyes. The cargo already unloaded, the river pilot and the deckhands gone ashore. But an old woman sitting at a pot of charcoal told him there *had* been one more arrival, savage he was, "In a blue cloth with a neckhole," she was saying as he ran on, now in joy too rebellious for him to hold in.

WHILE Willie was in Peru, Sara had had a telephone installed at the studio. It seldom rang except for business. But one day when Willie put the receiver to his ear, he heard old Edmund Foote's deep familiar South Carolina voice. The professor's style with the telephone was to talk, not listen. He told Willie his family was away and he was consoling himself by having some friends in to supper and gave the date and time and asked did Willie remember the address. A chance to decline the invitation was not proffered.

When the day came, Willie closed up shop at three o'clock and went to take a bath. He tried on four neckties before he found one he thought looked tolerable. Then for a while he thought he would not be able to make himself go.

On the gravel path up to the house Willie prepared himself for the usual face-off with the maid at the front door. But it turned out to be a black butler who answered at the Footes', and the happy old gentleman himself was right behind, getting his big thumb unhooked from his vest in order to shake Willie's hand.

The other guests were already gathered and talking with animation in the conservatory. Dr. Foote stopped Willie by a short, thick-set man with coarse hair brushed down across his wide forehead in the style of Benito Juárez of Mexico. Also like Juárez at least part Indian, Willie thought.

"I have been wanting you two to meet," Dr. Foote said. "Willie Hickler, Hap Meeker. Hap's my student in Greek. From New Mexico."

Willie put out his hand. The other man took it lightly and squeezed it. A sort of handshake Willie knew.

"Arizona," Meeker said, softly enough that Dr. Foote didn't catch it. "My father was mostly Papago."

Willie nodded.

He found a corner of a settee nearly obscured by the fronds of a great fern and hid there, surfacing only when Willard, the butler, passed by with his silver tray of drinks. There were ten or so men present, several slim tall blond boys, flushed and talking rapidly and smoking, a book dealer, his hair tinted brighter than when Willie had last been in his shop on High Street, a married professor of biology Willie had once made transparencies of moths' wings for. The rest Willie would not have guessed were men with any Uranian tendencies. For a time he wondered did *they* know what they had gotten into? Must have. All certainly more at their ease here than he was.

At supper a fellow who seemed to be a poet, or at least literary, maintained at some length that if we are to deify any human being, it should be the artist rather than the saint. Why? Because your saint has to concentrate only on loving the Good—or God, if you hold with there being one—whereas your artist must love everything, stand so far above good and evil that he embraces even his own sorrows and pains.

"Nietzsche!" one of the undergraduates exclaimed. "*Poo!*"

They were eating large red-skinned chunks of lobster in a sherry-rich sauce on trimmed triangles of toast. Dr. Foote, at the head of the table, touched Willie's hand and said, "You see? I promised nothing more than supper and nothing more than supper it is."

The poet put his hand to his breast and declaimed:

"*Sometimes with one I love I fill myself with rage for fear I effuse unreturn'd love,*
But now I think there is no unreturn'd love, the pay is certain one way or another,
I loved a certain person ardently and my love was not return'd,
Yet out of that I have written these songs."

Willard was filling up the champagne glasses again. Willie was getting very drunk. Unconcerned, content. He liked the poem.

"Written yours yet, my boy?" Dr. Foote asked.

Willie breathed out, smiling. "My song? Not quite."

"How far have you come?"

Halfway down the table the Papago man, Meeker, was sitting dead still, a rock in the to-and-fro breezing of the others. He was looking at Willie, appraising him without appearing to. Willie knew that trick. Hunting people all did it, and even the only sometimes hunters.

"How far? At times I recall how much we talked about ourselves, about the meaning of things, and then I think maybe that *was* the purpose of it all, for us to come together in the clear atmosphere of that high place to confer about our lives. Nothing more. Or less."

Dr. Foote nodded, a certain liquored solemnity. "Well, good for you, then. Your progress pleases me. Hiram couldn't find that wretched 'Vitcos' of his, but out of wanting it so badly he managed to dream up Machu Picchu."

"Like me inventing Ernesto Mena out of wanting someone *like* him so badly."

"Well, I rather think, don't you?" Dr. Foote didn't give Willie a chance to answer. "This Meeker, he's about thirty or so. Stays with us now. Got him a scholarship from stingy Old Eli. Beautiful mind, his grasp of Attic's better than mine ever was. And mine's nearly gone now, of course. Getting old, you become more a Hellene whether you want to or not. Comes from losing the belief in your body's great divinity, I think."

HAP MEEKER'S room in the Footes' home was at the top in the back above the kitchen and the servants' bedrooms. The ceiling folded down on two sides under the eaves and there was only one window, next to the bed. Outside slate roofs and, way beyond, like a separate principality, the university. Hap had a counterpane of interleaved, many-pointed stars. In the earliest morning gray, returning from down the hall, Willie saw the stars only as dark and light.

I had some blood.

Later under the gray clouds there was a kind of dawn, a band of cream poured out against the horizon, and Willie could see the counterpane was made of a hundred different colors of silk or maybe taffeta, purples and blues, reds and oranges put together in ways Indian ladies would match blouse and skirt or their hair ribbons.

I don't think I slept.

Me neither.

Is there some symmetry of our bodies which can tell us which one of all the others we by nature belong to? Ways we conform? Hard, Hap's penis filled Willie's mouth completely, comfortably. When they turned on their sides and Hap pushed back against him, his buttocks fit fully into the cavity of Willie's groin and Willie's penis rested just at Hap's opening.

What're you laughing at now?

Do you remember earlier?

Not much. I drank some last night.

When you asked would I sit on your cock?

Yes?

I didn't know what you meant. I thought it a funny request.

Hap stirred, raised himself on his elbow and gazed down at Willie. *That new to it, then.*

That new.

What must have been about eight o'clock there was stirring and clanking far below them and in a while the smell of bacon and coffee.

You're ready again.

Yes.

In a while the back door slammed. Willie looked out and saw Willard and his wife both in their Sunday best going toward the lilac-hedged back gate.

A little later, Hap down under the covers with Willie's penis in his mouth when the door eased open and two black children, a boy and a girl with a tray, came in. Willie was scared, but Hap came up from underneath easy.

Doctor say you'd be wanting your coffee by now, Mr. Hap. Who's that there?

His name's William.

Oh.

Hardly ever, Willie said.

Hap looked at him. *All right*, he told the children, *he's some man who's hardly ever William.*

THE MOVE to the west coast after the War came about as a result of a trip Willie and Hap took across the country one summer. They visited the remnants of Hap's family in Arizona and friends of Willie's in Flagstaff and Glendale. While they were in San Francisco Willie saw an ad in the paper for a teacher of Latin at one of the high schools. Hap got the job and had to begin almost immediately, so Willie went back to New Haven alone to close down the studio there. At first the new place he set up a little way out California Street did all right. But after a couple of years Willie noticed certain oddly familiar little quadrilles taking place again among the credits and debits and, as he told Hap, he began again envying anyone in trade who'd admit to 'getting by.' 'Scraping by' seemed to be more the term for Willie's life in business.

One evening during the Spring of 1926, Willie saw Hap leafing through the books about Peru he'd brought home from the Library and left on the hall table. In bed, Hap asked him, "Think there's a chance in the long run your loving that Peruvian fellow forced him to come to terms with himself any way like it did for you?"

Willie considered the question. "No. I don't think in the long run Ernesto was made to love men. I think if *I* had been more wholehearted about it, *something* might have changed in him. But I was still partly tied to Hiram. And for Ernesto it was always appealing to believe that nothing we attempt can ever come to fruition."

"How much longer will he be in your thoughts?"

"I'd guess I'm halfway through."

"How'd you figure that?"

For a moment Willie didn't know what to say. Then he remembered reading recently how the Spanish had been impressed by the appearance, well into the 1560's, of little groups of Indians in the streets of Cuzco bearing the annual tribute of flowers or produce it was their obligation to bring their Inca. As if, after thirty years, they still could not believe it was all over. Exactly as the heart will not believe.

"Should I try *not* thinking of Ernesto?"

"No, doesn't bother me." Hap kissed Willie's bare shoulder and turned onto his side to sleep. "Besides," he said, voice muffled in the blankets, "it wouldn't be like you to forget anything."

That night Willie dreamed of himself in the little house in Calle Las Minas he had not thought of for some time. It was a rainy Saturday afternoon and he was sorting negatives, the big ones from his old 8 x 10. A painful task because every one he found evoked not only the memory of taking it but a whole flood of other memories, and besides there were many he thought were missing, and that was more painful still to consider. Then he was coming out of the Angosta into the great plaza, into the Square of Joy, with his well-rubbed portfolio under his arm. The rain, unheard of for July, had stopped, and at the last moment the sun had come out from under the lowering violet-gray clouds. The light coming down the valley from Sacsayhuaman raked the plaza, creating a heavy chiaroscuro effect such as Tintoretto (or Max Reinhardt) would use for a Crucifixion, the light exactly as it had been the tired afternoon Willie had left Cuzco for good in everything but spirit. The Cuzqueños remained entirely indifferent to the magic at hand, of course, going about their business hopping puddles, street urchins cupping their genitals and fencing at each other like fighting cocks. The Indians peered in at the corners of the square, first fruits cradled in their arms. Willie hurried into one of the *chifas* on Plateros and there found Edmund Foote (in waking life his true confessor was many years dead now) waiting for him. On the chair next to Foote, half coming out of its brown paper wrapper, Thomas Eakins's watercolor study for his portrait of Walt Whitman. From its being there, Willie knew for sure what he had half known all along. The poem about the certain pay for unreturned love was Whitman's, and what Edmund Foote was demanding now was to see what Willie had to show finally. Hoping for a miracle, hoping against hope, Willie undid the strings and his portfolio drooped open. Black on one side, black the other too. The creator portrayed by emptiness. But wait. Better. Willie now fished out his wallet and presented Dr. Foote with a poor, unclear snapshot of two men in black swim trunks on the beach at San Diego, Willie's arm over Hap's shoulder, the hairy-chested and the smooth, Mutt and Jeff with tilted slap-happy smiles. "No song," Willie said without apology. "Only life as we've been able to make it up together." Which seemed for the moment, in the dream and afterward, sufficient.

TWO DEBTS

IN THE time of Hiram Bingham, it was still primarily William H. Prescott's history, published in 1847, which fired any imaginative attempt to understand the Conquest of Peru. Having read and reread John Hemming's 1970 *The Conquest of the Incas*, I can say almost more as a matter of fact than opinion that it is the comparable book for us in the present day. Hemming speaks of working in Prescott's "shadow," yet the added documentary richness and the leanness of his narrative alone make it clear that as an historian Hemming stands behind no one.

Several years ago I collaborated on a screenplay about a photographer with film writer–director Tim Hunter. In the process, I learned from Tim some incalculably valuable lessons about story and, more specific to this book, a great deal about how a photographer would think about his craft.

A NOTE ON THE TYPE

This book was set via computer-driven cathode ray tube in Janson, originally cast from matrices long thought to have been made by the Dutchman Anton Janson, who was a practicing type founder in Leipzig during the years 1668–87. However, it has been conclusively demonstrated that these types are actually the work of Nicholas Kis (1650–1702), a Hungarian, who most probably learned his trade from the master Dutch type founder Dirk Voskens. The type is an excellent example of the influential and sturdy Dutch types that prevailed in England up to the time William Caslon developed his own incomparable designs from them.

Composed by American–Stratford Graphic Services, Inc., Brattleboro, Vermont. Printed and bound by The Haddon Craftsmen, Scranton, Pennsylvania.